One Hundred
Years of
Vicissitude

One Hundred Years of Vicissitude

Andrez Bergen

PERFECT
EDGE
BOOKS

Winchester, UK
Washington, USA

First published by Perfect Edge Books, 2012
Perfect Edge Books is an imprint of John Hunt Publishing Ltd., Laurel House, Station Approach,
Alresford, Hants, SO24 9JH, UK
office1@jhpbooks.net
www.johnhuntpublishing.com

For distributor details and how to order please visit the 'Ordering' section on our website.

Text copyright: Andrez Bergen 2012

ISBN: 978 1 78099 597 7

A CIP catalogue record for this book is available from the British Library.

Design: Stuart Davies

Printed in the USA by Edwards Brothers Malloy

We operate a distinctive and ethical publishing philosophy in all
areas of our business, from our global network of authors to
production and worldwide distribution.

CONTENTS

For la familia
and 日本

酒なくて
何の己が
桜かな
Without saké,
what is the use of
cherry blossoms?
Anonymous haiku

Prologue | 序幕

It's swing time, and Fred Astaire and Ginger Rogers must be cooling their heels elsewhere.

In all honesty, I can't distinguish swing from boogie-woogie — styles my grandparents would be better equipped to judge. Though not wearing a tuxedo to match the music, I am blessed with a suave smoking jacket.

Anyhow, this jazz-inflected number continues to blare, doing seventy-eight rpm on brittle shellac, something warbled in Japanese about people having fun just by singing the zany song.

The whole package is strung together in a crackly, mono din that originates from a gramophone, housed in a lacquered wooden casket on the other side of the room.

Splayed on the floor before the music box lies a half-naked man, inert.

You'll find me propped up on the bed. It boasts a hard, uncomfortable mattress and the quilts are awry, but who would fret, seated next to a young, exquisite geisha?

Not that she doesn't have flaws.

This girl bears smudged makeup, a vivid red streak (blood) on one white cheek, and she's wrapped in a twisted, half-open kimono that's fallen off her shoulder.

I glimpse an ample amount of small, pale breast, as I reach over to light the cigarette she has pinioned between her teeth. Eyes off, you ancient rotter.

It's damnably humid in this small, spartan closet, and both of us are sweating. The temperature is something I doubt the fellow on the floor needs to concern himself with.

'He's dead?' I pipe up, in a blustering voice that startles me.

'As a doornail,' the woman says, unruffled, and then she exhales a plume of smoke toward the ceiling.

'So. What shall we do now?'

'I have no idea about you, but I'm enjoying the song and this cigarette.'

'You don't mind sharing them with a man you just murdered?'

'Well, I'd say he's far more functional in this state.'

She places her bare feet on the corpse's back, wriggles her toes, and then leans back to relax. There's a smirk on her cherubic mouth.

'That's better. Who needs a footstool?'

First up, a disclaimer. I suspect I am a dead man.

I have meagre proof, no framed-up certification, nothing to toss in a court of law as evidence of a rapid departure from the mortal coil. I recall a gun was involved, pressed up against my skull, and a loud explosion followed.

An ancient Chinese philosopher, whose bloody name escapes me, reckoned that 'A journey of a thousand miles must begin with a single step.' This was prior to the advent of gunpowder, so I'm wondering what fluff the fellow would have churned out concerning a single bullet.

Having proved my credentials—citing the crackpot savant while slinging in a footnote—allows me to get straight to the point.

There is no neat beginning with which to start things. And while debarkation here might be meaningful to the hoi polloi, so far as I was concerned?

Hardly.

My grand entrance in these parts elicited no dull, heavy, monotonous clang of a divine bell, let alone a jaunty toot-tooting of car horns. Festivities, it seemed, were off the agenda.

The climate? Well, this wasn't balmy enough to postulate the outer suburbs of Hell, but Paradise remained well and truly lost, and one saw nary a pitchfork nor harp. I suppose a better address would be the place to find the Pearly Gates, while Saint Peter must have been gallivanting on French leave. A blessing, since I'm not one for preachy types.

Lacking, to my mind, was a suitable background score banged together by Chopin—though with Frédéric François out of the picture, it was the opportune setting for Victor Laszlo to shepherd a rousing rendition of 'La Marseillaise'.

You might recall the suavely scarred, excessively honourable

Resistance leader, from the film *Casablanca*?

Sadly, the man was nowhere. At times I found myself humming the melody, deprived of Laszlo's guidance, but to be honest test pattern music would have sufficed. Alas, I was indulged with silence.

Not for my ears the faintest chorus of cicadas, wild squawk of ravens, or a reassuring rumble of distant traffic. Tiresome Christian Vespers and their Muslim stand-in, *adhān*, remained mute, and there appeared to be too few little darlings to belt out for me 'Oranges and Lemons'.

In the moments that I stopped humming as I hoofed it along, I heard scarcely a sound—a reminder of the hush that prevails with snow.

Hereabouts, we're fleeced of the sight of pirouetting flakes, so I initially considered hearing loss was a by-product of the hop, skip and lunge, from life to a possible demise. A rival thought that I'd alternatively gone insane later crossed my mind, but let's not go there now.

Although it was plain to see this domain went through the clockwork motions of day and night, and while the feel was more terra firma than Elysian Shangri-la, some aspects were awry. For one thing, the damned weather never committed.

Occasionally, the wind picked up or a light mist draped the horizon, but there was nought I could point to and declare, 'I say, there's the sun.' I marked an absence of rainfall, thunder, or hail. I missed the rain. Where I came from, it used to pour down by the bucketload.

The sky was a canvas of flinty grey looking like it was painted with a bold brush and careless abandon.

At one time, I spotted a sign writer at work up there in the heavens. If I expected 'Surrender Dorothy', I was thwarted—the baffling word 'Jihi' slowly dissipated and became nothing.

No matter how far I went, the venue otherwise refused to change.

Around me unravelled a vague, diminishing landscape with barren trees and otherwise no remarkable feature, no cities, no towns, no enticing attractions. Forget a parade or a semicircle of wagons overturned to dispel hostile assault by natives.

I was constantly struck by the dreariness of the place; as if a frumpy aunt's discarded beige stocking filtered the view. There was the odd shack, gloomy house, a lean-to or tent—nothing registering significant—and nary a rolled-out red carpet. Some of these places had a crucifix carved on their exteriors, with the added scraping of a vertical divot on the right side of the cross. This resembled less a religious symbol than a cretin's sloppy attempt at the number four.

The inhabitants, few and far between, hid behind rough-hewn curtains or skulked in darkened alcoves. Hence, their communication skills came across as altogether disengaged, and I thought, To Hell with them. Figuratively speaking.

So it was, amid these mundane individuals and across this scenery, dull as dishwater, that I first found myself trudging.

Which way I ought to have headed depended a good deal on where I wanted to get, and to be honest it didn't appear to matter which way I went. Despite sage advice from Lewis Carroll that getting somewhere should be just a matter of walking, no matter how much I walked I reached nowhere.

This pointless labour I undertook on shoddy paths made of clay and marked with washed-out, saffron-stained bricks, slapped down willy-nilly between the odd sprouting of wild Indian tobacco, white chrysanthemums, or rue. The surface of the roads needed a hearty levelling by one of those giant rolling pins you see at cricket matches, yet my inappropriate footwear remained grateful.

It was something else that irked me. Earlier on, I referred to the lack of visible riffraff.

Even so, up ahead on the odd occasion was a diminutive character, half my height, flitting through the scrappy woodland these paths trod. The blighter was never less than fifty or sixty feet away, so it was impossible to distinguish details aside from a scarlet anorak.

I found myself entertaining the bothersome notion that Big Bad Wolf is the role I was earmarked to play, yapping about and snapping on the coat-tails of Red Riding Hood. Let's cut to the chase here—while my age seriously hampered physical pursuit or a potential shining career in pantomime, the only achievable huffing and puffing would have been the rattle of frail lungs.

Oh, and there was another reason I let this individual be: I once saw a suspenseful Donald Sutherland film called *Don't Look Now*.

In that story Sutherland gives chase to another child-sized fugitive in red. He presumes this is his recently deceased daughter, but it turns out to be a homicidal dwarf.

Nothing is what it seems. Better to bide my time, chase nobody, and ramble solo. In hindsight, I could have easily fit into a hazy pastoral painting by William Turner: 'Man in Bedroom Attire Crossing a Bland Brook' or some such kerfuffle. It could sell for a fortune and add nothing special to an assiduously lit museum wall.

Artistic overkill aside, I do believe I was going to tell you a tale—but on second thought, let's chalk this implication up as bunk.

Rather than a depressingly singular account, it's going to be a mishmash of anecdotes, for neither the sake of brevity nor the saving of a few desperate trees. I don't aspire to be that kind of chap. I'd say, instead, my objective in doing a merge is plainly because these anecdotes happen to interlink.

Let's press on, shall we?

The death of a broken-down old man is, unquestionably, the least poetical topic in the world.

What then occurred, however, seemed curious at the time. Following up on brief, if considerable pain, pitch-blackness ensued.

No, I wasn't fortunate enough to see that old cliché, the beckoning white tunnel, offering rapturous fireworks aplenty. As I say, it was too dark to apprise myself of any such thing. Cursory entertainment like chess, a pack of playing cards, a neurotic white bunny with a fob watch — all of them failed to materialize. Even if they were there, I never would have spotted the things. As you may hazard a guess, said experience was unconscionably dull, yet worse was at hand.

I set up shop in these whereabouts.

For want of a novel tag, let us dub the place the 'Hereafter' since I'm here, after I allegedly carked it. Here/After. Yes, I agree, an infuriating moniker and miles away from quick-witted bon mot. You could always employ your imagination to dig us up a better one. In the meantime, we're high and dry.

After being here a while, a form of psychosis set in — I put this down to lack of stimulating company and the vapid wretchedness all about. This mental imbalance showed up in the way I harangued myself with incoherent soliloquies, a shade like this one. There was no orderly pattern to command proceedings in the old grey matter upstairs, and on countless occasions, I ended up exasperating me personally with puerile wisecracks.

Possibly it was one way in which I fended off the truth. There was no epiphany. In this particular Hereafter, Revelation had cleaned up, decamped, and taken with him all notions of figuring out the meaning of life.

I do concede a little grief that there was no Virgil, or any other Roman poet resurrected by Dante, waiting with a street directory. Neither was there a cowled footman out to menace tourists with a garden hoe — and manna was struck from the carte du jour. Perhaps Cerberus, the triple-headed guard dog of the Underworld, had fled his post to go chasing three sticks, while Charon, with his dinghy to Hades, was amiss.

This was actually a windfall, since I'd been marooned without

5

coinage in my mouth or anyplace else, so it would have been difficult to bribe the man or invest in steaks for the hound.

By the by, don't go fooling yourself about a handy hardcover ledger atop a podium made of gold, one in which we could tally up a person's lifetime pros and cons in separate columns—brandishing a baptismal balance and a funereal one, written with some celestial feathered quill. Such a tome was also amiss, and the only pedestals I came across were one or two decidedly out-of-place plastic milk crates, along with the random stumps of cadaverous cypress trees.

Talking of decrepitude, I felt I could pip Methuselah in the age stakes. Far older than the twilight years I'd lapped up in the land of the living, because at least in that place I had purpose. Here I meandered through the choice off-cuts of oblivion, and the ragged grey beard I had sprouted was a sign.

While I'll admit to having vaguely doubted the continuing growth of hair and nails after death, I was never inclined to think I would become proof of the pudding.

Well, disclaimers pushed to one side, a personal introduction is in order to avail you of the ledgerless bugger steering this monologue—since tawdry is how it may appear to others.

My name is Wolram E. Deaps.

The 'E.' stands for Evelyn, an appellation that can be applied to both men and women, dismally more often the latter. In the past I tended to share this middle name with few people, though reticence appears to have been scrubbed away after my bow-out from the mortal plain, last hurrah and all that. I'm quite unfussed handing it over to you now.

When I presumably kicked the bucket I was seventy-one years old, just a month and three days shy of seventy-two.

Even at my over-ripe age I kept track of the date—I was fond of celebrating my birthday and liked to mark the big occasion with panache. I'm not sure a single other soul shared the joy, but that's beside the point, is it not?

I'm trying to remember a conversation from before I expired, one that I had with my secretary, since she was in charge of organizing the all-important annual event. How did the chat go again...?

'Judy, cancel my reservation at Holberg's, will you? The place has been shut down since that nasty DLU business. Not the best atmosphere, should it ever reopen.'

I'm convinced I masked my inner-Wolram—the smug one that tends to behave poorly on the back-end of profitable mischief. Rarely clever to display that face to others.

'Let's shift the party to The Knave of Hearts,' I then suggested. 'Their service is more bohemian, it's spacious, and they do fine tarts. Get Tenniel on the line. He'll make it happen at this late notice.'

Now, what was her reply?

The words weasel in and out of my antediluvian memory. Their very triviality makes them harder to grasp—it was something she said repeatedly over thirty years of service. Was it 'Yes, sir'? 'Right away, Mr Deaps'? Perhaps 'Three bags full, Your Worship'. She was an excellent woman, very good at her job, never argued. Made a sterling cup of tea.

You know, I often now find myself wondering about Judy.

Here was a woman in her late fifties, unmarried I think, who had spent half her lifetime in my employ. What were her aspirations? Who was the real Judy behind the hard-working veneer? Why can't I dredge up her family name? When was her birthday?—I never thought to ask. Did she like working for me? Or did she spit in my teacup during the steeping, and then smile when I took a sip, smug on the rear-end of her mischief?

Anyhow, aside from the pricey restaurant soirée, a surreptitious birthday present to myself was the brave new world I had mapped out over the course of several years—a prize since rendered a vagrant pipe dream.

More irritating, and to exacerbate matters somewhat, I'd been knocked off in a wardrobe that consisted of a smoking jacket, a cravat, slacks, a pair of Jolly Roger boxer shorts, and lounge slippers. This apparel remained my only possession, along with an antique pistol brandishing the name Webley-Fosbery. I didn't know what I was doing with the silly thing, and had it shoved in my right pocket.

This does grant me an opportune moment to insert footnote number two, since possession of a firearm does wonders for a person's confidence.

I'll own up to being a pompous windbag, embarrassing underwear be damned—but let me tell you that having a cadaver perform the Greek Chorus on the side is a fairly good thing.

I need not lecture you that the moment we're torn out of our mother's womb, screeching and punting, we're held hostage by inherited behavioural kinks. Or that these are thereafter twisted by the irascible conduct of one's parents and the second-rate habits of everyone else—in collusion with the straitjackets of common culture, society, health, wealth, the goddarned weather.

Riding roughshod over these quirks are hidden agendas.

While I remained an aged bag of breathing flesh, I had these latter jewels to spare, with several sparkling ones proudly sewn onto the sleeve of my Harris Tweed, like military epaulettes, keeping fine company with the suede elbow patches.

A garden-variety example? That old favourite, an eye for an eye.

Hamlet dabbled with the notion, while the cantankerous people behind the Old Testament ascribed to this law of retribution. In life, sweet revenge assails us with intoxicating creative juices. Name for me one individual that hasn't, at some sour point, cooked up recourse against an adversary, former lover, a backstabbing friend, or blood-thicker-than-water-spilling family member.

Easier still, step back and take a gander at me. Go on, then.

If I were a spritely (living) person, brimming with the

decanted blend of vengeance, I might get rowdy enough to concoct a story—a little ditty about the demise of a gentleman I know named Floyd, my daughter's killer.

This is the same man who, I'm positive, shot me in the head in the middle of a lovely glass of bubbly.

Said 'ditty' would need to be penned in the debilitated pulp style Floyd embraced—I picture it sandwiched between two dog-eared, faded covers, with a gaudy image on the front of a mostly-naked lady. The name of the publication would be *Dime Store Detectives*, *Flotilla Magazine*, *The Noir Visage*, or some such nonsense.

You know, for someone at least half my own age, he certainly acted rather past his prime.

I'm not above giving it my best shot, however, to conjure up this fitting yarn—in the name of settling scores and of appeasing that sweet tooth I mentioned. While hardly leaving much up to one's imagination, I do like the coup de grâce, the vendetta appeased:

The first thing she does is she powders her nose.

She unzips her tobacco-coloured Louis Vuitton purse in the same manner a lioness, basking in the sun on an African savannah, tends to flick her tail—in a deceptive, lazy kind of way, but in reality it's a quick and precise gesture.

She drops her hand in the bag and fiddles about a few moments before her long, slender fingers emerge with a compact. Leaning toward the half-length mirror attached to the wardrobe, as I said, she powders her nose.

I've never seen anybody do it with such style.

Straight after her eyes in the mirror shift to mine, she smiles a fraction, then changes her mind and blows a kiss.

I'm pretty certain it misses, and that was the point. Attention returned to herself in the mirror, she adjusts the bra strap on her left shoulder, straightens out the dress strap next to that, rotates both shoulders to make the ensemble sit better, and pushes her hair back.

'What're you looking at, babe?' she says in a distracted kind of way.

I don't answer. I just stare at the beauty in that reflection and find it remarkable that such a serpent could sit so pretty.

'Snake got your tongue?' She seems to know my every thought, and I find that spooky. Not that it matters now, I guess. Her laughter is husky and it drifts around me. I loved that sound. I loved her. I thought the feeling was mutual, but I'm beginning to cotton on that I was wrong.

She's on top of me now, the aroma of lilacs intense, pressing her face as close as possible to mine, so that our eyes meet and her two hazel peepers become one in my struggling vision.

'Cyclops,' she whispers—it's our age-old game of affection, yet right now her tone sounds more vicious than vivacious.

Straight off the bat she breaks away, sits up, and stares down at me. 'Well, you are boring today, my love. You could put in a little more effort.'

She eases herself off my lap, heads into the kitchenette, and pushes two slices of bread into the pop-up. The cap's off the tequila and she's swigging straight out of the bottle. She's wandering that savannah again, eyes pushing wild, before a return to civilization and pouring a shot into a glass.

She paces the kitchen waiting for the toast. The way she walks takes her out of my sight every now and then, but I can hear her breathing and can smell the perfume.

'You got any Vegemite?' she asks. 'Oh wait, found it!' Her next pace takes her to the fridge, where she peers inside. 'Oh crap. Margarine? I hate margarine, you know that. Why couldn't you get Western Star butter? A girl might get the feeling that you don't care about what she wants.' The toast pops, and then she's laughing to herself as she spreads condiments. In her next breath she's singing Foghorn Leghorn. 'Oh, doggy, you're gonna get your lumps. Oh, doggy, you're gonna get some bumps…'

The way she stands there on the linoleum floor, I'm watching her from behind. She definitely knows how to move that body of hers in that tight satin dress—truth is she always did, especially in my field of vision. Her hips sway as she spreads and serenades, and it's a mesmerizing sight.

Finally breakfast is over, followed by a sizable slug of tequila, and she comes back into the bedsit—with the bottle— to stand before me.

'I'd offer you some brekky,' she says, 'but I have a feeling you'd just play mum. You know?' After she swirls the tequila around, she glances at it and back to me. 'So, what's your poison? …Oh, wait, you've already had it.' She leans over me on the couch and pries away the empty tumbler that's been stuck in my mitt for the past half hour. 'How's that paralysis coming along, babe?'

She puts a playful finger to my mouth, though I can't feel it. At all. I also can't catch the lilac any more.

'No need to answer. Shouldn't be long now. Probably your vision will start botching up next.'

I can see her clearly enough, but the edges of my sight are starting to get haggard, and that haggardness is creeping in from all sides. She sniffs the glass that she took from me and frowns.

'Say, you can smell the extra bonus stuff a mile off. You really have only yourself to blame. Someone who was a bit more cautious would've whiffed this before the first sip. But you just love your booze, don't you? Down the hatch before you even stop to breathe.' She sighs. 'Well, I was nice anyway—at least this concoction isn't as painful as others. It's also not very quick. Sorry about that.'

She's right. At the moment I'm feeling nothing, my senses

numb, but as I say it's been over thirty minutes according to the big, kitsch, 3D crucifixion-scene clock on the wall.

There is a query nagging away at the back of my noggin. I just wish I could enunciate it through dead lips, or express it to her via some kind of mental Morse code. Hell, sign language would be fine, if my fingers still worked.

The question was a simple, one-word no-brainer: Why?

She picks up the phone and makes a call, and right about then the lights go out.

Ahh, revenge.

The thing is, as I mentioned to you, I'm presumably dead. This situation renders pointless such exercises in an imaginative dénouement. It's passive aggression without a punch line.

John Milton and old Gandhi had their merry thinking caps on when they asserted that revenge festers old wounds and/or makes one blind, and personally I do like to think Mark Twain receives his tick for the quip that revenge is a lot of unnecessary pain hanging onto anticipation of the beast.

It's also not good business, and death, as it shapes up, is a great leveller.

Living it up here, I'm not in a position to affect comeuppance—I very much doubt I'm capable of haunting anyone. Place a sheet over me and I'd scare only Little Miss Muffet.

Hence, roiling with post-homicidal notions of reprisal is a wasted effort, and a far better recourse—in truth the only decent one available after that gentleman so kindly (probably) placed a bullet in my belfry—would be to leave Floyd altogether out of the picture. To ignore the man. To deflect all memory of his uncouth inanities and twee judgment calls of *liberté, égalité et fraternité.*

Sad, really.

Shall we tarry forth—tally ho, and all that jazz?

2 | 二

While you may not like me, you can place a smidgeon of stock in what I have to say.

I think the reason for doing so is obvious. Probable death sabotages irate desires like revenge, regret and anger.

Aspirations I polished up in life—audacity, pugnacity, ambition—have sadly scarpered, fortuitously taking with them qualities I found irritating or just plain feeble.

One thing that has survived is an appetite for the treasures omitted here.

Oh, how I'd thoroughly enjoy Eggs Benedict, followed by an aged Johnnie Walker Black Label, served neat at room temperature. Unsurprisingly, perhaps, given recent experience, champers I could do without.

This mind-numbing successor to life goes on and on.

Perhaps to keep me a fraction amused since I bit the bullet— a turn of expression I'm certain would appeal to someone who shall, henceforth, remain mostly nameless—I met a woman who stood out from the vacuous crowd.

She was awaiting her knight-errant.

Yes, I well realize how absurd the idea sounds. Before I died, I would have thought the woman stark raving mad, yet here things have a natural disorder that renders the obscure commonplace and the idiotic reasonable.

The woman's hovel, or 'cottage' as she more kindly referred to the place, was perched on a windy bluff that jutted out two hundred metres above a raging, steel-grey sea. There was, in fact, more rugged pizzazz in that locale than I'd experienced in an age.

The first time I beheld it, I thought of Ireland or the coast of England, or some nameless rural borough in Scandinavia.

This makes the setting sound terribly Emily Brontë, but the

house belied the notion. The building was a dysfunctional architectural graft of medieval European peasant cottage and a tall-ceilinged, thatch-roofed Edo period farmhouse in Japan.

No other structure, person or wraith wandered into view as far as the eye could see—which, to be honest, is not saying much since I'd been shipwrecked here without my bifocals.

I'd never once before felt the need to pay a house call on the residents of the insipid landscape elsewhere, so I don't know why I adapted my policy here. Perhaps it had something to do with the underlying moxie of the elements and the kooky setting.

Before me stood a peeling white picket fence that surrounded a lush herb garden, protected by a hedge seemingly bent at right angles by the gale.

Nearer the dwelling, in a small plot of land serving as a yard, was a scarecrow propped up beside an abandoned wagon wheel. A brown and white Jersey cow chewed grass around this, while next to the entrance lurked an old statue of a comical raccoon dog with a party grin, a wide-brimmed hat, and rather enormous testicles. He held a bottle in one paw and a book in the other— possibly it was the missing ledger I mentioned earlier.

The track leading up to the house detoured around a gnarled tree I took to be a hazelnut, embalmed in honeysuckle vines, and nearby leaned an empty kennel where a rooster poked about.

I don't exactly recall how I arrived.

One moment I wasn't there, the next—*voilà*. Since the feat lacked a puff of cheap stage smog or the disorientation of parlour mirrors, it was refreshingly simple.

I peered at the face of the scarecrow, troubled that it knew things I didn't, before a gust of frigid air picked me up like a kite and deposited me on the doormat, right next to the jocular raccoon and a brass sign saying 'Chevrefoil'.

Then the door opened to inky depths and I heard a woman declare '*Yōkoso!*'

I fathomed—and counted on—this being some type of word

of welcome, since she grabbed my right elbow; I was yanked inside, and then shuttled over to an ivory leather couch positioned close to a fire in a pit. Thankfully, said blaze gave out no smoke, yet my sight was taking its jolly time adjusting to the switch in illumination.

'Welcome, Mr Harker.'

'My name is not Harker.'

'Of course it isn't. I was just having fun, playing up the Dracula angle—gloomy chalet, and all.'

'Not quite the chalet,' I grumbled.

'Well, excuse me. Mr Deaps, isn't it?'

'That's right. How did you know?'

'Ahh, if I revealed that, we would lose half the mystery.'

'Mystery? What mystery?'

'Just wait and see.'

I felt an acidic sensation in my throat, but once I'd sunk down into the settee I discovered a cup of a warm liquid in my hands, and took a cautious whiff—I have no idea why. Conceivably my surly, hardboiled tale about Floyd was ringing in my ears.

The odour was unique, the faintest vanilla tossed with fruit, flowers and something else I couldn't hope to identify. Still, I recognized the combination. Not bitter almonds, no carafe of haemoglobin, and by no means poison. It was Japanese *saké*.

Heavens above or below or wherever they were, I needed no encouragement.

I mentioned that this pitiable excuse for an afterlife has in no way deprived me of my love for creature comforts, even if some of them—such as a nice drop of Camus Cuvée, or one of my prized Havanas from the final box of Coronas del Ritz—were no longer on the menu. And for someone with minimal feelings left to call my own, I felt chilled to the bone.

'Marvellous! I like saké.'

Straight after I sipped the alcohol, an errant thought occurred to me, a silly recollection from a film I'd seen decades before. My inaugural experience was when it screened at our neighbourhood movie theatre, and I wasn't out of short-pants.

By God that comes across geriatric—I refuse to accept I would stoop to such a broken-down commentary. Where was I? Ah yes, the film.

I was aged about seven (and you can forget the short-pants), a student at a primary school called Gardiner Central, located in Gardiner—a leafy, often drizzly eastern suburb of Melbourne.

We lived three minutes' walk from Gardiner Station, around the corner from Gardiner Newsagency, and next to a tiny stream named Gardiner's Creek. I think the cinema was called Gardiner Picture House, or something of the sort.

All the Gardiners in the area were ratcheted up to honour John Gardiner, a nineteenth-century Irish-born banker and pastoralist of no actual note.

As with a marriage, the area may have remained bound to the Gardiner name, yet it gradually shed all the visible romantic charms I recalled from boyhood.

The school was torn down to erect a glitzy elderly citizens' home, the theatre demolished to make way for a petrol station, and a concrete freeway was thrown slap-bang on top of the waterway. So, on second thought, perhaps I *am* fossilized—that was sixty-odd years before I settled down here.

Anyhow, I digress.

There was this resuscitated film memory to share, a throwaway quote continuing on from 'I like saké', to 'especially when it's served at the correct temperature, ninety-eight point four degrees Fahrenheit, like this is'.

While my impromptu adaptation lacked flair, I'm certain I nailed it verbatim.

Age does, however, continue to play featherbrained—my eyes were taking a month of Sundays to get accustomed to the dim inside light. I looked up from the drink to focus on the woman's silhouette, stoking the fire. There were small flames, but again no smoke.

'*You Only Live Twice*,' I heard her surmise.

'Well spotted,' I chuckled.

'The Japanese title was *Double-O-Seven Dies Twice*, odd given that James Bond "died" only once in the movie.'

'That is strange. It's remarkable how much is coming back to me—I haven't thought about the film in years! Let me tell you, I was marginally beguiled by Kissy Suzuki. It's likely dated, but—ahh—my first taste of Japan. The sumo and the Shinto wedding, exotic pearl divers, Bond's counterfeit Oriental makeover, those bungling ninja at the training school next to Himeji Castle. And of course the saké. It's no surprise I ended up with a skewed opinion of Japanese culture, women in general, and an affection for fine drinks.'

I stopped for breath, and then remembered my breeding.

'By the way, wonderful to meet you.'

'You too, Mr Deaps—it's nice to be able to squeeze a word in edgewise,' the woman laughed.

'I apologize. That was a complete ramble. Put this down to lack of decent conversation for, I don't know, far too long.'

'Never mind. I've been looking forward to our meeting. In particular, I do like your beard. It gives me something to hang on to, if need be.'

'Er… Righto. Returning to Sean Connery's splendid turn as Double-O-Seven, have you ever heard the rumour?

'My answer would depend upon which one.'

'Now, there's a fine point. I'll tell you about a political associate of mine, a fellow named Denslow. Someone in-the-know when it came to Japanese cuisine, but a blockhead in most else. He mentioned that Roald Dahl, the scriptwriter of *You Only Live Twice*, may have got the saké thing wrong—but he didn't sound confident. I put it down to scuttlebutt.'

'All right, now you're losing me. "Scuttlebutt" I'd expect from a retired sea captain.'

I chuckled. 'There's a reasonably salty ring to it, yes. Perhaps we should take out my private yacht for a spin? Scuttlebutt is a rumour—in this case, that saké served at such a hot temperature, thirty-seven degrees Celsius for those of us who are Fahrenheit inept, is an inferior blend, lacking in quality.'

With a shrug, the woman stood upright and collected together a few utensils including scissors and a box cutter. If I wasn't dead already, I might have been concerned.

'Fascinating,' she finally declared in a tone so thoroughly flat I could detect no sarcasm—which is not to say it wasn't there. 'Yes, I remember that was the case in the middle part of the 1960s, round the time *You Only Live Twice* was filmed. Certain breweries fortified their *nihonshu* with distilled alcohol—an extended hangover from rice shortages in the Second World War.'

'Crooked.'

'I always had a soft spot for "dodgy".'

'Not such a bad turn of phrase.'

'Right?'

Things around me were starting to take on an orange-tinged visual clarity. The woman's hair, the same colour as the charcoal on the brazier in that smokeless fire pit, was long and tied back in a bun. She had a low nose and an oval face, without makeup, devilishly pretty, and eyes of a burnt sienna hue flecked with chestnut. She was wearing a shift of fabric, like rough cotton or linen, that hung down one very narrow body to her ankles, and her feet were bare.

This drew me to my own, and I realized I wasn't wearing footwear. For the life of me—or lack of it—I could not remember removing my slippers.

The woman scooped up vegetation and laid it out on a round white table, a couple of metres from me. I noted sweet briars, yellow carnations and asphodels amid other flowers I didn't recognize, and leaned forward to get a better ringside seat.

'Do you know *hanakotoba*?'

'I don't know. In what context? Is that the name of some Russian gymnast?'

The woman looked amused. 'Sorry, sometimes my "b" sounds like a "v". Hanakotoba is the language of flowers.'

By return, I opted for facetious—'They have their own language?'—since I felt the topic deserved it.

'Funny. No, we have one for them. Special meanings, symbolism. A Japanese thing, but I believe it was also popular in Victorian England.'

'I don't know anything about that. I thought we were talking up saké.'

'Oh, I haven't forgotten. It's just that you seemed interested in my work here. *Gomene*—sorry. My mistake.'

She bunched some flowers together, looked at them, and then shook her head, pulled them apart, and laid each kind in a separate pile.

'That's not really right. The colours don't work. Now, where precisely were we with the saké?'

'Dodgy distilleries.'

'Ahh, well, by serving the drink steaming, those people could veil any sharp or unbalanced flavours caused by the illicit practice.' She segued on while her hands moved at a rapid pace. 'But that was years ago. Neither your friend Denslow, nor Mr Dahl, was wrong. Ninety-eight point four degrees Fahrenheit isn't a "correct" temperature for all saké, but it's perfect for cheap brews like Ozeki One Cup, as well as some premium blends.' Her gaze flicked over. 'I prefer not to serve up dregs to my house guests.'

'Never the intimation, my dear.' I indulged in the rest of my drink, downing the cup's contents in seconds. After that I licked my lips and I'm fairly certain I beamed. I felt warm and relaxed inside, a new experience in this great beyond. 'As a matter of fact, the temperature and taste suit me to a tee.'

'Good for you. This is "Kimono Sleeve", an *onnazake* from

Fushimi, down near Kyoto.'

'I'm sorry—it's a what?'

'The name, or the style?'

'The style, I believe. Onna…?'

'Onnazake. Feminine saké.' There was a curl at the corner of the lady's mouth—faint to be sure, but clear enough to observe with my mediocre sight, and worry some. 'This kind of saké takes longer to produce and has a sweeter, softer, more delicate flavour. Most sakés are harefooted, harder, less sophisticated—the male variant.'

'It figures I'd favour a woman's drink.' I sighed.

'Don't fret. It's even worse when your supply runs dry. There's a haiku poem I love, written by Kobayashi Issa, about the experience: "Saké nomanu waga mi hitotsu no yozamu kana" which translates as "Out of saké. Such is my life—a cold night." Touché.'

I wasn't sure if this touché was a shiv meant for my cheek, or a prop for the abbreviated Japanese metaphor, so decided blindness was the best path to take.

'You appear to be very well set up here. How do you do that? The deities supposed to run the place have absconded, leaving me empty pockets and a predisposition for road trips in a pair of Royal Resort Collection slippers.'

'Would you care for a top-up? Or are these theological musings a more pressing concern right now?'

I was annoyed the question needed asking, but deduced this was her intention: to rattle frayed nerves.

'Pour me another one, there's a good girl,' I said, holding up the cup like a golden chalice pilfered from church service. In seconds, a handcrafted tokkuri flask was working its special magic, doing the refill.

Like half the house and the drink, my hostess was surely Japanese, and more teenager than adult. I would have right then surmised her age to be fifteen or sixteen. She later said she'd pipped one hundred the day she died, making her old enough to be my mother, yet she looked fifty-six years younger than me.

This didn't seem fair.

But I do cherish my tea, and her voice drifted across to me in the form of a warm, beguiling collusion of well-steeped Lady Grey, with a dollop of Sidr honey. Likely, such fancies boiled down to the simple fact I was desperate for someone to talk to. There was barely a trace of an accent in her English—not foreign, not bona fide native, or something of the sort.

It would appear that human frailties like a language barrier have no point here, making it more of a shame the effects of age were not so liberal.

'Mr Deaps, have you read Sir Thomas Malory's *Le Morte d'Arthur*?' she asked as she carefully arranged flowers and branches in a vase.

'That's a peculiar question to throw at someone you have just met.'

'True, but I don't live up to the idealized perception of Japanese womanhood—what they call *yamato-nadeshiko*, and otherwise referred to in English as a wallflower. I pride myself on a more... um... atypical nature.'

'Good for you.' I shrugged. 'Now, let me see—oh yes, I do believe I touched upon Malory a lifetime ago.'

While this woman prized nonconformity, I on the other hand had obviously embraced tomfoolery, and found myself chuckling at the half-witted word play. 'A lifetime ago'. Get it? Good Lord, no wonder she was unmoved, plausibly even bored. I had to gather together severed wits.

'At university, among other needless texts. None of which made any impact.'

'Clearly.' This was a tart comeback, completely deserved.

'I'm not one for intellectual snobbery,' I fudged.

'I thought you'd be the type to appreciate it.'

'Why, because I'm old?'

'No, more because of the airs you put on.'

'Well—I think it's safe to say I've shelved most of those. They're difficult to circulate when one has an unruly beard and very few people to entertain. You could say I have a passing knowledge of the subject you mentioned, however, since King Arthur is scarcely an unknown.'

'I should hope not. *Le Morte d'Arthur* was first published on Caxton's presses in 1485, meaning you've had well over five hundred years to catch up.'

'That long, you say?'

'Donkey's years. And it may be a bridge too far, but there's the ring-in story of Tristram and Iseult.'

'Ahh. A flask of love-dram gone astray, unrequited amour, and much associated histrionics. Why yes, it seems I can cross that one.'

If the lady took offence to my flip, she wasn't disclosing a flicker.

'That was my favourite bedtime story when I was a girl,' her voice steamrolled on, with bulldog bravura. 'The star-cross'd Cornish knight and his Irish paramour.'

A yawn escaped my beard—I'm fairly certain I suppressed it before she noticed, but I decided to duck for verbal cover. 'Begging your pardon, but aren't you still a mere child?'

She rolled her eyes and breathed out loudly. 'As if. What an idea.' Then, it appeared, she did give the matter some thought and giggled. '*What* an idea! Wow! Anyway—where was I?'

'I believe we were on the topic of cloying melodrama.'

'Oh yes, that. Melodrama. In this case, the doomed nature of their relationship, undercutting old-fashioned elements of honour, love, and chivalry.'

'"Old-fashioned" being the key word here.'

She acted deaf and dumb to my barbs—in all likelihood a natural skill that set me on edge.

'There was a selfishness about them, about the way in which

they carelessly destroyed other people's lives for the sake of their own lust. Compelling stuff.'

The girl's hands worked a kind of magic on the flora that I hadn't before witnessed, and felt I never would again. Leaves and flowers intertwined to embrace one another.

'Of course I grew up on a sanitized version that was poorly translated into Japanese. I only realized this once I was able to read the original French and English. For years, I called the lovers "Tristan and Isolde", since those names were easier to pronounce with a *katakana* inflection: *tu-re-tsu-ta-n* and *i-su-o-re-de*. Purists tend to call them Tristan and Iseult, or Isoud, but these days I like the sound of "Tristram and Iseult" much better. I'm not sure why.'

'Interesting.'

'Meaning, not at all?'

'I said no such thing.'

'I heard the implication in your tone. You're not very good at hiding contempt, are you?'

'Never my intention.'

The woman cut a long bare twig, and then started to trim another branch. She did so with a patience and calm that relaxed me into the spectacle. The conversation may have been a mite mundane, but perhaps this she now understood as she no longer spoke.

That gave me the opportunity to stickybeak about.

The interior of her lair was spacious, much larger than one assumed outside, with tapestries on two walls that depicted Richard I era rampant lions. Suspended on a stand before another wall was a superb rectangular banner, predominately a golden orange in colour mixed into washes of cream and yellow, with a couple of small triangular bites taken out. The material— was it silk?—had pearly and aquamarine storks in flight woven across the surface. It shimmered.

'Not storks,' the girl cut into my inspection. 'They're *toki*—

otherwise known as the Japanese crested ibis.'

'Right you are.'

The material's bookend at the other side of the room was a suit of polished armour that had a woodcutter's axe leaned up against the right leg—incongruously crossing swords with a battle-scarred cricket bat. Behind the tin man were four closed *shōji* paper lattice screens that intimated more space beyond, and there was a steep, well-worn wooden staircase leading to an upper level.

I understood the living area doubled as a kitchen.

Cupboards, over-stuffed bookcases and a secretaire lurked at orderly attention in the shadows. I made out a cedar coat rack mostly obscured by a hat, black and wide-brimmed, beneath which dangled a long, dark cloak. Praise the Lord, it wasn't red.

The floor was covered with worn, tidy straw *tatami* mats, except the area around the fire pit, which was paved with colourful *pietra dura* tiles of entwined birds, monkeys, tigers, and bears.

There was other knick-knackery scattered about in minimal fashion, including an authentic inflated blowfish that dangled from the ceiling, and a thirty-centimetre statuette of Godzilla on a shelf.

On a small round table next to the sofa was a pile of books, at the top of which sat a hardback titled *Dead Yellow Women*. Peeking out beneath that was a cartoonish goat with a cigarette, on a dirty brown cover.

A framed black-and-white photograph stood next to a small shrine portraying what looked like a World War Two military man, beside a geisha with a parasol. From that distance and with my second-rate vision, I couldn't make out their faces.

The place looked lived in. Not my taste in décor, but not terribly shabby either.

My hostess stopped what she was doing, briefly inspected her handiwork, and wiped her hands on a tea towel that was covered in Scottish highland tartans. Then she looked at it. 'Why on earth this is here, I'll never understand.'

'Part of the charm of the place,' I mused.

The girl pulled up a classic pillar-box red Arne Jacobsen Egg chair and as she reclined into it she curled up her legs. She produced a French enamel cigarette case and slipped out a long brown cigarette with a mesmerizing gold tip.

'Do you mind if I smoke, Mr Deaps?'

'Not at all, though I'll have to press you for the name of your supplier—I was stranded here with nothing elegant whatsoever.'

'Help yourself.'

She leaned over with the case and I prised one free. I tried my very best to be blasé about the manoeuvre, but I saw my hand shake and I can't blame age or the liver spots for that. Eventually, I held up what I suspected was a South American number, and she lit it with a dull chrome Zippo that had the word 'MONTE-VIDEO' inscribed in capitals across its surface.

Settling back to enjoy the moment, I could feel those jangly nerves of mine wind themselves down. I hadn't realized how much I missed this simple custom.

'You seem to have me at a disadvantage, my dear,' I said. 'You know my name, but I'm not certain how I should address you.'

Her mouth made a casual 'O' shape and four smoke rings spiralled up with finesse toward the high, gabled ceiling. That settled, she piped up again.

'In my time, I've answered to a few different names.'

'So what shall it be, or should I get creative and ascribe you another nom de plume to add to your collection?'

She smiled, a gesture so thoroughly overwhelming that her eyes disappeared into diagonal lines on either side of her face. The girl had large teeth, straight as a whisker and beautifully arranged, aside from a tiny gap between the two top front ones.

I realize that, all up, this likely sounds anatomically fractured. To the contrary, it was a beautiful, disarming sight, bordering on perfection—and I'm hardly one to gush.

When the beam subsided, she looked over my way.

'There's no need to be so generous. You can call me Kohana. In English, it translates as Little Flower.'

Fair enough.

'I wonder, Mr Deaps—do you think time doesn't exist in this place? You'll notice I have here neither clock nor watch, and I'm presuming you're without one as well.'

'Ah. That.' In answer, I held up my arms. The worn crimson sleeves of my smoking jacket slid down to reveal two bony, blotchy old wrists. 'No timepiece, and I find it liberating. No deadlines to abide by. Half the time I looked at the watch, I wasn't reading the thing. Force of habit, and all.'

'So we seem to have an abundance of time on our hands,' Kohana decided. 'May I tell you a story?'

'That depends.'

'It does?'

'It most certainly does. If the story involves Grail Knights, flagons with dragons, or much ado about jousting—well, Kohana, I'd much prefer you continue with the humdrum commentary on saké. So long as you keep pouring the stuff for dramatic effect.'

The woman gave out a laugh, and then started to examine my face. This scrutinizing made me bloody uncomfortable.

'Please stop that. I'm becoming self-conscious. What are you doing?'

'What, it's all right for you to stare at me, but not vice versa?'

'Why on earth would I bother staring at you?'

'That's what you were doing a little while back. No harm in admitting it.'

'Nonsense—you're imagining things.'

'I see. Fascinating. You *do* look like him, only you're not very nice, are you?'

'I beg your pardon? Look like whom?'

'Chiefly, I think, it's the high, straight forehead, which is unusual. I can picture when you were a young man, you had similar eyes, though I'm sorry to say the green in yours has washed out with age. His were the intense darker shades of Fei Tsui jade—but they're alike all the same.'

'Alike? What the Devil are you babbling about?'

'Oh, your grandfather.'

I stared back at her.

The eyes she'd just character assassinated felt like they bulged in their sockets and I swear my heart, if I had one and antiquated as it would be, skipped a couple of beats. I knew straight away which male ancestor Kohana meant, don't ask me how. It took a ridiculous effort to put into three simple words the furore buffeting my senses. 'You met Pop?'

'Cute. I knew him as Les—but in answer to your question, yes. We were somewhat acquainted.'

'How on earth...?'

'Part of the story. Of course, we could always settle for something else, since it doesn't rate as a pot-boiler.' She smirked in a mischievous manner. 'Shall I tell it to you, or would you prefer that one thousand, three hundred year history of saké?'

'I think it's safe to say you've sufficiently whet my appetite. Has this story any decent food in it?

'Are you kidding? *Sushi*, blowfish, *senbei*, *soba*—you might be relieved to note that a tart or two are tucked away in there as well.'

'Then it doesn't sound too bad. I'll endeavour to stay awake.'

3 | 三

What transpired next was like the opening reel of the old film version of *Henry V*, starring Laurence Olivier, although we can dispense with cast and crew lists here.

Instead, picture an artificial, very grounded stage play that has a velvet curtain pulled back to reveal the real world, within the story. The set vanishes and becomes 1415, with Prince Hal rallying his English troops for the Battle of Agincourt against the pesky French.

Dorothy Gale secured a similar location reboot when she traded Kansas for Oz, and so it was with Kohana's tale—minus lions, tigers, and bears. Plush drapes were amiss, a wild tornado failed to threaten, and sadly there was no trusted steed to lord it up on.

The switch also scared the willies out of me.

One moment we were comfortably seated in her hovel, sipping saké, and the next we'd lost the drinks and were forced to stand on pebbles in a shadowy archway. My kingdom for that horse. Fortunately, I was once again wearing my slippers, even if they weren't made for this kind of outdoors adventurism.

I looked around us, getting a better feel for the Devil's details.

The structure looming above us, an aqueduct of some kind, was so tall you could steer a double-decker bus through it. This stretched from one set of trees on the left to a forest the other way. I couldn't see where it ended, but that's not saying much.

Black moss spattered sections of the uneven, pale pink brickwork, in contrast with other splashes bleached white. There were odd bits of green vegetation clinging to an upper parapet and the bricks looked handmade.

I'm not sure how it would compare in scale with famous European aqueducts like the Pont du Gard, which I'd studied in art class during the final year of high school, since that was a four-by-five-inch photo neatly tucked away in a textbook. This one was more imposing if only because it dwarfed the snapshot.

Surrounding a small, flat expanse of gravel were maple trees, and I believed I could make out the sounds of a stream. A stone's throw distant was the grand black silhouette of a temple or shrine, with winged roofing that pointed this way and that, uncertain in which direction Heaven lay.

'This is enchanting. Where on earth are we?'

'The aqueduct above us is named "Sosui", and it was constructed between Lake Biwa and the city of Kyoto in the nineteenth century. It runs through Nanzen-ji, where we now stand: a Zen Buddhist temple in the foothills of Kyoto.'

I had a hunch I hadn't forgotten my guidebook. This was convenient.

'An odd place to put a European-style waterway, slap-bang in the middle of this Asian religious house. Then we actually are back in the real world? I was joking.'

'Not exactly. We're lodged in a memory of the past, circa World War Two. It's reality on rewind, I suppose.'

This morsel threw me, so I unspooled my attention to check more closely than before, dubious thoughts running amuck. 'A memory? My grandfather's?'

'Not his. Mine.'

'Is he here?'

'No. We'll get to that part—just not now.'

'In which chapter, then? Or do I have to wait for the epilogue? At my age, it would more likely turn out to be the requiem.'

'Charming—and you take other people to task about over-dramatics. Have you forgotten that you skipped through the pomp and circumstance of your own funeral rites? We'll get to "Pop" at another stage.'

'When?'

'Soon. Trust me. Time is on our side, since we no longer have to fret about the concept. For the moment, I have skeletons to address and I need an outsider's perspective. I hope you wouldn't mind being chivalrous enough to escort me through the maze.'

I squinted at her. 'I have reservations. Chivalry is not my strong suit.'

At that point in the conversation—in spite of said squint—I noticed something in the corner of my eye. Strangely, this called to mind a peacock.

I loosened my lids to focus properly and saw it was another woman. I have no idea how I missed her before—she stood out well enough, hovering in the bright sunlight about ten metres away.

The woman was wearing a mostly orange kimono, with sleeves that hung down past her knees, and she had hold of a salmon-pink parasol. When I noted the serene, alabaster face shading itself beneath, I decided chivalry might come to me.

'Is it vital for me to know who the geisha is?'

'Not geisha. Not yet, anyway. In Kyoto, they called them *maiko*, apprentice geisha. In Tokyo, the epithet *hangyoku* was used. You don't recognize me?'

I do have to confess the tidbit trounced me, yet once she made the remark the evidence became discernible, as I started to see the structure of the face. It had Kohana's excellent symmetry written all over it, buried beneath the paint.

'Kyoto. Geisha. It fits.'

'Actually, I was only visiting Kyoto on this occasion. I was from Tokyo.'

The focus of our conversation had her gaze set somewhere in the middle distance. I glanced over that way, but could find nothing remarkably magnetic. 'What's she—you—looking at?'

I whispered the query, and can't opine why. Perhaps I did so because the lady was oblivious to our presence here in the archway shadows.

For her part, Kohana wasn't concerned how far her voice carried.

'Tell me you're kidding. You can't honestly expect me to remember minor details like that, can you? This was all the way back in 1944.'

'Really?' I did some quick finger counting, which isn't as easy as it sounds when your digits are semi-arthritic. 'But that would make you… I say, about…' I was at a complete loss. It was impossible to calculate such things in our current state. 'How old are you? Or were you, when you—?'

'Died? I'd hit one day past a century when I gave up the ghost. Can we get back to the here and now of this place?'

'I'm not sure I'd employ those words. "Elsewhere and past the use-by date" would better apply, with some kind of superlative thrown in to stress how far back we are. I hadn't been born yet.'

'My, aren't you young?'

'Well, I wouldn't get all hysterical about it.'

Right then, I recognized the gown the other girl was wearing. It was the sheet of fabric Kohana had hanging on her wall, the silk number with the embroidered storks—sorry, wrong bird. The ibises.

'I wore it today, for him,' Kohana said beside me in a more subdued voice. 'It was his favourite.'

She motioned at the approaching figure of a man with a strong profile, dressed in Japanese military uniform, a vintage Second World War number. He stood to attention before the geisha with a superbly straight posture, and bowed formally.

'Hangyoku,' Kohana whispered, so close that I could feel her warm breath on my neck. 'Not geisha, not yet. I told you.'

'Sadly I will never, ever be able to remember that word,' I murmured in return. 'Geisha's easier. What does it matter? Call me a heathen.'

Back on stage, the geisha gave the pilot that entrancing smile I'd witnessed earlier. Even the makeup couldn't disguise it. Then they talked together, but we were too far away to get the gist.

'It's a stunning gown,' I admitted.

'This kimono was lost during the firebombing of Asakusa in 1945, when the *okiya* I lived in was destroyed.'

'But I believe I saw it just now, on the wall of your hovel.'

'Cottage.'

'Cottage. Right you are.'

Like that kimono, questions hung unanswered. I detest such moments. As I believe I mentioned, a mystery leaves a sour sensation in my throat—unless, of course, I'm the architect of said whodunnit.

To compensate, I tried to focus on the girl chatting with the man, and studied her mannerisms. She occasionally laughed in a controlled, subtle fashion, and when she did so she sheltered the lower half of her face with an elaborately opened fan. Once composure was regained, the fan would close up shop with a deft flick.

There was a scarlet-fringed collar poking out above the gown that set off her white throat and upper shoulders, although I noticed a couple of patches on the back of the neck were left exposed to the elements, sans greasepaint. Tassels and not-so-hidden extras adorned an elaborate, glossy, brunette hairdo.

'Grant me one request.'

'What now?'

'Is that a wig? Or did you really have hair like that?'

'It was my own.'

'How did you make the hair so shiny, and what did you do to cause it to defy gravity?'

'Shhh.'

The other girl had a bright, colourful sash wrapped tightly around her waist and tied together in elaborate fashion, yet it dangled to her ankles. On her feet were white socks, with wooden clogs that looked like precarious miniature towers.

'We call the shoes *okobo*—but sometimes you may hear the term *geta*. Foreigners generally use that. They were worn to prevent our kimono from touching the ground. This pair was thirteen centimetres in height. They took a lot of practice.'

Tall, yes, and eye candy, to be sure, but I had no clue why we were here.

'Is this a pucker-up and make-out memory?' I asked, with some suspicion.

Kohana barely registered the query. 'Patience.'

'Well, when does it get otherwise involving?'

'Keep your smoking jacket on, and allow it to unravel.' She clicked her tongue. 'My gosh, you have too many questions.'

'Of course I do! Bah. It feels off. Not only are there connotations that this is going to be courtship bunk, it's also voyeuristic. Here we are studying you, yet you're right beside me and refuse to fill in the gaps. You wouldn't like me when I work myself up into a lather of pedantry, Kohana, and I have to assume you're already impartial to my charms.'

The girl looked fed up. 'Yes, yes. He left me today. In a few minutes from now, if you must know.'

'Ah-hah, so we are adrift in tear-jerking terrain. Due to some fit of bizarre nostalgia, or am I to take it you enjoy rehashing misery? The scoundrel was married, am I right?'

It seemed Kohana couldn't detach herself from the scene of the couple, not even while I needled her with a shoddy insult or two.

'He wasn't married. No, I suppose his was a different kind of commitment. Y was a pilot, a lieutenant, with the Japanese Imperial Navy. He was here on leave from a posting in Taiwan.'

'Which "here" are we looking at? What's the date?'

'It's 1944. I told you.'

'When, precisely? Humour me.'

'September 17.'

'About a year before the end of the Pacific War. How long had you known the man before today?'

'Almost three weeks? We met at an officers' party in Tokyo in late summer. We spent two of those weeks there, and then, at his invitation, the final one here in Kyoto in order to visit his family in Fushimi.'

'Where the feminine saké comes from.'

'You remembered.'

'I'm not completely oblivious. So, correct me if I'm wrong: you entertained notions of deep affection for this man within a smattering of days?'

'We were in the middle of a war and time was scanty.'

Kohana frowned, though her face was too confoundedly young for the expression to have definitive meaning.

'If we move closer, perhaps we can hear what they're saying.'

'And why on earth would I do that? I don't take to eaves-dropping. I mean this in my case, of course—you've heard all the sweet nothings before.'

'Oh, put a lid on it.'

'Temper, temper.'

She seized my hand and tugged me after her, out of the security of shadow, to be closer to our colour-mismatched lovebirds. If I'd tried to drag my feet, I doubt I could have stopped her. My withered bag of bones had nowhere near the stampeding vitality Kohana gave off in presumed death.

'Aren't we likely to interrupt things?'

'How? We're just ghosts—so much for not being forgetful.'

The voices became clearer as we neared, and true to my slave driver's suggestion, they paid no heed.

In all honesty, I doubt the pilot would have noticed us if we were flesh and blood passers-by. It was apparent that his attention was devoted to the jewel before him, and fair enough too.

'You wore it. You look exquisite,' the man remarked, in a hearty baritone.

He struck my ear as a young Gregory Peck. The fact I could understand him at all was a fortuitous bonus—when had I picked up Japanese language skills?

'I'm flattered that you appreciate my kimono.' Kohana's voice came from a different source, this time the student geisha, with a softer, more singsong inflection.

The man touched the girl's cheek, taking care not to spoil her makeup.

'Without this face, the garment would be sorely lacking.' He blinked a few times, and the hand dropped. 'I must tell you something. I'm being transferred to the Philippines and will be leaving on a flight this afternoon.'

'This afternoon—? Why?' His escort's intonation lacked the strength and confidence of the one I'd lately become accustomed to. 'I thought you were a training instructor, that you were out of combat duty.'

'Things change, Kohana-chan. This is war.' He looked past her and stroked his chin. 'You wouldn't understand. You're a child.'

'Is that so? I've been woman enough to this point.' That was more like it. Not in any way shrill—it was a deserved reproach, uttered with a tad of dignity.

Obviously the barb also made its mark. The man's gaze drifted to hers, but I fancied he was holding something back.

'Very well. I'll tell you as much as I can, which I'm afraid is very little, about the new posting. It's an idea of Vice Admiral Onishi's: the *shinpū tokubetsu kōgeki tai*, a special attack group.'

'What makes it special?'

'This is a new weapon the enemy won't expect. A divine wind, like the one that stopped the Mongols invading our land.'

'Seven hundred years ago? I thought military technology had improved since then.'

'The same wind blows.'

Well, that was disengagingly cryptic. I yawned.

There were lead-grey tufts of clouds in the nearby hills that threatened to despoil a marvellously sunny day. For now, the light was so bright it felt like the world was overexposed and the colours—particularly of the kimono—incandescent. Probably this was down to my inability to adjust to direct sunshine, after years without.

'Is it dangerous?'

The girl's face was nowhere near so blinding as the kimono, white-washed aside from a pert red mouth and watchful eyes. If there were an incorporeal being hereabouts, the geisha would be a better candidate for the role than myself. Even so, her façade was composed and her tone wonderfully steady. It was the question that came across strained.

'There is always danger in war, my flower. If I had the freedom of choice, I would stay here with you—but, alas, I do not.'

I recognized the lofty, patronizing overture, since over time I'd availed myself of a barrelful of like-minded gems. On top of this, he had squirreled away something, believing her too naïve to get the gist.

'I am not going on the mission for Emperor or for Empire. I am simply going because I was ordered.'

'What if I ask you to belay the order, or insist that you stay?'

'Such an enterprise would have the same impact as my parents' attempt. If we were to place it on a numerical scale from one to ten, I'm afraid it would rate only as—'

'Zero?'

'Zero is a powerful number to bandy unwisely.'

'Oh, rubbish,' I muttered.

Thunder rumbled somewhere, but there was neither lightning nor rain. The air felt heavy around us and it surprised me a shade could be so sensitive.

'I may be unwise,' the girl was saying, 'and yes, I am young. But I comprehend the truth when it blows my way, like those laughable winds of yours. Besides, you people bandy about "Zero-sen" enough on your own—isn't it what you call your silly airplanes?'

Bravo.

In answer, the pilot bobbed his head. He may have been as starched as a dinner shirt, and the movement conducted almost imperceptibly, but I noticed.

'He nodded,' Kohana assailed me in the left ear, 'didn't he?'

'To my mind, yes.'

'I thought so then, and I believe so now. But I never knew whether he was acknowledging the point, making some kind of vague apology, or if he did so out of politeness. I still can't fathom the gesture.'

'I got the impression the man was more acknowledging the sting in your words.'

'What's the use of returning here if nothing is clear? Isn't it a complete waste of time?'

I patted her shoulder. While I instantly twigged that, in doing so, I was treating her in the same condescending manner as the heel of a pilot, another option escaped me.

'Kohana, my dear, are you forgetting we have a lot of time to waste?'

'No. Don't be stupid. Of course not.'

'Just double-checking.'

She pushed her arm around my waist and this time manhandled me away from the two people, back toward the shadowy arches of the aqueduct. I may have been put out, but was grateful she showed some discretion and hadn't yanked me by the beard.

While we walked, I felt her arm tremble a fraction, and I made up my mind a shot of levity was in order.

'So, as you implied, he was married to his job, a depressingly familiar lark. This all took place a very long time ago—what happened to the rotter?'

'Y was killed the following month.'

'Ah.'

'He was sent on a one-way mission to fly a *tokkō*—kamikaze—attack.'

'Self-immolation was this ingenious new weapon he boasted of?'

'Most likely. The Japanese love to sacrifice themselves for stupid things.'

'I wouldn't know. I do wish I could convey an appropriate homily—you know, "He died with honour", or with his boots on, or whatever Hallmark classic you gift to a war widow. And yet—'

'There's nothing honourable about nose-diving an airplane, packed with explosives, into an enemy ship? Have no fear, I'm there with you.'

'Where did it happen? Near Japan?'

I was thinking of Okinawa—I'd read about the battle years ago. Oddly enough, Kohana read my mind.

'No, no, Okinawa was the following year. Y killed himself in the Philippines, at the Battle of Leyte Gulf. Right here.'

In a flash, we were standing on the flat deck of a monstrously huge vessel, with a twisted bundle of burning metal nearby and Caucasian-looking sailors running about, screaming and shouting. Others sat and bled, and some lay prone, burnt, blackened, or missing limbs. Perhaps some of these were included in the collection embedded in the metal walls.

Water cannons sprayed everywhere, yet missed the blaze itself, and airplanes buzzed high above. There was the muffled, far-off sound of machine guns and explosions.

Thrown all together like this, it was madness.

'Jesus wept,' I managed. 'He was not selfish in death. It looks like he took a crowd of other people with him.'

To my consternation Kohana, standing beside me, had commenced on one of her fancy cigarettes. I hadn't seen her light up. I looked around at puddles of gasoline on the deck nearby.

'Should you be smoking here?'

'Once again, you forget. We're *yūrei*—what do you call them, spirits?' She exhaled a liberal plume of smoke as she surveyed the wreckage. 'What a mess. What a stupid bloody waste.'

'Kohana, might I remind you that we're supposed to be paying a social call on your memories? It's impossible for this to be one of them.'

'Did I say that? I must have a vivid imagination. There's his plane,' she said quietly, nodding to the jumble of twisted and torn kindling the sailors danced around with their huge hoses.

'I presumed as much.'

You would never have known what it once was. This was genuine spectacle, but thankfully the decibel level of the yells had been taken down a couple of notches. The only things missing from the entertainment were the debilitating heat of the flames and the smell of burned fuel, gunpowder, and flesh.

The woman flicked away her cigarette.

'He was twenty-three years old. The news travelled lethargically to my ears—there was no wind to whisper the truth, not even a polite breeze. I heard about it from one of his fellow officers that December, and I carefully closed up shop in my heart.'

'Oh, poppycock,' I cut in, determined to bang the ticker back open. 'How ridiculous. This reminds me of something pilfered from an overwrought romance novel: "I will never love again." Surely you can't believe such tripe.'

Kohana's abrupt laughter cut through the melancholy.

'Wow! I knew there was a good reason I dragged you along with me,' she managed to say, clapping her hands, 'and it wasn't for the convoluted vocabulary.'

This was when I realized I was back on the leather sofa, cradling a cooled-down cup of saké in my fingers. She was opposite me, again seated on the Egg chair, smiling. I felt my left eyebrow rise of its own volition.

'How the Hell did you—?'

'That old trick? Who knows? Nifty, though, don't you agree?'

'Allow me to reserve judgment.' I sat there for a few seconds, untamed thoughts and a modicum of distress taking turn to storm the ramparts of what passed for good sense. Finally, I found words. 'I have some silly questions.'

'Of course you do.'

'How is it possible that I can understand what people are saying, when they're clearly speaking a language I never studied?'

'I don't know.'

'I see. Well, how do we jump, or teleport, or flip channels—or whatever it is we're undertaking—between each setting?'

'I have no idea.'

'Am I insane?'

'Are you?'

'I hope not. Are we dead?'

'Maybe.'

'Oh, the Devil with you, this is ridiculous. You evade answering a single question, hit me with unsweet nothings, or lob back interrogatories! It's maddening, and let me tell you—I am not one to be treated this way.'

Kohana looked straight my way, her eyes sparkling. 'Are you threatening me in some obscure, geriatric fashion?'

'Take the comment whichever way you prefer.'

'All right, Wolram. If you want free-range interpretation, by all means. Let's look at you. For starters, you like to be in charge, am I right? You ran your own company, your own city, your own world. In bed, in the missionary position, I bet you're the one who has to be on top—dictating proceedings while stark naked.'

'If it were a paying position, why not?'

'So you'd be up for prostitution?'

'I'm not certain many people would be up for a seventy-one-year-old gigolo.'

I don't know why I blushed, but it was obvious that's how I reacted, since I could feel my ears and cheeks burning.

'And, by the way, if you are saying I am a control freak, I resent the implication.'

'If I said you were a control freak, it's not an implication—it's a statement.'

'That's damned well pedantic.'

'It's damned well proper word play.'

'Well, are you?'

'Am I, what?'

'Implying? …Stating?'

'Neither tangent entered my mind.'

'Pfaw!'

Kohana laughed. 'Oh, Wolram—what does that mean—"pfaw"? Isn't it something more appropriate between the covers of a Charles Dickens?'

I was too annoyed to see any wit behind the comment. 'You tell me, since you're the avid reader. In fact, why is this important at all? Let's return to everything right here, right now, about this place and what on earth we're doing. What exactly *can* you tell me?'

'Very little.'

'Oh, rich.'

'I'm sorry. There's no instruction manual here, no convenient cheat-notes. I can't skimp on the book by watching the movie version, like you did at university with *The Name of the Rose*.'

I'd been moodily staring at the floor, rubbing an index finger along my right brow, an old habit when grumpy, but glanced at her when I heard this last comment.

'That's not entirely true. I read some of it.'

'How many pages?'

I shifted in my seat. 'Thirty-odd?'

'Then you only missed the next five hundred.'

Kohana pursed her lips—it seemed to be her own pet mannerism when thoughtful. The two of us were full of them.

'Anyway, I may have been here longer, but like you, I'm mostly flying blind.'

'Making it the mystery you were talking up earlier.'

'Much of it, yes.'

'A lot of good that does me.'

'I agree. So, stop thinking so hard and go with the flow.'

'The flow? I'd say it's more like inserting my head into a strobe machine.'

'A neat analogy.'

'Thank you. May I ask a different question?'

'You can try.'

'Will you grant me an honest answer?'

'I don't know. That would mean my turn to try. Bother.'

'Are you a religious person?'

'Far from it. Life taught me otherwise.'

'Putting inconsequential lessons to one side—are we ghosts?'

'Well, the thought crossed my mind that we might be Buddhist *Preta*.'

'Eh?'

'In Japanese, we call them *Gaki*, and I think the English expression is "hungry ghosts"? But all the pictures I ever saw portrayed these creatures with bulging tummies, and an otherwise emaciated look—neither of us has to worry there. Also, we're by no means aflame like Gaki, let alone smoky—unless we take the cigarettes into account.'

'Gaki?'

'It's an Asian thing. Spirits of jealous or greedy people, cursed with an insatiable desire for the good things in life.'

'That sounds like me before I died,' I groaned. 'One last query.'

'Yes?'

'Are we merely passive observers? What do you call those non-memories, like the burning kite on the American ship? Bonus extras? Are we ethereal, no more than ghosts?—and, if so, how can we touch objects? How can we walk on solid ground, for that matter?'

'Sorry, I'm swamped.' Kohana got to her feet and crossed

silently to a cupboard. 'Are you hungry? I have some rice crackers, though you probably won't much like them. *Wasabi* flavour. It's my favourite, aside from *yuzu*.'

'Look, at this stage of affairs I'd partake of grasshoppers in soy sauce—'

Kohana wrinkled her nose.

'—and, yes, I do know they were considered a treat in some parts of Japan, though from your expression, I'd wager they're scarcely your cup of tea. Not that I have an appetite. I never do these days, but at my advanced age I need to keep my hands from clawing up out of disuse.'

'Zounds,' the woman muttered as she placed a bowl of tan-coloured crackers nearby. 'Give me a few weeks and I'll be combing cobwebs out of your hair. You really are obsessed with your age. When will you get it through that brain of yours that I'm older?'

'Probably, I'll allow further consideration when you look the part. By the way, I'm not happy about the situation we're in, or the lack of concrete answers. I refuse to budge from my high-horse until I'm satisfied.'

Without thinking, I took a bite from one of the crackers.

I knew what to expect—I was well enough acquainted with Japanese horseradish—but it took its own chomp out of my palate, and I swallowed the bugger as quickly as I could.

'By God, you weren't joking. This finger-food is running rampant across my taste buds.'

When I looked up, I was blessedly able to forget all about wasabi, since we'd swapped locations in an instant.

This time, the two of us were deposited at a low table in some kind of restaurant that didn't believe in chairs. We were forced to sit cross-legged on prickly tatami mats, which played havoc with my problematic left hip.

There was a cup of murky, frothy, green-coloured liquid before us both. I presume I blanched at the sight.

'Do we really have to go through this now? I was looking forward to a toilet break—my bladder isn't what it used to be, my girl.'

'Later,' she shot back, all serious again. The woman was like a revolving door.

Turns out, the adolescent geisha and her pilot beau were 'seated' at the next table. Surprise. My Kohana scrutinized them closely, like someone absorbed in a thoroughly gripping Korean telly drama. Of course I had to join in and watch. The ratings must have flown through the roof.

Our ring-in Kohana, starring in this nonsense, wore a different kimono, a ravishing emerald-green number with a lemon-yellow *obi* sash.

Since we were much closer to her and the light was gentler indoors, I could better see charcoaled brows with a touch of crimson, and gently arched eyes outlined with red and black. The sienna irises, with flecks of chestnut, stood out a league or two.

I should have hoped the pilot would notice them, but on this occasion he was preoccupied with the bland meal before him, a dish of grey pasta slapped down on a bamboo mat.

'*Soba*,' Kohana mentioned. 'Buckwheat noodles. They're far better than they look to you.'

'I'm sure.'

'By the way, just so you know, wasabi isn't horseradish.'

Once he finished some disturbingly loud slurping, the pilot dabbed at his lips with a napkin. 'I'll take you today to see Nijō-jō,' he announced, with all the pizzazz of a gherkin.

What had Kohana called him? Y? Didn't the man have space for a full name?

'I was under the impression that this Y-character had flown the coop,' I said, muzzling another yawn.

'We had lunch together here, the day before our final meeting at Nanzen-ji.'

'You're flipping the narrative around? You could grant me fair warning next time.'

'I'm doing so now. Isn't that enough for you?'

'No, it's not—I'm bursting to go to the loo, and of course I'm going to get cranky.'

'Shush.'

'You shush.'

Meanwhile, the young man droned on, despite the better attempts of a rousing baritone. Oh, hurrah. How I craved the ability to override my newfound language decoder.

'Construction of the castle was begun by Tokugawa Ieyasu, and completed by his grandson Tokugawa Iemitsu in the 1620s. It's more palace than castle, but what fascinates me is the *karamon* gate. It was plundered from Fushimi Castle'—cue wry twinkle, bordering, I'll admit, on debonair—'and is one of the most beautiful castle gates I've observed.'

Throughout the one-way discourse the geisha kept her gaze more often downturned, with a charming smile on cherubic, plum-red lips.

'Chiefly it's the inlay of the toki in flight, above the heavy gates themselves,' he went on. 'There is a sense of otherness that reminds me so much of you and that kimono you once wore. The magnificent one also graced with ibises.'

At that, the geisha's eyes looked up and sparkled.

I swivelled to the girl's doppelgänger, triggering a dull ache in my hip. I knew we would not be overheard, but spoke to her in a low voice. 'What's he waffling on about?'

'Is your hearing worse than your memory?'

'Whatever. Is this sort of oratory romantic to you people? Does he seduce you with a line like that?'

'Well, I'd hate to hear what you consider lovey-dovey,' Kohana whispered back. 'For such a ladies' man, you exhibited some shocking courtship choices in your time.'

I glared at her. I could feel my face getting hot, something I'd not experienced in years. 'What the deuce do you know of my life?'

'This and that.'

'Meaning?'

'A portion of this, and a smidgeon of that.'

I think I was prepared to leave the table, then and there, if my troublesome hip hadn't locked.

'I'm becoming very tired of this circular discourse, getting no straight answers. Please don't let you be the Ghost of Christmas Past, or some such nonsense.'

'I'm Japanese. The only thing we celebrate at Christmas is fine wine and dinner with a paramour. Occasionally, we get tipsy and sing Christmas songs at karaoke. Poorly.'

'Well, good. I'm not one for Scrooge and all that morality claptrap.'

Kohana beamed. 'I can't believe you said "claptrap"—isn't that a bit grizzled? Why don't you road-test "humbug" for effect?'

Her bonhomie disarmed my anger, and went so far as to provoke a grin. 'Well, I considered using "mumbo jumbo", but it doesn't roll off the tongue so sweetly, and—I don't know—it sounds provincial. I don't want to come across as a bamboozled old fart, even if that's what I am.'

I looked at the two people we were supposed to be here to observe.

'Speaking of which, is he still prattling?'

'I believe so. He talked for over an hour. Y cherished his traditional Japanese architecture, and I loved listening to him "prattle" on about it. How else do you think I learned about the aqueduct at Nanzen-ji? There was such affection and passion in his attention to detail. Whatever you make of him, Mr Deaps, he showered that on me as well.'

'Wolram, for Heaven's sake.'

'May I call you Wol?'

'No.' I sized her up. 'Ko.'

'How would you like a chopstick in the eye?'

'Would it make any impression in our current state? I could become accustomed to the wearing of an eye patch.'

'I really don't know. I doubt we're capable of injury, but I'm not keen to try out the theory.'

Kohana had conceivably forgotten the monologue at the next table, and I was not going to remind her.

'Well,' she mused, 'a different question: do you entertain any regrets?'

'None whatsoever.'

'A quick fire response.'

'I appreciate what I am, and strive to keep things uncomplicated.'

'Oh? Good for you. Like your vocabulary, I suppose.'

'Is that sarcasm I detect?'

'I have no idea. You tell me.' The girl rotated her cup in both hands before taking a long sip.

'How is it?' I had been too cagey to try my own.

'Wonderful. I'd forgotten how perfect the *matcha* was at this teahouse.'

She placed the cup on the low table.

'You might be foolishly frightened of green tea and foreign noodles, but I think we're similar. Both of us have lived self-centred lives that harmed other people, and we did it with a careless—no, make that deliberate—ardour. The other thing we have in common? We're both murderers.'

I felt as if my stomach had been bludgeoned.

'You?' Somehow, I motioned to the docile twin at the next table. '*Her?*'

'Yes. Us. And you. We all do what we must, and live with what we've done—isn't that right?'

Though I couldn't mark it, the comment sounded eerily familiar. I felt discomforted, a sensation not entirely caused by my aching hip. 'Go on,' I murmured.

'Ends up, you're not the only miscreant with a fractured Iago complex.'

'I'm not sure I understand what you're saying.'

'About murder in general, or the amateur analysis I tagged on the end?'

'The *Othello* part.'

'Oh, so you bothered looking at a book?'

'It was compulsory reading material at school—but anyhow, Shakespeare has more pull than Sir Thomas Malory.'

'Possibly because he smote closer to home.'

'Possibly.'

I stared at her, as I tried to gauge in what direction she was corralling the conversation. Her face may have suggested itself as an open tome from which I could ransack meaning while her guard was down, but, as with Shakespeare, I couldn't come to grips with most of the content right there in front of me. I wished I'd paid more attention in class.

'Let's back-pedal to Iago, shall we?' I suggested. 'While the man did have his moments running rings around the Moor, and his amorality is an intriguing beast to explore, at a baser level the man lacked confidence.'

'You think so?'

'I do. The man shot himself in the foot pursuing a course of self-sabotage, and he was hamstrung by—what should we call it? ...Meaninglessness? A long-winded word, to be sure, but you get the gist.'

'Relatively.'

'So, these are things miles from my character. I'm willing to take the punt that the same applies to you.'

'Oh, very kind.'

Her voice had wandered across in a glacial monotone. I was impressed, but in return guffawed out loud. I hadn't laughed so boisterously in an age or two, and ended up having to wipe the tears away, in order to see properly.

'Murderers? Well, for goodness' sake. Would you care to know the misgiving that's been whizzing about in my head? I was worried you'd be an artless princess-bride, enamoured with the dashing, cardboard cut-out aerialist.'

'There's a zany idea, Wolram—do you make up these things for a living?'

'Frequently.'

'Then this is one time you don't have to fret.'

'I stand, or sit, gratefully corrected.'

Sashimi had appeared before us on a light blue ceramic platter, decorated with shredded radish and a flower. Kohana poked at the fish with a pair of chopsticks.

'The real deal,' she confirmed. 'When I was alive, people would have been aghast to see me playing with my food this way. Now, who's to stop me? I wish I were hungry. Think of Y as an adolescent phase I went through. I was immature. He died on October 25, a day after the sinking of the Japanese aircraft carrier *Zuikaku*—but also the day after my fifteenth birthday. I mean, really, I was too young. Good riddance.'

The girl watched me as she spoke. While there was not a single moment that her gaze failed her, I experienced doubt all the same. Probably it was the amount of detail padding out the sentence. I wouldn't have been surprised had she rehearsed the disavowal.

I glanced at her likeness, seated beside us with the ironing board posture.

The fan in her right hand occasionally spread its wings to send a cooling breeze across an absurdly pale face. I studied those made-up eyes as she attended her pilot. I don't care how well someone is trained to behave in a certain way, no matter if they're a geisha, an actor, a politician, or a high-stakes businessman—the truth is always there.

When I looked back to my Kohana, there was a similar glint.

This glint was minute, cleverly hidden behind trapdoors and

pulleys, and I'll admit it was more difficult to smoke out. But in the end, I could see precisely how she felt.

'You're still in love with the miscreant,' I said, affixing a degree of venom that surprised me.

4 | 四

I snapped to, on a toilet.

It was a well-appointed commode, to be sure, with a warm seat and a device attached called a Washlet S-1900—though I couldn't read the instructions beside each button, as they appeared to be written in scrambled Japanese.

This remote controller also had the word 'TOTO' printed on it in Roman capitals.

Beside me, there was a roll of floral-pattern double-ply toilet paper hidden under a lace doily, just like the ones my grandmother used to crochet. Marcel Duchamp's cistern this was not.

To be honest, I have no idea if I had relieved myself. Despite my quip to Kohana, I could not recall a prior necessity of doing so here in this limbo—but I was open to change. Perhaps the lavatory break was also designed to remind me of my infantile choice in undergarment. Several white, grinning skulls on black flags peered at me with undisguised mirth.

I hastily pulled up my pants, worked out how to flush, and then washed my hands at a nearby sink.

Kohana's cabin was empty. Even the fire had scarpered. I walked the length of the living space, listening for some sign, but all I could hear was the wind whistling outside. It was like the set-up to one of those chilling Hammer films from the 1960s, right before Frankenstein's monster barged in.

Annoyed, I went to the door and swung it open.

It was bright out there, with no breeze at all. Curious. I found my slippers by the entrance, slid them on, and walked out into the warmth.

I found my hostess seated on a grassy knoll, over near the edge of the cliff. She'd changed into a cotton robe with spacious sleeves, pink and grey and decorated with lotus flowers. There was a taut, saffron-yellow sash tied round the waist. The bun on top of her head had been unravelled and the straight hair now hung down past her hips. She also had a fringe that sat at a charming, minimal distance above the eyebrows.

Otherwise, the woman had her elbows on her knees and her chin in her hands. She was staring out over a sea that was much calmer and had a blue tinge to it.

In absent-minded fashion, I broke off some honeysuckle leaves from around the hazelnut's trunk.

'Don't do that,' Kohana said, without looking over. 'There's already enough love lost in the world.'

I didn't reply, possibly because there was nothing to say to something so harebrained. I dropped the leaves in exaggerated fashion, looked around at the emptiness in all directions, and decided to mend some fences.

'Would you overly mind, if I sat with you?'

'Not really. No, not at all.'

Kohana edged over, in order to allow me space to unravel my old body into a reasonably comfortable position beside her. I believe I was getting used to the lack of chairs.

'You have flowing water here. Where does that come from?'

'The pipes?' I could not tell if she was being glib.

'Well, that's apparent. And where do those pipes get their supply?'

'I haven't the foggiest.'

'There's a surprise.'

'We're really lucky this isn't Yomi, a gloomy underworld—like Hades—that we learn about in Shintōism. Here, we have a view. A sky and an ocean to ponder.'

It was a splendid view. I decided to shut up and enjoy the moment.

To be fair, I was also trying to shake the sounds of the screaming on board that wartime ship.

Within moments, I had my limbs composed identically to Kohana's and gazed over the sea to the hazy point where the horizon should have been. Of course, I couldn't remain silent for long.

'I have to mention something. You can desist with all the references to *The Wonderful Wizard of Oz*.'

'Excuse me?'

'The toilet: Toto. The scarecrow back there, the allusions to the animals from Oz that are littered throughout the house, numerous other hints. I'm not myopic. I have noticed.'

'Fascinating. Toto was once a famous toilet manufacturer in Japan—the name is an abbreviation of the two words making up the company's name, Tōyō Tōki.' She wasn't looking at me. 'I'm not the type to pay homage to a book I never picked up. Yep, I've seen the movie *The Wizard of Oz*—who hasn't?—but it didn't leave a lasting impression. Either you're reading too much into matters, which I find dubious, or you brought baggage with you.'

I remembered the toilet roll doily.

'Ahh.'

I rubbed my forehead. I thought I smelled a combination of salt and kelp in the air, but couldn't be sure. It might have been the scent of a spit-roast.

The girl was right. Nothing here was what it appeared to be— and that, as sure as punch, put a spin on things.

5 | 五

'I was born on Black Thursday.'

'Oh, indeed?' I scratched my chin, beneath the straggly beard.

'You know it?'

'That depends. If you are trying to frighten me, it's not working. Black Thursday—boo! I'm tempted to toss a "humbug" right back.'

'You're peculiar. I'm not trying to scare you. Black Thursday was on October 24, 1929. The first day of the Wall Street Crash in the United States, and the beginning of the Great Depression.'

I seized the moment right after the girl finished giving her pint-sized speech to return a warm round of applause.

'Wonderful! What a way to recall one's birthday. It's highly unlikely friends and relatives could forget a date like that, by gosh. In my case, I was nowhere near so fortunate. I shared my birthday with Armenian Independence Day, on the 21st of September, and wouldn't be able to point out Armenia on a map.'

Kohana had her eyes fixed on the placid water far below. What she thought, I couldn't tell, and to be honest I did feel the tiniest amount chastened by her silence.

'Oh well, I must apologize,' I ventured. 'Did that rain on your parade?'

In answer, the woman ignored me.

'I was not born alone,' she took up, acting as if my babbling had never transpired. 'I arrived four minutes after my sister. And the only thing that crashed for us on that date was our mother's uterus. Seconds before, I had no name, and my mother was alive. Then, my sister had a twin. I came out screaming, and my mother's womb collapsed. She died giving birth to me.'

'Yes, I see.' I felt a minor chill. 'I do get your point.'

Spread out, on the sandy lawn beside us, was a thin mattress on which a dead woman lay. Of course, I recoiled.

The skin around this woman's bare chest and neck had an ashen tinge to it, but I could not make out her face, since it was shrouded beneath a mess of black hair. The lower half of her body was covered with a quilt drenched in blood and sweat. Two lively, naked, screaming babies lay next to the woman.

'Really, Kohana, this is too much. If you want an apology for my impertinence—you have it.'

I looked away, but after some seconds passed, I sneaked another glance at the diorama. It had packed up things and vanished. I assumed I had to make a comment of some kind. My remaining semblance of good manners demanded it.

'So, you had a twin sister.'

'I did.'

'Did you look the same?'

'Are you asking if we're identical? Yes. On the outside. But our innards were cast in completely different foundries—she had my mother's healthy ones; I often think I inherited her dismembered, post-natal self.'

'Eloquent? For sure. Far-fetched? Extraordinarily.'

'Most likely you're right.' Kohana examined her lap and used fingers to smooth out the material of her dress.

'I suppose death in childbirth was a far more common occurrence back in—when was this? 1929, you said? Ancient times?'

Again the girl ignored me. This was getting to be a diabolical habit.

'My father refused to be called "Papa". He held to the more formal *Oto-sama*, and he regarded me with an expression that said "You killed my wife", or something close to it.'

There was no poignant, carefully choreographed picture-show this time. To all appearances, Kohana preferred to keep the old man out of frame.

'How does one do that?' I asked.

Deathlike silence, like talking to a wall.

'Excuse me?'

'Hmm?' The girl looked over.

'Aren't we having a discussion here?'

'Yes, of course.'

'Then how does one do it?'

'Do what?'

'My original question, of course—devise a facial bearing that conveys so much? It would be rather useful. The poker face was a breeze for me to master, but I'm certain I could have closed the odd engaging business deal, with a filicidal scowl.'

'I doubt it's something you can flip on and off.'

'Surely there's a switch?' I meant something emotional, but the woman went off tangent for material.

'Wolram, my father wasn't a power point.'

'Do tell.'

'But now I think of it, he had only that one expression—sustenance enough for the remainder of his life. Yes, the switch was left on. That would make Mama fortunate. Not only did she escape an exceptionally negative marriage partner and a brace of clutching kids, but she was in good company.'

'How so?'

'She relinquished life on the same date Christian Dior did in 1957—though I've heard tell that this is debatable. May I use your word? Scuttlebutt has it Dior died on October 23, not October 24 as reported.'

I honestly didn't care one jot which day Dior kicked the bucket. I feigned interest for a couple of infuriating seconds, and then gave up. Bad enough that she'd tarnished scuttlebutt's good name.

'What does some Frenchie fashion designer have to do with your mother? Unless I'm missing an elemental clue here? If so, pray enlighten me.'

Kohana refused to answer, and I couldn't tell whether this was because she was being truculent, or just damned well depressed. Either way, it made me irritable, so I turned my attention elsewhere.

'There are no seagulls here,' I muttered. 'In fact, I've seen not a single bird since I arrived. Aren't ravens and crows and other carrion supposed to be signifiers of death? All we have are those ibises on the kimono in there.'

I shifted in my squatting position to place my hands on my thighs. My lower spine was aching—an old complaint I'd come to term 'art gallery back', principally because I suffered it at insufferable exhibition opening parties.

A cold, gusty breeze had started up and I spied white tips on the waves below. Despite its non-committal nature to this point, the weather looked like it was about to turn brutish.

'Shall we go indoors?' I had in mind velveteen pillows and warm saké.

As I pushed to my feet, I could have sworn I heard the old bones creak. Once I'd achieved the amazing, I looked down at my hostess, but she hadn't moved a muscle.

Her choice. I shelved any plans of playing it suave and walked unsteadily back to the hovel. Once I reached the door, I took off my slippers and went inside.

Somehow, the fire in the centre of the room had restarted and it gave off enough light to see by—if you didn't mind a stubbed toe.

I felt hungry for the first time in an eternity, ravenously so.

I popped over to the pantry against the wall, the one where the rice crackers lived, and searched for a treat. There was a bar fridge set into the woodwork beside it, and inside that I discovered perfection. Sushi. A whole platter of raw fish of various colours, assembled purely for my satisfaction.

I took out the plastic tray, placed it on the table, and snapped apart a convenient pair of wooden chopsticks. I had no idea where to find soy sauce, but the situation offered deficient impediment.

Without further ado, I dug in—or gave it my best shot,

anyhow. One chopstick strained, and then snapped, while the other slipped from my unprofessional fingers. I do believe I swore out loud.

'What are you up to?' Kohana asked from the doorway.

'Trying my best to look competent.'

I picked up the stray chopstick, wondering whether I should give it a rinse, or go with the flow. I doubted bacteria would indulge in an afterlife and tried to use the utensil as a scale-model harpoon on an enticing chunk of orange—the salmon—beached atop a bundle of white rice. The devil was hard like leather, and I had all the competence of Captain Ahab.

'You do know, that's plastic?'

I stopped mid-lunge, to glance at her. 'What do you mean, plastic?'

'It's fake. Made at Kappabashi-dori, a place we call Kitchen Town, near where I used to live in Tokyo. They specialized in realistic plastic display food for restaurants—like the sushi.'

'Then why the blazes do you have it in your refrigerator?'

Kohana shrugged. 'Where else would I put the thing? I don't exactly have a restaurant, and it looks out of place on the secretaire.'

I thought this over for a moment. 'True.'

The girl waltzed my way, whisked from my hand the counterfeit cuisine, and placed it back on its shelf in the fridge. 'Are you really suffering from an empty stomach, or just bored?' I heard her ask.

'How could I ever get bored, my dear, with all the surprises you keep dropping off in my lap? It's busier here than a department store bargain sale.'

Openly yawning, I leaned over so I could better see the framed photo of the military man and geisha that was propped next to the altar.

'You and your inamorato Y,' I deduced at this closer angle— but then checked myself. 'Just a moment. How do I know the girl in the picture is you? Didn't you just mention an identical twin?'

When I looked to my hostess, the doubt was hardly abated.

She had her head tilted to one side and gazed at me with a fathomless expression. One could imagine dropping depth charges there and never hearing them explode. Being reminded of the sham sushi, the whole package struck me as unnerving.

'There's a fine question,' she said, at last.

Ill at ease, I returned my attention to the photo.

'So, now we potentially have three people who all look the same—this is bound to become confusing. Or is this fake too?'

In the photo, I noticed a classic Japanese triple-storey villa on the other side of a pond behind the couple, and even in monochrome it boasted an unnatural iridescence.

'Kyoto, right? I believe I recognize the building.'

Kohana had sidled up next to me.

'That's Kinkaku-ji and, yes, it was in Kyoto. It's likely you remember the place from a computer wallpaper image that once popped up everywhere—you're old enough for that. But, like the sushi you were poking just now, the building in the wallpaper was a phony. The one in this photograph is real.'

'You're losing me.'

'I suspected as much—hang in there, tiger.' Kohana smiled one of her big, rich numbers, and I felt my legs go unsteady. She knew how and when to allocate those prizes.

'You really are dangerous,' I grumbled.

The girl winked at me. '*Deshō?*'

'What?'

'*Deshō*—um, how do I put this? *Deshō* has many meanings, usually things like "right?", or "isn't it?"; it's used as a confirmational tag, for agreement, or when one isn't sure. In this case, I was agreeing with you.'

'Well, yes, whatever.'

'*Deshō.*' She laughed to herself. 'Getting back to Kinkaku-ji, let me also explain that a little clearer. You do know the twentieth-century Japanese writer Yukio Mishima?'

'One Q&A I can tackle, with complete conviction—he killed himself via ritual suicide, am I correct?'

'*Seppuku*. That's right. Kudos, Wolram. How did you know?'

My invisible victory punch fizzled in midair. I ought to have been accustomed to that.

'Denslow, again. Remember the Japanophile? He always had his nose in a book by some Japanese author. Mishima popped up. One of his favourites, he said, when we were sharing a cup of tea and the conversation was flailing.'

'Did you look at any pages inside?'

'No need, my dear. I answered your question. Deshō?'

Kohana looked dubious. 'Delightful. Mishima penned a famous novel called *The Temple of the Golden Pavilion*. You wouldn't have heard of it.'

'Sorry. Not on any of my reading lists.'

'Don't worry, I assumed as much. The story revolves around a mad monk who adores beauty—yet, at the same time, loathes it—and he ends up setting fire to one of the most beautiful buildings in Japan. A place that, until then, had survived six hundred years, some particularly violent centuries. Mishima based the novel on real life. Kinkaku-ji burned down in 1950, and was rebuilt in 1955. The building on the Apple wallpaper is the remake, but in the photograph here, you can see the original.'

'Which you visited? Or was it your sister?'

'No, no, me. Tomeko never went to Kyoto.'

So. The sister did have a name.

6 | 六

'I'll drink to that.'

I'd seated myself on the couch again and was thinking a toast would be in order.

'Would you happen to have any more saké?'

Kohana returned and stood over me with the flask, her hair swinging around my face. A more pleasant way to get a refill and have my view obscured, I'd never once encountered.

I had not realized it, but she was a good two centimetres taller than myself—more due to the fact that age had shrunk my height, than any Amazonian stature the girl possessed. Plus, as I do like to insist, I was seated, whereas she was standing up.

'Are you thinking about making an offering?' Kohana asked, after she finished filling my cup and stood back.

'To whom? You?' Frankly, I was confused.

'Not to me, Wolram. It's an old Japanese custom to make an offering at a shrine or temple, as a token for departed souls, and often we leave saké.'

'Oh, I see. Fair enough.' I raised my cup. 'Well, here's to the gods of abundance and creature comfort.'

'Perhaps you should check behind you?'

Taking her cue, I looked over my shoulder.

'Oh dear. I see I will have to put on hold my old friends abundance and creature comfort, at least for the time being.' That said, I turned back to my budding cruise director. 'So where are we now—and is this before, after, or in-between the two other times?'

'Later. Roughly six months.'

'Kyoto?'

'Tokyo.'

'At this rate, I'll have seen all of Japan before I die again.'

I was happy to note I had travelling partners aside from the woman: I was comfy in the ivory-coloured sofa, and had that cup of saké in my right hand. Admittedly, I was now slap-bang in the middle of a narrow, quiet street some time after nightfall, but I'd managed to haul along a couple of creature comforts.

Kohana had abandoned her plain attire of the other visits and taken this opportunity to arrive in resplendent form—making me feel more the sore thumb.

Her hair, which had so recently tickled my nose, was tied up and laminated into that geisha working girl style—the same as her younger, living self, the first time I saw her in Kyoto. You know, the golden kimono with ibises on it, fluttering about, and a snow-white face. In other words, a life-size Japanese souvenir doll, only she seemed a little older and somehow sadder.

The girl turned around slowly, in mincing steps on those hazardous clogs, gazing with thawing warmth that replaced the sorrow. I took this to be affection for the rows of dark brown, compact, double-storey wooden houses on either side.

'This is Asakusa. I lived here with my sister from the age of six, in that okiya—a geisha house—right over there.'

Kohana pointed out an innocuous building before us that had a red lantern dangling from its balcony.

Its dark, downstairs window was made of wooden lattice and paper, but the one on the second storey, above the tiled verandah, was round, with diagonal slats, and softly lit. There was a small sign with a freestyle painted *kanji* symbol next to the front door, which consisted of two sliding screens.

'The okiya was called Kiri—Paulownia Tree—and it was owned by a woman named Oume-san. She ran a house that was a cooperative, dividing the profits among the girls, after overheads were covered.'

'Is that so? I heard somewhere that geisha houses were strict, disciplinarian places.'

'You've been reading too much fiction by foreigners.' The girl unfurled a fan in quasi-coy manner. 'Oh, wait, did I say *reading*?

Perhaps I should infer you've watched a few too many movies-of-the-week.'

'Side-splitting.'

Kohana snapped shut the fan.

'I know, I know—flimsy. Surprisingly, you're not far from the truth. This was not the norm for okiya, and Oume-san was nowhere near the norm for its management. Personally speaking, we had the best mama-san in the trade—but she wasn't so good at business. We barely stayed above water.'

'So you worked here? It looks a little small.'

'It's not a brothel, Wolram. These were our living quarters— we mostly worked in tea houses and at restaurants.'

'How many people lived in the building?'

'There were eight of us. Oume-san, two older geisha, three hangyoku, including Tomeko and me, and our maids. Space was precious.'

The wooden structures along the street, to left and right, looked dull and interchangeable. 'Are these all geisha houses, then?'

'Some are.'

'How good was business?'

'Before the war, I hear it was booming. By 1945, we were scratching to survive, and most of the other okiya had been closed down. I hit my prime at a dreadful time. We were fortunate that Oume-san had high-up contacts in the military— as much as she privately despised them.'

I sipped at my saké. The street was quiet and peaceful enough, and we were the only people about. One could get used to lounging here, even if the temperature was a trifle crisp.

Right then, however, my leisure time was interrupted by... What the Devil was that annoying sound? Bees?

'As a wise man once told me, danger always strikes when everything seems fine. Listen, Wolram. You hear it?'

'How could I miss the commotion? What is that?'

'Speculate.'

'Oh God, I'm not in the mood for guessing games. Bees, or wasps, come immediately to mind. So, I don't know—the Wicked Witch of the West, sending down a horde of emissaries?'

'Not the Wicked Witch.'

'No?'

'The Allied Forces.'

It clicked, then. 1945.

'Oh crap. A bombing raid?'

7 | 七

I was sitting on a three-legged stool, next to that glazed raccoon dog on the hovel's doorstep. I couldn't recall how I got here.

I peered in all four directions.

The ocean. Nothing. Nothing. The hovel. And that was it—a realm so darned mundane, I believed I might scream.

'You know, given the state of the place I was ejected from when I was shot in the noggin, I never thought I would admit this—but I yearn for city life. I miss the amenities, the wining and dining, the twenty-four-hour convenience.'

'Those things mean a lot to you?' Kohana asked from where she sat on a large, flat rock in the yard, sketching impressionistic cats with elongated necks. They reminded me of the cats my mother used to draw for me when I was a child, and looked like bottles lined up to fall. 'You miss Melbourne that much?'

'I can't say I've mentioned Melbourne to you before. Have I?'

'I don't know. You shouldn't expect a centenarian to have the best memory.'

The girl was shading one of her drawings green. A curious colour for a cat.

'Did you ever visit Melbourne?'

Kohana sniffed and wiped her nose. 'Visit?' Then she looked right at me. 'I lived there half my life. Deshō?'

Being caught off-balance by this infuriating woman was turning out to be a commonplace experience, but this time the disclosure was perfectly reasonable, in light of recent world events—or at least the recent ones, before I expired.

'I assumed,' I said, 'well, I meant to say…'

'You assumed I lived and died in my country? I wasn't through-and-through Japanese by the time I kicked the bucket. I'd spent several decades living abroad—most of that in Australia.'

'Why didn't you say so?'

'You didn't ask.'

'This changes everything!' I was suddenly delighted.

'How?'

'Well, if you were born in 1929 and died when you were a hundred, that would have meant you did so—'

'In your brave new world.'

I checked myself. 'Oh.'

'I died there not long before you pulled up stumps—well, that's not especially true. A few years before. Enough time to get acquainted here.' Kohana sharpened a pencil. 'So I knew about Wolram E. Deaps when we were both alive and kicking. Couldn't really help it—you were a famous man.'

She stood up and dusted down her backside.

'I feel grimy. I think I'll take a bath. How about you?'

'What, together?' I chuckled to myself, having dared so brazen a quip. Somewhere, sight unseen at the back of my mind, I etched a few notches. Wolram—3, Kohana—0.

'That's what I presumed. Why is it amusing?'

Those notches were straight away erased. 'No, no, to the contrary, I assure you,' I panicked. 'Not funny at all.'

'Then why are you acting so weird about the idea?'

'Weird? What's weird? It's not weird.'

'More weird. Right. Good. Come with me, then.'

'Now?'

Kohana frowned. 'No, tomorrow. What do you think? Come on, buster.'

I grudgingly followed Kohana on a dusty path around the hovel, skirting the herb garden and the scarecrow. At the back of the building, in the open, with no roofing or sense of discretion, was a cast-iron contraption that looked like a barrel in which you'd usually press grapes.

This was not intended for making wine. It was a bathtub, and beneath it smouldered a wood-burning stove.

'Now you get to take off your clothes,' Kohana announced as she turned around to look at me, with a cheeky beam. 'Kohana — 3, Wolram — 0.'

The Devil she knew. 'What, all of them? Now?'

'Whenever you're ready.'

'In front of you?'

'All right, all right. I'll turn around. Unbelievable.'

As she did so, the girl slid off her cotton dress and an undergarment, and before I could think to avert my eyes, I saw a large tattoo on her back — a winding dragon with eight heads, stretching from her neck to her naked buttocks, cavorting right down to the left thigh.

I twisted away. I was staring at the back wall of the hovel, a side of the place I'd not seen before. No wonder. It bored me senseless.

'Come on,' I heard Kohana urge.

I swallowed my slaphappy pride, took off the smoking jacket and folded it neatly, swept the residual gunk off a banana lounge, and placed it there. Then, I removed my slacks, shirt and cravat. I was stark naked, aside from pirate underwear — which I attempted to disguise with my hands, when I slowly turned back to the woman.

Kohana stood there with no clothes and no shame. I stared at her face, refusing to look an inch beneath the chin. The girl had no such qualms. She ran her eyes over me, and then guffawed.

'Oh dear. Why on earth are you wearing such silly short-pants — those are Jolly Roger flags! How old are you again?'

'Laugh all you want, my dear. Modesty prevents removal. May I point out, I'm an elderly gent?'

'Gent? That's questionable. And don't you don't think I've seen an old rump, or three, in my time? I lived to be one hundred.'

'I don't know how you lived the remainder of your years — you may well have become a nun, so far as I'm concerned.'

'Do I look like a nun?'

The tattoo sizzled in my mind.

'I don't know. What does a nun look like? The last one I saw was when I was five years old—a middle-aged lady of Greek origin that I saw on a tram, with a black habit and black moustache. Apparently, I pointed out the facial hair to my mother, in a very loud voice, causing embarrassment all round. She never allowed me to live it down.'

'Well, you don't have to worry about the occupation or the facial hair, in my case. Your legs are so skinny. Did you eat at all before you died?'

'Like a goat, only better. I do appreciate my gourmet grub.'

'Such as plastic sushi?'

'They looked right enough.'

'They have brothers in the fridge.' Kohana stared at my boxer shorts. 'You're going to have to take them off. They hurt my eyes. No clothing is worn in Japanese baths—and relax, I'm not going to take advantage of you.'

'Look away then.'

'Really?'

'Really.'

She did as requested, and after much ado I kicked off the underpants—but kept my hands down there, to cover up.

'We have to rinse first,' Kohana said, now all business-like.

The woman grabbed a wooden bucket and washed herself with water from a tap, and then passed it over to me. I filled it up, poured it over my head—and shouted. The water was bitterly cold. As she climbed into the tub, Kohana sang something.

I was trying to keep my teeth from chattering. 'Might I inquire what the song is?'

'It's "*Tsugaru Kaikyō Fuyugeshiki*", "Winter Scene of Tsugaru Strait", an old *enka* standard by Ishikawa Sayuri—sorry, Sayuri Ishikawa. A favourite of mine that I used to sing at karaoke. When I say it's "old", however, I lie—she released the song in

1977, when I was already forty-seven. It was conjured up by lyricist Yu Aku, with composer Takashi Miki, aka Tadashi Watanabe, who was also responsible for the insanely catchy *"Anpanman no March"* theme song for the kids' anime series *Anpanman.'*

'I have no idea what you are rattling on about.'

'Come on in. You'll freeze to death standing out there.'

Surprisingly, I didn't need to be asked twice.

With great difficulty, and much shame, I scaled the wall of the tub in a backwards manoeuvre, my private parts turned away from the woman. Of course I fell in. Once immersed, I felt like I'd been scalded.

'This is too bloody hot!' I objected.

'It's supposed to be. Almost the same temperature as the saké.'

'If you dare say *deshō*, I'll whack you one.'

'Never crossed my mind.' Kohana smiled.

So, we crouched there in the water, inches from one another — and silence ensued. I had no idea what to say. After a few minutes, I became accustomed to the heat, and in fact could feel my muscles relaxing. That was something.

'Would you mind giving me a shoulder massage?' Kohana asked.

Cue: muscle tension. 'Why on earth would I do that?'

'Go on, W. I have sore shoulders. No hidden agenda — nothing you could pin to your Harris Tweed jacket. Jeez.'

I scrutinized her face. 'A quick question, and if you can answer it, I'll grant you the massage. What colour was my favourite Harris Tweed?'

Kohana was gazing at the black, empty sky. No stars shone. 'There's a toughie. Let me see — grey-green, with subtle flecks of camel?'

'All right. Certainly. Turn yourself around.'

When she did as told, I came face to face with that multi-headed dragon. All the eyes scowled, and I wondered where I had misplaced my white flag.

'Any time you're ready.'

'Not a problem. I used to do this all the time.'

'I bet.'

'I did, you know. I massaged my daughter's leg every morning of every day. It was part of her therapy. I did that for two years.'

After hesitating some more, I placed my hands on the woman's shoulders, between the heads, and began to knead.

'Say—not bad. I thought you'd complain of arthritic fingers or some such nonsense, just to wriggle out of it. Thank you. I feel so tense.'

'You're welcome.'

'And so formal too,' she sighed.

'I have to ask, since these brutes are staring straight at me— they're not very friendly chaps. What's the story with the tattoo?'

'Yamata no Orochi? A story within a story.'

'There's an opaque answer if ever I've heard one.'

'Well, he does relate to our earlier diatribe about saké. There's a Japanese myth that adds depth to the drink. Would you care to hear it?'

'If it eventually leads to why you have him on your back.'

'Eventually.' I heard her snigger. 'This is a well-known Japanese fable that starts out with some parental hand-wringing. The eight daughters of an elderly couple are being devoured, on consecutive years, by a dragon named Yamata no Orochi. This roughly translates as Eight-Branched Great Snake, or Eight-Forked Serpent.'

'So—dragon or snake?'

'The difference gets lost in the translation.'

'Another tragedy.'

'Let's call him a beastie, to keep it simple.'

'This works for me.'

'Good. Ow!'

'Sorry.'

'Your hands are stronger than they look. Anyway, this annually ravenous beastie flaunts eight heads and eight tails, and size-wise stretches out over eight hills and eight valleys. While this may play havoc with the Japanese notion that eight is a lucky number, things straighten out just prior to the consumption of daughter Number Eight, named Kushinada-hime — Rice Paddy Princess.'

'An engaging name.'

'Are you being facetious? Do you want to hear this story?'

'I'm all ears.'

'I'd prefer you to be all hands.'

'I'm trying. This is highly embarrassing.'

'Why? There's nobody around to watch.'

'Still.'

'I don't know. Imagine if your old mates could see you now — naked in a tub, a seventy-one-year-old massaging the shoulders of a fifteen-year-old. Just don't let on I'm old enough to be your mother.'

'Stop it. Get back to your ho hum story.'

'Okay. Things do get more interesting, fear not. It transpires that our grandstanding hero here is Susanoo no Mikoto, the banished Shintō summer storm god.'

'Very Thor-like.'

'I suppose. I don't know who Thor is. I remember Toshiro Mifune played Susanoo in the 1959 movie. Having met the old couple, Susanoo gets the hots for Kushinada-hime and offers his assistance — in return for the daughter's hand. There's always a catch in these tales. Both parents accept, since I don't think they have much choice, and Susanoo swings a magic trick that transforms Kushinada-hime into a comb he hides in his hair.'

'So he moonlighted as a magician?'

'I think all gods can do the comb trick. He then ordered a barrier built around the house, in which there were eight gates.

At each gate, a cavernous tub is placed upon a bench, and the eight tubs are filled with eight-times-filtered saké.'

I noticed that one of the beastie's heads, on Kohana's right shoulder, was split in two, with a raised scar of about four centimetres between the eyes. I stopped massaging and, with care, touched the area.

'What happened here?'

'A story for another day,' Kohana said.

'You and your secrets.'

'A girl has to keep some things under the cuff.'

'I have grave reservations about that.' My fingers were aching, but I said nothing. I doubted she'd let me off the hook.

'Fair enough. So, as I was about to tell you, when the beastie makes his lumbering eight mountain/eight valley arrival, he finds his path blocked and, after much huffing and puffing—like the wolf in the three little pigs story, really—Orochi finds that he can't breach the barrier.'

'Baffling.'

'Very. To make matters worse, Orochi's acute sense of smell takes in the saké, which the polycephalic dragon loves—like you, really. So, the eight heads entertain a dilemma: they desperately want to guzzle the delicious saké that calls out to them, much like the Sirens from Homer's *Odyssey*, yet the fence obstructs their path, blocking any easy access to reach the precious booze.'

She stopped, and groaned.

'Too hard?' I ceased with my pressing.

'No, no, perfect. Don't stop.'

'Could you keep the groaning to a minimum?'

'Oh you.'

'Story.'

'Well, when one head suggested they simply smash the barrier down, the consensus was that this would knock over and waste the saké.'

'I don't think it needs a consensus to work that one out.'

'He is a beastie, remember. When another head proposes they combine their fiery breath and burn the fence into ash, they agree that the nihonshu would potentially be evaporated.'

'What was the temperature of the saké?'

'Not part of the tale—deshō? As Orochi looks closer, he finds that the gates are actually unbarred and, pining for the saké on the other side, his heads are keen to stick their necks through to go guzzle it. But here the eighth one, which is the smartest, warns his cranial brethren of the folly of such action—then volunteers to head through first to make sure the coast is clear.'

'I'm not sure if that's brave, selfish, or downright stupid.' My thumbs, smarting as they were, found a knot, and I focused on that.

'Ouch! No, no, don't stop. Good pain. Of course, it's a cruel trap, as Susanoo skulks in some shadow, hiding, and allows that single head to drink the alcohol in safety. The head, buzzing by now with the carefree abandon that saké imparts, reports back to the others that there is no danger. With a "Whoopee!", all eight noggins plunge through a different hatch, greedily skulling every last drop in the vats, and then revel in the effects of the drink.'

'That, I can imagine.'

'I'm sure you can. Alas, it has a sad finale. As the heads reel, Susanoo launches his attack. Drunk from slurping too much saké so quickly, the great serpent is no match for the wily, tee-totalling hero, who decapitates each dazed crown in turn and thereby slays him—a fitting lesson for all eight-headed beasties out there with a taste for the hard stuff.'

'Was this hero of ours wielding a sickle, or a sword?'

'I really don't know.'

'Sounds like Orochi could've done with some lessons from the Lernaean Hydra. Eight heads are not so useful if they don't grow back.'

I took my hands off Kohana's shoulders, and leaned back.

'There. Penance paid for my stupidity with the Harris Tweed. Are you going to tell me why you got the tattoo of an under-achiever like this?'

'I felt for his loss.'

That answer fizzled. I felt somewhat cheated. 'Righto.'

8 | 八

The lights dimmed abruptly.

There was darkness, and definitely no more hot water.

We're not talking the pitch black that greeted me after I was dead and buried, or cremated and scattered—or whatever the case may be—when I first landed, slap-bang, in that miserable place I call the Hereafter (have you dreamed up a better moniker yet?).

My fingers had stopped aching, for which I was beholden, and I was completely dressed, in a relatively comfortable seat, and heard the subdued murmur of people around me.

There was a gathering rumble of sound, a slowly advancing noise that came from what I recognized as an orchestra pit below, in front of closed stage curtains.

We were in some kind of large theatre, and although most of the lights were out, they slowly grew back, along with the sound.

'Richard Wagner's "Vorspiel", the prelude of *Das Rheingold*—we're listening to the low E Flat beginnings,' said a childish voice beside me.

As my sight adjusted, I found myself face-to-face with a six-year-old. The girl peered back from beneath a cute, pageboy haircut.

'We're at the bottom of the Rhine,' she said lightly. 'The music builds slowly, to a stirring drone in E Flat major. Can you hear it?'

How a child could dissect something that was, for me at least, wonky pedestrian noise, came across disconcerting. For all I knew, she was making it up and hoodwinking the old man in the next seat.

'Wolram, it's me.'

'Kohana?'

'You were expecting Little Red Riding Hood?'

'I haven't the faintest idea. So, what's afoot this time? And why the kiddie get-up?'

'It's early 1936.'

'Of course it is.'

'So, you get to meet itsy-bitsy me.'

The girl stood up, all of one hundred and ten centimetres, in a taffeta party dress and big bow, and curtsied to me. Then she grinned and sat down again.

'Very polite of you,' I remarked. 'Tell me, is this where the Arthurian nonsense started?'

'Actually, *Das Rheingold* isn't about King Arthur at all. It's the story of water-sprites in the Rhine River, some coveted gold, and assorted characters from Norse mythology.'

'Don't they go hand-in-hand?'

'No! ...Well, I suppose they could, if you choose to be completely ignorant.'

'And we're backtracking this far because you wanted to give me a better musical education?'

'Why not?'

As Kohana kicked back, I noticed her feet didn't come close to touching the floor.

'To fill you in, when I was six years old, the world famous Freigedank-Dummheit Opera Company came from Dresden, to tour Japan for several performances. They were a hit. Germans were popular here in the 1930s.'

'Likely, this had something to do with the kindred authoritarian bias.'

I looked around the theatre. The walls were gold and the ceiling had a huge chandelier, as well as a big picture of a nymph. There would have been over a thousand people there, many in Western clothes, but most in traditional Japanese garb.

'We're in the Teikoku Gekijo, also known as Teigeki—the Imperial Theatre in Tokyo,' Kohana held forth in her new, disquieting child's tone.

'You didn't have your Orochi tattoo at this age, did you?'

'Wolram, I'm a little young to go getting tattoos.'

'Well, you brought me here, true, but aren't you also, then, too young to be allowed admittance to a prestigious event like this?'

The girl pouted. 'I guess.'

'Who brought you?'

'My father. He loved opera. I used to come here every summer as a child. You know, before the war.'

'Which war?'

She slit her eyes.

Curiosity definitely got the better of me. 'Where is your old man?'

'You're sitting in his seat.'

I almost jumped out of the thing, worried I'd been reclining on some poor fellow, but there was nobody beneath me.

'Good gosh, Kohana—don't scare me that way. He's not here?'

'He's not important.'

'You're desperate to hide the man from me. Why is that?'

'Not desperate—I choose to spend no more time with him.'

'Your drama, I suppose.'

About three minutes had past since the orchestral thrum began, and I will admit it had something rousing and zippy about it. Of course, I'd heard the music before—I just felt like playing it dopey.

The waif-like Kohana had turned away and was gazing at the nymph on the ceiling. It took another half minute for me to notice the tears on her cheeks.

'This was the most sublime, moving music I had ever heard,' she said, so softly I barely took in the words. 'Beautiful, isn't it?'

'What is?'

'The music.'

'What music?'

'The music they're playing.'

'Oh, yeah.'

'To be honest, the opening four to five minutes were the best. The rest of the opera, well, I could have done without it. Straight after the performance, my father flagged down a rickshaw, we stopped by Oume-san's okiya—and he left me there. For good. I never saw him again, but I am grateful for this parting gift.'

One thing occurred to me—where was Kohana's sister Tomeko, in this memory? If she were taken to the geisha house at the same time, after the grand finale, wouldn't the girl logically be here? A frumpy, middle-aged woman with far too much makeup occupied the seat next to Kohana.

That was the moment I remembered something.

Another concert, another six-year-old. Not Wagner. What were they playing? Mozart? No, Tchaikovsky, something from *The Nutcracker*.

Corinne beside me, watching and listening in awe. She adored the ballet, even if she would never be able to dance.

Me, checking text-messages, bored senseless. Ignoring the girl as much as I did the music. Her sad expression, when I finally found the time to take a look.

I brushed it off and started texting again.

9 | 九

'1939, I think. Looks like a spiffy spring day for Tokyo.'

Kohana breathed out loudly.

'You don't sound so happy about it.'

'Oh, I am, I am. But it's a mixed blessing.'

I followed her into a small garden, with high wooden walls on all four sides. There was a cautiously dripping bamboo doohickey in one corner, and the elderly woman of the house stretched back on a recliner.

Music came from somewhere inside the house.

'It's "*Natsukashi No Bolero*" by Ichiro Fujiyama,' my companion said. 'Oume-san's favourite record at the time. She played it over and over, and wore the thing out.'

'Sounds like a hoot.'

'What actually is a hoot?'

'I'm not sure. Fun?'

'Pfff.'

Before me was the rather storied mama-san, Oume. Sadly, I was not impressed. The woman appeared to be a skinny bag of bones aged somewhere from fifty to ninety—it was impossible to tell how old—and she was not an attractive sight.

Her face was crisscrossed by lines, and her scraggly hair a mix of white, grey and shreds of black. The woman's teeth were crooked and the mouth lopsided. But those hooded eyes twinkled with a solid combination of good humour and intelligence.

The woman was reading from a novel that had on its cover two roughly painted soldiers, sharing a cigarette, on a plain yellow background. Also gazing at that image was a nearby young girl with a long ponytail, seated on the ground next to the old biddy.

'Me. About nine, I'm fairly sure. I remember this. Oume-san, in the back garden of the Paulownia Tree, with a pipe and this book. She sat like a queen in that flimsy chaise longue you see, next to the tree stump.'

'Queen' wasn't the word I was clutching for.

'What are you reading?' the girl asked.

'*Mugi to Heitai. Wheat and Soldiers,*' said the old lady, in a gravelly tone. 'It's by a writer I like, Hino Ashihei, a novel that touches upon the evils of war. There should be more of this, but with the new edicts coming through, and this rampant government militarism, soon all we'll be allowed to read about will be the beauty of bloodshed. In *manga* form, with silly pictures.'

The old woman set down her book, took a pinch of shredded tobacco, and filled her long-stemmed pipe.

'Never believe what these people ram down our throats, Kohana-chan. The government is roosted by *piman.*'

'Capsicums?' I queried.

'What's inside a capsicum?'

'Very little.'

'There you go. Picture their heads as little green peppers.'

'Oh, I see. A nice touch.' That sorted, I returned my wandering attention to the lady on the couch.

'I loved this old tree,' she was saying as she patted the amputated stump beside her. 'It was ancient like me, a real survivor. But it got too big and the neighbours complained, and we had to chop it down. One of the saddest things I've ever done. But there's a lesson in there for you, little one. Never let yourself get too big.'

I leaned forward. 'Er—I hate to break the moment, but was she talking up your weight, or your possible future success?'

'I was never quite sure,' Kohana admitted. 'I like to believe it was a more philosophical moment and she was referring to the latter. I'd hate to think the moment was lost on an observation that I might be getting chubby.'

She turned full circle in the yard, and sighed.

'I also remember the day our father brought us here.'

Oume, and the girl, and the recliner vanished.

The trees and plants around us back-pedalled three seasons in as many seconds, and a tall tree stood where the stump had once been. It was wrapped in summer foliage.

I could make out chatter inside the house—a man's voice, deep and gruff, and an elderly woman's growl I recognized as Oume's.

'I want to be rid of the one, I tell you, only this one,' the man's voice said, annoyed. 'The other is not for sale.'

'I'll take them both.' That was Oume. She sounded stubborn— one of those people with whom you don't want to do business. 'They're perfect bookends. Individually, I'd make a quarter of the profit that, together, they will bring. I'm sorry, but that is my single condition. Both, or neither.'

I stole a look through the open window, into the gloom of the house, but could make out nobody.

'Are they discussing what I believe they're discussing?'

'It's obvious what's happening,' Kohana muttered, as she leaned against the wall. She looked up and fingered the old wooden boards there. 'My father wanted to offload me to an okiya he frequented. I think he was sick and tired of the constant reminder of his dead spouse. But Oume-san refused to take just one—she wanted the two of us. She may not have been a terribly astute businesswoman, but she could see a pot of gold when it appeared in front of her, and my father folded quickly.'

A marginally younger-looking Oume emerged from the doorway, leading two children by their hands. She seated them on a bench and gazed at them.

They were beautiful girls, dressed identically with short bob hairstyles and taffeta dresses. I recognized them from Kohana's look at the opera. Bookends indeed.

One of the pair had a blue and yellow flower tucked behind

her right ear.

'*Ne m'oubliez pas*,' Kohana said in a soft voice. 'Otherwise known as a forget-me-not. We call them *wasurenagusa* in Japanese. Same meaning. When I was a child, I adored flowers.'

Oume cleared her throat, not that it made her voice any prettier.

'So, now we are a family,' she said, as she squatted in front of both charges. 'Shall we get acquainted? What are your names?'

'My name is Tomeko,' said one of the two, the one without the flower, in a small, shy voice.

'A pleasant enough name. And yours, my dear?'

The other girl bobbed low. 'I'm Akuma.'

Oume whistled. 'Oh, no, no, no, that name won't do. Not at all. It will scare potential customers half to death.'

The woman studied the girl for a few moments, and it seemed her scrutiny came to rest on the flower behind the ear.

'I think we'll call you Kohana. What do you say?'

'A bombing raid?'

I shook my head to clear it of unnecessary nonsense. Hadn't I been here before? Déjà vu, and all that jazz? I felt like I'd been kicked in the behind.

Minus the couch, this time around.

I was nestled on a stool, on a dark footpath, next to a wooden dwelling I recognized, despite the poor light. Not Kohana's hovel—her okiya. Oume-san's place. No doubt the lantern aided in identification.

'Not any garden-variety bombing raid, my sweet,' Kohana was saying as she walked around me with small steps, surprisingly steady on precarious-looking geta. Yes, she was the almost fully-grown geisha again.

'Hangyoku,' she reminded me, suddenly very close to my ear. I nearly perfected the jumping-out-of-one's-skin manoeuvre. She'd covered ten feet in less than a second, clogs or no clogs.

'I get you,' I assured her, tense.

I was also annoyed, because I could make out those bees again. It was an irritating sound. Would I be allowed no peace? Give me Wagner any day.

Then I made up my mind to do something.

'Do you mind if I explore? I know this street well enough, though last time I was comfy in a couch. The stool is a bit hard.'

I stood up, stretched my back, and eyed off an alley three doors down. I don't know about you, but I've always had a fascination for lanes—something that stems from growing up in Melbourne, where there are fascinating laneways aplenty.

'No.' Kohana's arm stopped me.

'Just a brisk walk.'

'Not now.' She sounded adamant. 'Focus. Listen. You hear that?'

'Yes, yes, the bees, or the Allied planes, are whatever they are.'

'It's the sound of over three hundred American B-29 Superfortress bombers.'

I glanced at her. 'As many as that, you say?' I walked around her arm. 'So why are we here, again? Would you like to fill me in on something poignant?'

'I'm getting there. Give me time.'

'Time, time. That's all we ever seem to talk about.'

'Wolram, this one does take time, believe me. There's so much I need to tell you. There are three hundred and thirty-four B-29s on their way here, right now, powered by one thousand, three hundred and thirty-six twin-row turbocharged radial pistol engines, manufactured by a company founded by aviation pioneers Orville and Wilbur Wright—you must know them?'

'Of course, I do. I'm not thick.'

'Never the implication.'

'This is the second time we've been here. When are you going to tell me what this is about? I detest a mystery.'

'Well, where do I start? There are so many facts and figures to relate to you, before we arrive at the big event. I wouldn't want to overwhelm you. For starters, these aircraft carry three thousand, seven hundred crew-members and have two thousand tons of an experimental device, incendiary explosives, neatly tucked away in their bellies—a hotchpotch of white phosphorus and napalm.'

'Napalm? The munitions used in Vietnam?'

'Invented twenty years earlier, during World War Two. This street will be one of its first testing grounds—along with all the other roads you can picture, in every direction, for miles.'

Kohana punctuated the sentence with a sweep of her huge, hanging sleeve. I was impressed with the flourish.

'That includes the laneway over there?'

'What do you think?'

'Yes?'

She was apparently not listening. 'Napalm was a brand new,

jellied-gasoline mixture, concocted from a wonderful Harvard University recipe of oleic acid, naphthenic acid derived from crude oil, palmitic acid derived from coconut oil, and aviation fuel.'

'How do you know these ingredients—let alone remember them, off the top of your head, this way?'

'I read a lot about it.'

'Obviously. You and your reading.'

'Yes. Me and my reading.'

She gave me a lively look, before rattling off more data.

'The mixture was placed inside M-69 cluster bombs, nicknamed "Tokyo Calling Cards", which were designed to spray napalm over a one hundred foot area, before or after impact, then explode—sending flames rampaging through the densely packed wooden buildings.'

The houses here were, indeed, densely packed.

'Asphalt will boil in the one thousand, eight hundred degree warmth; super-heated air is going to suck people into the flames. The fires can be viewed one hundred and fifty miles away. Operation Meetinghouse, as it's dubbed by the Americans, is going to be the most devastating air raid in history.'

The urgent wail of air raid sirens began.

'Tonight?'

'Tonight.'

'Can we leave now?' I asked.

11 | 十一

'Snug?'

'Extremely. Especially now we've fled the sirens, the bees, and those bluntly annoying B-29s.'

There I was, loafing back in the familiar cradle of the couch, with a hot toddy in one hand and my feet up on a medieval footstool. My head rested on a soft pillow and I even had on nice woollen socks that Kohana had kindly donated. It would be difficult not to be comfy.

'Would his lordship like a pipe?'

'By God—you wouldn't have one handy, would you?' Right away, I twigged she was teasing me again. Typical. 'One of those South American numbers will do fine.'

The enamel case was whisked out of some pocket, sight unseen, the lighter flicked, and I was presented with a cigarette my hostess had pre-lit. Service, with a whimsical smile to boot.

'Now you're all battened down,' she was saying, 'I think I'm going to assail you with a good lecture.'

'Another one? Dragons? B-29s? I'm exhausted.'

'None of these things.'

'It's not regarding my recent behaviour, I should hope?'

'No, no, a different kind of lecture—a throwaway one on Japanese history.'

'That tedious address on saké you warned me about?'

'Fear not. I'll steer you there another time.'

Kohana smiled again, as she sat back on her Egg chair, facing me.

'Now, try to imagine me as the teacherly type in a white lab coat, scrawling stuff across a patchy-coloured old blackboard—in green chalk, mainly because I can't find the nicer yellow or orange pieces.'

'Is the chalk important?'

'No, shhh. I write this simple question, circled twice for effect: "What is the oldest novel in the world?" Straight after, I look at you, my star pupil, and await your perspicacious response.'

'I haven't the faintest idea.'

Kohana looked bothered. 'Would that be regarding the novel, or the word "perspicacious"?'

'May I opt for both?'

She blew out her cheeks. 'Moving along, if you were to toe the Anglo-Saxon line, you might end up clutching at a name like Shakespeare.'

Here I threw up my hand, as I felt I had something solid to add to the conversation.

'Yes, Wolram?'

'Dubious, to be sure, Miss—I know there's something older. By Chaucer? Please don't tell me it's Thomas Malory's Arthurian drivel.'

'You'd be backing the wrong horse, either way. They're too recent. You could opt for *Beowulf*—anonymously put down on parchment some time between the eighth and eleventh centuries—but it's a poem, not a novel, and if the original inscription did fall into the eleventh century, then it's also too late.'

In spite of the whisky, I was beginning to feel drowsy. Lectures from other people tend to have that effect on me, no matter what the subject matter. This one was feeling particularly dusty.

Kohana, however, was on a veritable roll.

'The earliest contestants for "prenatal novel" bounce between *Satyricon*, possibly written by Gaius Petronius in the first century AD, and Longus's *Daphnis and Chloe* in the second century—yet, while there were a couple of other novels hacked together in archaic Greek and Latin tongues around the same period, these in no way relate to the modern "classic" novel, with more emphasis on character psychology.'

'Is that so?' I noticed my nails were getting long and needed a trim.

'This is where *Genji Monogatari*, better known in English as *The Tale of Genji*, slinks in.'

'Oh, of course it does.'

'Wolram, have you heard of this book?'

Now she did sound like a teacher. 'No,' I admitted.

'Then be a darling, shut up, and listen. Where was I?'

'Something about slinking.'

'Oh, yes. Nice try with the red herring. Here, we have to introduce Murasaki Shikibu. She was a noblewoman at the Japanese imperial court, who composed *The Tale of Genji* in the early eleventh century, during the Heian period. Murasaki first mentioned the story in her diary—in the midst of an otherwise dull day's activities—on November 1, 1008. The tale is supposed to have been finished in 1021.'

'You've really done your homework.'

'Actually, to be honest, I never read the book itself.'

I looked up from my nails. 'I beg your pardon?'

'It's enormous, it weighs a ton, and my other excuse is that the original text is illegible to contemporary Japanese.' She leaned over, performed a theatrical glance to either side, and whispered in conspiratorial fashion: 'I did, however, read the manga series *Asakiyumemishi*, which was published in the 1980s. That's how I brushed up on the story and the characters, though it's a modern adaptation.'

'Are you sure that counts?'

'In my opinion it does—there are thirteen volumes of the manga. Anyway, we're veering wildly off course. Let's get back to Murasaki's original work.'

'Which you haven't read.'

Kohana cleared her throat. 'Exactly.'

'Do we have to?'

'Yes. Hang in there. I'll try to make it quick and painless.'

'Can I anaesthetize myself with another drink?'

'That will be your reward at the end of the lecture.'

'Oh God, I'll die of thirst well before then.'

'Nonsense, I'm on the scoop's home stretch. This yarn may have taken over a decade to complete, but the ink was dry forty-five years before the Normans invaded England, *Harold Rex interfectus est*, the arrow through the eye, and all that nonsense. *Genji* is also the first full-length novel still considered a classic—though some cranky people decry the honorary status, and whether or not Murasaki wrote all fifty-four surviving chapters. I think that's something you might be able to relate to.'

'How so?'

'Well, armchair critics continue to insist that the real writer of sixteenth-century England's best-known plays may not in fact have been John and Mary Shakespeare's wee tacker.'

'Oh, that old rumour.'

'Yes—scuttlebutt.' She winked at me. I was impressed. This wink had flair. 'There was also a rather infamous piece of legislation written in Australia not long before either of us died, with rumours circulating regarding its true authorship. Isn't that right, Wolram?'

My head lifted from the pillow.

Kohana, for her part, took up right where she'd left off, with Genji.

'While he might be the dashingly handsome son of an emperor, for political reasons—namely, that his mum was a low-ranking concubine—Genji has no hereditary title, and he ekes out life as an imperial officer. As the tale unfolds, we quickly come to realize just how much of a womanizing character this man is, tempered with a debonair edge that leaves the womanized swooning.'

'As fictional characters do.'

'Unfortunately, the impact isn't always mutual. Genji finds the dalliances dull, and sometimes said romps are fatal affairs for his partners.'

'Ouch.'

'Yes. And, in an iddish twist worthy of Oedipus and Freud, our hero has a penchant for his father's new wife, the beautiful, responsive Lady Fujitsubo, while forced to deal with his own cold, haughty spouse, Aoi no Ue.'

'Could I have that drink now?'

'Almost.'

'Please?'

'Soon. Allow me to finish. The *Tale of Genji* is a mix of James Bond's bedtime antics, which you would like, with a dash of Don Juan histrionics, which you may not—distilled into a Romeo and Juliet pot-boiler. There's also kidnap, court intrigue, danger, chronic infidelity, deaths aplenty, and other plot contrivances recently found in dramas on the other side of the Pacific, like that whipped up by the Bill of Deviations.'

'Unsubtle hint, number two,' I muttered.

Kohana shrugged. She took my cup from me to refill it, saying, 'Subtlety tends to be pointless on occasion.'

I recognized the line from one of my business motivation speeches.

12 | 十二

Air raid sirens were blaring and a dark, empty street beckoned.

'Oh, for Heaven's sake. Are we back here—again?'

I leaned against a bamboo pole on the street corner, as I'd now lost both the sofa and stool—and then decided to go for a walk to exercise my legs.

There was always that alley a few houses down from Kohana's okiya, the one I had a hankering to explore. I considered strolling straight in, but Kohana's arm barred me.

'Not there.'

'Why?'

'Don't get distracted. It's not the reason we're here.'

'Well, what are we doing?'

'You're so impatient.'

'Absurd. I'm far more bored, and annoyed.'

'And I pray for considerate.'

Aside from distant buzzing and the loud bawl of the sirens, I could make out light chatter. This time, a few other people had ventured outdoors, moving slowly here and there around us.

'Friends of yours?'

Kohana skipped the question. 'Most people had become accustomed to nightly visits by the B-29s, since in practice they dropped few or no bombs, so we paid scant attention to the sirens this specific evening.'

I decided to play along. Perhaps if I did, it would be easier for me to get to the bottom of things—and then get back to the hovel for a spot of bed rest.

'All right. What's the date?'

'March 9, 1945, almost March 10.'

This didn't ring any bells—and since we were in Tokyo, there was no need to get over-excited about atomic antics.

'No,' Kohana agreed, interpreting my train of thought, 'but

more people will die tonight than at either Nagasaki or Hiroshima, where the atom bombs were dropped six months later. Those B-29s you hear up there are on their way over to kill a hundred thousand of my neighbours.'

'One hundred thousand?' I stared at her. 'You're pulling my leg?'

'The master of the appropriate comeback,' she muttered. 'Sadly, I'm pulling nobody's leg. I may be off in my stats—you can give or take twenty thousand. No one knows for sure. The exact figures are unknown, probably because a lot of people simply disintegrated.'

'Here? Tonight?'

'Now.'

13 | 十三

Our two porcelain saké cups, pressed up against one another, began to rattle in collusion.

Kohana was up from her seat in a jiffy, and hovered beneath the staircase as the room began to do a merry jig. Odds and ends around me proceeded to swing, jump, smash, and topple.

'What's going on?' I asked, trying to repress panic. 'That air raid?'

'No, intermission—it's an earthquake.'

'An earthquake? Oughtn't we to duck and cover?'

'You really are a Cold War child. Come over here, or you'll get yourself conked on the head by something.'

I didn't require much persuasion. I quickly found myself in an inappropriate position, pressed up against my hostess in the small stairwell, and attempted to cover the impropriety—and my fear of the tremor—with mindless prattle.

'I thought, by the setting outside, that this hovel was supposed to be somewhere in northern Europe, where earthquakes don't happen.'

'Well, it also reminds me of northern Tōhoku and Hokkaido— where earthquakes do. What can I say, I'm Japanese. These things hit with shocking regularity.'

'This hard and this long?'

'Sometimes more so.'

'You called me a relic of the Cold War,' I said as I watched the walls continue to sway and the axe skittle over. 'Aren't you as well?'

'I was a teenager before anyone knew anything at all about splitting the atom,' she reminded me. 'There. I think it's subsiding.'

'Look at us. Acting like it's real, or that it matters.'

'Old habits die hard. What's your excuse?'

'I'm not an earthquake veteran.'

I could feel her warm breath on my neck and was cosy right where I was. To be honest, I didn't want the temblor to end.

'Don't get too comfortable,' Kohana said. 'Now we have to clean up.'

'You ought to invest in a maid.'

'Well, now—there's a job opportunity for you.'

14 | 十四

'The planes didn't come together.'

Kohana, geisha'd up, stared at a black sky that this time did have some stars in it.

'Not like the Valkyrie, swooping to select the dead on some Norse battlefield. The B-29 bombers arrived in formation at five thousand feet, three planes every minute.'

There—and back again.

I was mesmerized by her speech, in spite of better judgment. 'God, is there no time for rest? I'm still getting over the quake.'

The few high-school world history lessons I recalled had skipped over this part. One hundred thousand people dying? Napalm being used?

Then again, this shouldn't have surprised me, since we were on the winning side of the war. The victors write the history, remember? George Orwell put it perfectly: 'Who controls the present controls the past.' I had had that quote framed up and placed in my kitchen in the latter years of my previous existence.

Kohana was riding a pulpit of self-indulgence to match mine.

'Two percent of Tokyo's residents, most of them civilians, perished,' she said in a voice that wavered. 'The lucky ones died quickly in the initial explosions; others would be burned or boiled alive. Twenty-five percent of the city—three hundred thousand mostly wood-and-paper buildings in the downtown Shitamachi quarter, right around here—was destroyed. One million people were made instantly homeless.'

I felt like my head would implode, and I wasn't certain I could blame the whisky I'd enjoyed earlier on. 'All these facts and figures confuse me. Can we fast-forward a tad, preferably in mute, and get to the conclusion?'

'About to happen.'

She took bitty steps around me. Due to the restrictive kimono, or because she was becoming increasingly upset?

'Like most of the Asakusa I loved, this entire street will be destroyed—not by the bomb-loads but by the furnace that follows. Oume-san and our two maids were victims. We found no trace of Oume, but discovered the charred remains of Midori and Naoko in a strange, desperate embrace. They were younger than me, you know. Midori was eleven. My best friends – Noriko, Yuki, and Harumi – perished. The two geisha lodging with us, Miyoharu and Eiko, died. My dresser Iwabuchi-san survived, with burns to sixty percent of his body. I—I found—too much.'

Kohana had closed her eyes. There were tears, but she wasn't crying, per se. She brought her hands together and appeared to pray.

'I don't mean to interrupt you,' I spoke up, 'and forgive me for doing so, but what about you? How did you—?'

'How did I survive? *Me?*'

The woman spat out the pronoun, threw down her hands, and this time glared from eyes that glistened in the streetlight. I would have ducked for cover if there had been anywhere convenient.

'I was lucky.'

'Unquestionably. How so?'

'Simple—Tomeko and I weren't here. I wish I could say a book saved us. Rather, we were saved by a booking. Ta-dah.'

15 | 十五

First impression?

In Egypt, I once saw the conjoined statues of Ramses II and his wife Nefertari, and this pose was similar, except that the faces of the two marbles were female and identical—as if Ramses had been given a very public flick, and the queen inducted her mirror image to sit atop the throne beside her.

The statues were Kohana and Tomeko, seated with perfect posture next to one another on tall wooden chairs that were pressed up against a wall.

On either side of them was a set of leather-bound Encyclopædias Britannica, standing upright across the floor. People lurked nearby, mere silhouettes. Even so, I believe I could distinguish officers' uniforms.

The girl to the right was dressed in a plain white kimono, the colour of snow. Her partner, on our left, wore a robe of fathomless black silk. Both had their white geisha masks identically applied, and their hair shone, with paraphernalia inserted.

There was a red strip of undergarment poking out a few millimetres above their kimono, making their throats look whiter. Neither moved. I barely made out their breathing, and the blinks were so discreet they would be easily missed.

'Which one is you?'

My Kohana stood beside me, dressed far more simply. 'Can't you guess?'

'Honestly? I have no idea. The one in black?'

She fidgeted beside me. 'Why do you assume that? No, I'm the one in white. This was one of Oume-san's gala gimmicks, a play on matching, inanimate bookends—with the twist being the opposing colours, and the books arranged to either side, not between. She also occasionally had us dress in identical kimono, but this was her favourite routine, one Tomeko and I regularly performed at functions while we were hangyoku. The guests delighted in it—they made a sport out of judging which one of us was which.'

'Was there anything to give the game away?'

'Only when we performed. Tomeko was the far better *shamisen* player; I was a marginally better *tachikata*, or dancer. Also, to the intrepid observer, the colours. White was always going to be Tomeko's colour, and black mine, just as you presumed—though sometimes we exchanged the robes to keep people guessing. This was one such occasion.'

There was a sudden, piercing wail that began outside the room, far away. Other sirens joined it, closer by. The two bookends glanced at one another, terrified girls, their ethereal image shattered.

Then the lights switched off.

'The same night the B-29s bomb Tokyo,' Kohana said. 'March 9. This is the booking that saved our lives. The very night Asakusa was levelled and we lost Oume-san, along with the rest of our slapdash family.'

I could hear a muffled thump-thump in the near distance, and the overhead chandelier rattled.

16 | 十六

Kohana looked wonderful as usual.

This bothered me.

'Let's say we flip proceedings,' I decided.

'Sounds fresh—I'm always up for that. Something different.'

'Fine. How about describing what I wear, for a change?'

'Why would I do that?'

I held up my hand. 'Indulge me. I seem to go into a great amount of detail regarding your costume changes, whenever—and wherever—they transpire. Usually in places I don't care to be.'

'That's because you're enamoured with my wardrobe.'

'Hogwash. Stop leading me astray—back to my question. Why don't you have a shot at describing what I wear?'

She gave me a quick once-over. 'What, a smoking jacket that's seen better days and needs the left elbow mending, worn-out slippers, pants that don't flatter your figure and are threadbare round the knees, and that charming, accidentally off-colour cream cravat?'

'Exactly. It doesn't change.'

'Of course it does. The outfit gets more tatty.'

'Ahem. Hardly fair. You know Fred Astaire was buried in a smoking jacket?'

'That's news to me. I liked his movies with Ginger Rogers.'

'I thought they would be your vintage—my grandmothers' generation.'

'Oh, Wolram. You like to decry "Frenchie" fashion designers, but were you aware that the smoking jacket on your back right now was designed by a Frenchman?'

'What? Nonsense.'

'Believe me, it's a classic Yves Saint Laurent. Why not check the label? I met Yves Henri, you know.'

'I wouldn't care if you met Napoléon Bonaparte.'

Try as I might, I couldn't rotate my head enough to see the tag, not while I was wearing the thing, and I did not want to give this girl the satisfaction of espying such doubt.

The smoking jacket had been a Christmas present from Judy — my secretary, remember her? She knew my anathema for things French. Why would she gift me something designed by one of these people? A smile, smug on the rear-end of mischief, worried me.

'This was when I went to Paris in 1965,' Kohana trawled on, oblivious, 'to rendezvous with my friends Chimei Hamada and Kenzo Takada. Yves Henri and I became avid pen pals—until I told him that his pantsuit design was one of the ugliest things I had ever laid eyes on. Even so, he dressed Catherine Deneuve in Buñuel's *Belle de Jour*, so you have sizeable shoes to fill.'

She tilted her head.

'Of course, you really don't have to believe me—perhaps you should consult your grandmothers.'

I felt bruised. This woman didn't just fight with kid gloves; she used them to bludgeon one's senses.

'My kingdom for a dry-cleaner's and an Italian shoe store,' I muttered as I peered at her. 'You don't happen to have any men's clothes in that excessive closet of yours? It seems to have a larger capacity than the Magic Pudding's.'

'I'm sorry.' She gifted me a saccharine expression. 'None that would fit—and nothing to match those Jolly Roger boxers of yours.'

'Desist,' I warned her. 'We've already aired that dirty laundry. Shall we move right along.'

'Aye, aye, skipper,' she saluted, damn her. 'Anyway, aside from your dress-sense, Wolram, could you tell me one thing? How long did it take you to cultivate this image of yours? You know, the smoking jacket and cravat, and the plum in your mouth?'

'Eh?'

'The "My dear" this, and "Good Lord" that, ad infinitum.'

'What are you gabbling about?'

'Well, it's hardly genuine, is it?'

'How do you mean?'

'You know precisely what I mean. A sham.'

'Oh,' I chose my words carefully, 'you noticed.'

'It's pretty obvious.'

I grinned in a manner that I prayed touched upon predatorial élan. There was an image to uphold, but I had no mirror to check.

'Brownie points there, my dear. The process took a few elocution lessons. Years of them, to be honest, but I persevered. I couldn't lead the world while sounding like an uneducated oaf.'

'The greatest leaders are honest ones,' Kohana said.

'An airy fairy ideal, to be sure.'

'You went to university.'

'Yes, but I sounded colloquial, too kitchen-brand, working class "Aussie". People respect those who use words they cannot understand.'

'Really? I thought they laughed at them.'

That made sense. Damn. Why hadn't the simple thought ever occurred to me? 'Perhaps that's why my political career never got off the ground?'

17 | 十七

'So, as I mentioned, this particular night, Tomeko and I were two miles away, entertaining military clients the way we did most often during the war—together. Not a single bomb hit the street where we kicked off our okobo, and the fires blew in the opposite direction.'

The two of us were in the Asakusa street again, entertained by a chorus of bees that had become a monotonous drone—more like cicadas in high summer. They were a season early, but just as distracting.

Kohana was considerate enough to allow me use of the couch, but I felt unsettled. 'There were winds?'

I looked round at all the clapboard buildings, stretching out along both sides of the road. Ready-made kindling. Why weren't there brick buildings?

'In an earthquake-friendly country like Japan? Wood and paper were safer.'

'Surely you had air raid defences around a city as vital as Tokyo.'

'We did, but this was 1945. The country was exhausted and most of our best soldiers were dead, missing, or fighting elsewhere. The raid happened at night, which made things more difficult, and the B-29 pushed the throttle to three hundred and fifty-seven miles per hour—making it faster than our fighter planes, such as the Mitsubishi A6M Zero.'

'The same plane Y flew into that ship?'

'Mmm.'

The girl sat down on the sofa. I looked at the alley not so far away. Surely, it would be quieter there. I could feel a breeze starting to gather.

'No, don't go there. Sit here, with me.' Kohana patted the leather.

'I don't want to.'

'Are you being pedantic, my sweet?'

'Don't call me that. I'm not your sweet. I would like to go home.'

'Home?' She laughed out loud. 'Where on earth is home? Do you mean my "hovel", those shacks out in the Hereafter, or some place more luxurious back in Melbourne?'

'You're an evil woman.' I scowled.

Kohana absent-mindedly fiddled with the odd accessories in her hair.

'Perhaps you're right. I do often wonder. Am I?'

I refused to say a word.

'In this instance, I can see both sides of the equation. The American fliers didn't get off scot-free. Forty-two of their bombers were heavily damaged, and most of them returned to base with blistered paint beneath. Fourteen B-29s crashed; two hundred and forty-three US airmen were lost.'

'Stop it,' I muttered. 'Just stop it with the facts and figures. I've heard enough.'

'You think so?'

'I know so.'

'But I have only a few more to share. Some of the stats are interesting.'

'How?'

Kohana misunderstood that I was registering disbelief, and set about explaining 'how' she found the folly intriguing.

'Well, while some planes were shredded by flak, several had non-combat related technical problems, and one aircraft was actually struck by lightning. Vortex updrafts from the fires tore the wings off one bomber. A B-29, nicknamed "Tall in the Saddle", crashed in Ibaraki—killing nine crew-members. Three survived. One of them was executed by the military police, and the other two were interned to Tokyo's military prison, where they burned to death in another air raid.'

Kohana breathed out heavily.

'I'm not going to sit here and tell you that the men in these bombers did wrong. There were too many diabolical feats during the war, enacted by both sides.'

To be honest, I wasn't paying the best attention. I'd almost finished my drink, had tried to blot out most of her diatribe, and was distracted by the reverberation in the air. I felt exhausted and overwhelmed. I sat, with brutal finality, next to the woman.

'There was a certain amount of evil adrift in the world, and some individuals channelled it more effectively than others.'

'I know.' More than she knew.

'In this case, I'm thinking of the man who organized Operation Meetinghouse.'

'Douglas MacArthur?' I guessed, lacking enthusiasm.

'No, but one day I'll have to tell you about the time I pinched Douglas's famous corncob pipe.'

'You were on a first-name basis, yet still stole one of his accessories?'

'Your grandfather Les asked me for a souvenir.'

'He did?'

'He did.'

'And that excuses everything?'

'Well, when I had my chance—puff! Gone. But not forgotten. The general had another dozen stashed in his quarters. He replaced it in minutes, and was tamping tobacco, then lighting up, as per image.'

'Douglas MacArthur? Did you—'

'Sleep with him? No, I was still undefiled then.'

'Far too enlightening.'

'Douglas preferred a quiet smoke and chat. I had a better grasp of English than most other geisha, so we met on some occasions. I found him kind of sad and lonely.'

I'll admit to being flustered. 'But he's the one who organized the bombing?'

'I said no, already. It was American Major General Curtis LeMay.'

'I haven't heard of him.'

'Lucky. Did you ever see the Kubrick satire *Dr Strangelove*?'

'A long time ago.'

'The gung-ho character of General Buck Turgidson was based on LeMay. I read something he said to his crews before departure on this mission: "You're going to deliver the biggest firecracker the Japanese have ever seen." This is the same man who, in the 1960s, turned his bombing attention to Vietnam and recommended the use of nuclear weapons there. Our Japanese government saw him in a different light. On December 7, 1964, with much pomp and ceremony, they conferred the First Order of Merit, with the Grand Cordon of the Rising Sun, upon General LeMay. A reward for fine service.'

I could barely hear her now. The buzz had become a relentless roar.

'So this LeMay was an evil man, and the Japanese officials were cowards. So what? Please, Kohana, shouldn't we now beat a path away from here? I believe I've seen and heard enough. I listened to your rant. You must have had your fill as well.'

She took my cup from my hand, sipped, and gave it back. I looked at the trace of cherry red on the rim, and then investigated her face.

There was no fear.

'This time, I'm staying,' she said. 'I need to be where they were. Where my real family died.'

'I can understand your feeling guilt—it's a survivor thing. But you have to close that chapter and move right along. Personally, I'd prefer to evacuate us—or I can go, you can stay. Be my guest. Just tell me, how do I get the Hell out of here? For God's sake. Do you understand what I'm saying?'

I was raving. Why? Think utterly terrified.

Here I was, already a dead old man, terrified of what was

about to happen. I could not begin to picture three hundred Superfortresses crowded together, in one sky, at the same time.

I pored over the black heavens, taking in the searchlights that swept to and fro, darting in and out of low-flying clouds. Straight after, I polished off the saké.

At the very least, I'd stopped whining and grown a balsa wood backbone. Thank blazes for the alcohol. I could feel my eyes were far too wide.

Kohana took my hand in hers. She smiled.

'Be brave.' Her voice steadied me. There was a degree of affection that soothed my nerves, rather than smothered them. When had that changed? 'And thank you for being here, at my side.'

'I don't think I have a choice,' I managed.

'Hush. Don't ruin the moment. What are you afraid of? We're on cheat-mode—a little bombing won't harm us.'

Straight after, I heard the payload whistle of three hundred-odd B-29s, and the air pressure switched.

18 | 十八

Which was when we ended up in a minimally decorated reception room, with the soundtrack of sirens and explosions at a safer distance.

I was standing up, but I had to fling out a hand to stop myself stumbling, and with that leaned against a wall. My heart was pounding.

'Wolram, are you all right?'

'I'm fine.'

I hung my head for a while, steadying the old nerves. When I finally felt up to it, I straightened and patted Kohana, who was right beside me, on the shoulder.

'Don't worry about me. It will require more than three hundred bombers to take me out of the picture this time around.'

I expect the quip made her happy. She had on a plain white dress that reached just above the knee, and it looked like something my mother would have worn back in the late '60s. I wondered if this was the intention—to inject something reassuring for me, a fond sensation, after the recent histrionics.

'What's happening now?' I asked. 'Is it the same night?'

'Same night, same ongoing drama, I'm sorry to say. A different perspective. Are you up for more?—or need a rest?'

'No, no, it's okay. Given you lived these experiences, I'm thinking that playing the inactive ghost is not so terrible. Lead on, Macduff.'

'We don't have far to go. Look.'

The room was dark.

A group of nearly transparent people had formed a ring around two far more substantial girls, dressed in polar-opposite black and white kimonos that were decorated with geisha regalia. The teenage Kohana and Tomeko.

The girls were identical, each wrestling with her mirror

image. The one in white pulled herself free, and slapped her sister—hard.

'Get your hands off me,' she hissed. 'I'm going back there, to see if I can help.'

The other child held her cheek, which looked pink under the heavy white greasepaint. 'It's too dangerous,' she warned. 'There's nothing you can do; the sirens are on!'

'*Kutabare!*—Drop dead! You can play the coward, a role you're made for.' The fleeting look, from the girl in white to her partner in black, was a venomous one.

'Tomeko tried to stop me,' Kohana said at my elbow.

'Apparently.'

'I ignored her.'

'That is one way to put it.'

'And I ran all the way over.'

'All the way, where?'

'To Asakusa. The air raid. We were here, at this function, when it happened. I think I told you. As soon as the sirens started up and we heard the explosions, I made up my mind to go straight back to our okiya.'

'In the middle of it?'

'Headstrong, I know. Stupid. Selfish. God, I should have listened to her.'

The girl in white swept straight out through a sliding door, moving surprisingly swiftly for someone restricted by her kimono.

I glanced at Tomeko. She was frozen to the spot, as if the lights there, just like the ones above, had been turned out.

'Come on.'

'We're going?'

Kohana grabbed my hand, and tugged me along after the other girl.

In another blink, we had changed location from a plush, orderly living room to a devastated, fractured street where sheets of wildly swinging fire soared hundreds of metres into the air and encircled us.

Yes, there was most certainly a wind.

I couldn't feel the heat as we picked our way through fallen walls and over the debris of smashed rickshaws and cars and signage. Bursts of blinding light flashed in the distance, as well as nearby. The earth buckled and groaned beneath my feet. A kind of mist started to fall, catching fire as it descended, setting alight every object under its path. Roofs collapsed, glass exploded, paper screens ignited.

Over all of these, the buzzing sound came in waves.

The whole world was on fire.

A huge awning above us made a cracking sound and started to tumble my way, at which point Kohana grabbed my beard and yanked me to relative safety.

'Did you need to do that?' I muttered, rubbing my chin, grateful all the same. 'I thought danger didn't matter—in cheat-mode?'

'We haven't proved that little theory.'

She started on again, this time leading me by the arm.

At one point, we passed an elderly gent seated on a huge chunk of concrete. The man was clad in scorched, smoking clothes, but was otherwise unharmed—he looked sufficiently relaxed to kick back and read a newspaper. I saw him light up a hand-rolled cigarette from the flames of a former house, just to his right. A few metres away, a young woman knelt outside a collapsed building, dressed in a torn cotton kimono, with an empty baby sling on her back, screaming and sobbing as she repeatedly struck her head against the cleaved surfaces of the road.

A soldier staggered into view, his bloodied face raised to the sky. 'The enemy is right here before us!' he railed to nobody, aside from a couple of ghosts. 'Rise up immediately, and take revenge for this—!' A falling electrical pole ended the speech.

All around, blackened, smouldering shapes littered the place, and it took me time to realize they were the remains of people.

Down a narrow side street, dozens of their neighbours pushed and shoved like cattle, skirting curtains of fire, and threw themselves into a river, most of them already aflame.

Enter the girl in white, the teenage Kohana as I knew her to be, trudging beneath glowing ash that rained like furious snow. She charged straight past us, through the rubble and carnage, in a pair of borrowed wooden clogs and that restrictive silk kimono.

Somehow, in the middle of this carnage, I rediscovered my voice.

'Isn't silk flammable?'

'Not really, not as much as wood.'

Kohana grasped my arm and guided us in pursuit of the other girl. A religious building stood nearby, untouched and lonely.

'Asakusa Shrine, the same one where we prayed with Oume-san and the others from our okiya,' said Kohana. 'It survived somehow.'

The other Kohana's mad dash was progressively hypnagogic, as we flitted on her heels from place to place. Somehow, the spotless white kimono remained that—spotless—with nary a scorch mark, soot stain, or blemish.

She paused for a moment before a cart, shorn horizontally in half, with four horse's hooves that stood a metre or so apart. There was nothing left of the beast from the ankles up.

Seconds later, a huge, round red paper lantern bounced down the avenue, afire. Unseen people screamed while the sirens wailed and the bees sang.

Finally, the girl reached a street in which a huge aircraft had parked itself, its wings sheared off. A propeller was stuck, motionless, in a nearby roof, and the fuselage of the plane was torn in half. There in front of us, near the nose with its shattered windows, we saw a huge painting of a half-naked chorus girl, waving an American flag, the words 'Miss Jupiter' inscribed above her glorious, smiling face.

A boy sat on the ground beneath the picture.

A crew-member of some kind, not out of his teens, with an unruly head of blonde hair peppered with red. More of that red was splashed on his face and neck, but he was still alive. He was playing fetch, with a dog and a rubber ball.

After a feeble toss and the hound's return, the boy's arm dropped. 'I'm sorry, fella, I don't think I can throw it any more.'

The dog, some kind of Spitz, sat down next to him and panted.

Blood began to trickle down onto the boy's shoulder as his head fell forward—just as Kohana, in her white kimono, entered the picture.

She stood over the airman for a few seconds, likely indecisive, and then knelt, lifted his head, and felt his forehead. The boy stirred, and he took in this sight before him, wrapped in white silk, with that overly made-up face shining like an apricot moon in the light from the fires surrounding us.

'Are you an angel…?' he asked.

She smiled, and then he died.

'I never understood what he asked me, until just now,' said the older Kohana beside me. 'Funny. An angel.'

19 | 十九

We were strolling together, along a wooden verandah that appeared to stretch on forever—well, at least the end of it was somewhere beyond my short-sighted range of view.

Kohana, promenading on my arm, had switched clothes.

She was again dressed as a geisha, with all the makeup that entailed. Her kimono was a deep burgundy colour, decorated with white flowers and mint-green leaves. The wide obi sash boasted a mix of light green and gold, and the paraphernalia in her hair matched all these hues.

Although together, we couldn't have been further apart.

Both of us remained silent and barely exchanged eye contact. It was not awkward, but it was necessary. I don't pretend to know what she was thinking. For my part, I believed I required time to digest and escape the things just witnessed—then I realized it was far easier to just plain waffle.

'Do you mind talking?'

'Yes, please.'

'Out of curiosity, back when you were doing the kimono-and-greasepaint profession, how long did it take you to get ready to go out?'

I looked at Kohana's face and was surprised to see a smirk. Even the false front could not hide it.

'A lot depended on whom I was going to see,' she admitted. 'When I was a geisha, the process was quicker. While I was still hangyoku, it took more time because the presentation is doubly elaborate. The apprentice always looks showier than the master.'

'Which one are you now?'

'Can't you tell?'

'My dear, I'm rough around the cultural edges and learning the ropes.'

'Excuses. By this time, I was a geisha. The hairstyle isn't so elaborate, as you can see, and did you notice I've lost my crimson collar?'

'I did. Which year is this?'

'It's 1946. November 27, in late autumn, to be exact. Hence the colours of my wardrobe.'

'Thank Heaven for the minor details. Weren't you a little young to graduate?'

'Thanks to the war, there weren't many of us left. Concessions were made—call it fast tracking. I slipped through the system before the Americans introduced an age limit to the profession.'

'I thought you lost your okiya.'

'I did. I joined another one.'

'And Tomeko?'

'Her too. Our new mama-san, Otsuta, was a lot stricter, a frequent alcoholic and a bit of a bully, but she had some wonderful kimono stored away, as you can see. We lost all ours in the bombing.'

I stopped and looked around at a leafy, beautiful parkland view. Behind me was the dark wood of the huge old building.

'This isn't Asakusa.'

'No. Kyoto.'

'Ahh, Kyoto, again.'

The place was beginning to feel just like a second home.

'You might remember that Y died two years ago?'

'Vaguely.'

'This was my second visit to the old capital. I'd been invited down to view the changing colours of the leaves—Kyoto was famous for the transition. This afternoon, the rest of my party were indoors, gazing at row upon row of religious statues. I'd stepped out for some fresh air, and to appreciate the trees we came here to see. I had just turned seventeen. Now, you can get excited—this, Wolram, is where I met your grandfather.'

I snapped to attention, in as much as I lifted my head up straight. It's difficult, at my age, to execute much more snapping than that.

The area around us was empty.

The endless verandah, the gravel-covered space beyond, and the trees lining it—with plumage that was indeed a multitude of colours—seemed to me deserted.

'Like Y, he was a soldier,' Kohana was saying. 'Otherwise, they could not have been more dissimilar. The war was over. Whatever had transpired over the past six years, Les was not likely to stoop to any overblown heroics or silly self-sacrifice. He was simply a member of the Occupying Forces, based in Saijō— near Hiroshima—with the Australian 34th Brigade. As with Y, he was also on leave, when I first met him.'

'Here?' I think it's fair to say I was stupefied. The place was like an antique warehouse in the middle of an orderly estate.

'You must know your grandfather loved history?'

'I had no idea.'

'Ah. Surprise. Turns out he that was also smitten with traditional Japanese culture, so Kyoto appeased both curiosities.'

The woman stopped, her trademark, all-encompassing smile bloomed, and she nodded.

'There he is now.'

A robust part of me did not want to look.

That side beat my conscience with a stick. 'This is aberrant,' it wailed. 'This is obscene.' It took me some effort to smother the ridiculous complaint, and in that time Kohana had equally quelled all unnecessary emotion on her face.

Finally, I checked in the direction she gazed.

Where, before, there had not been a single soul, standing there on the verandah was a tall, slender man. He was wearing army khakis and polished-up boots, and had a slouch hat at a jaunty angle on his head, with its brim turned up on the left side—the archetypal Australian World War Two soldier.

A big door spellbound this particular archetype.

Kohana went ahead of me—my feet were pinned to the floorboards—and as she moved, I heard only a vague swish of silk, and the light tapping of her wooden clogs making small, rapid steps.

The man was so intrigued by said door that he didn't notice the pearl approaching him, until she was essentially on his lap. Finally, he registered her presence, turned, grinned, and inclined his head in awkward fashion.

'*Konnichiwa.*'

God, how I remembered that voice—and yet, here was a much younger man than the Pop I'd known for too brief a time.

Kohana was right about the high, straight forehead and the intense green eyes. He was freshly shaved, and his face and arms were tanned and healthy looking. All up, this was a handsome man. I could never have pictured it.

'*Konnichiwa,*' Kohana returned in a lovely tone.

'It's a beautiful day.'

'Isn't it?'

'Hang on, hang on.'

This was I, interrupting the picturesque moment. Having managed to lever my feet and my jaw off the ground, I'd caught up with my companion.

'Is he speaking Japanese or are you speaking English? Linguistic details like that aren't so clear to me in this ethereal state of ours.'

I got the impression Kohana reluctantly withdrew her gaze from my grandfather to look at me. 'Does it matter?'

'I believe so, yes.'

'Well, all right, we had a stab at both languages. I thought it a good idea to learn the language of our conquerors, but his Japanese was initially superior to my English—we ended up teaching one another the in-betweens.'

'So. I can conclude you got to know him well.'

'Decidedly well. Les was not what I'd been indoctrinated to expect from a member of the Allied forces. Most of my life, I'd grown up surrounded by a propaganda machine that painted foreign soldiers as devils or ogres, hungry to rape and pillage the fertile soil and women of Japan. To the contrary, Les was an incredibly kind man, with a grounded sense of humour.'

There was a sparkle in Kohana's demeanour that I couldn't account for. I had a feeling high jinks were involved.

My grandfather was oblivious to our ancillary conversation.

'I don't mean to be a pest,' he was saying, 'but could you tell me something about this terrific building?'

'Oh, not more architectural banter,' I muttered.

'That is not being a pest in any way.' Kohana pushed me aside, annoyed. 'Your interest in our culture flatters me.'

'Not at all. I'm overwhelmed by the strength and age, as much as its beauty. And the size of the place is staggering.'

'This is the longest wooden building in all of Japan,' Kohana breezed, 'a Buddhist temple we call Sanjūsangen-dō. It was established in the twelfth century, and the temple houses one thousand life-size statues of the Thousand Armed Kannon. It's also said that the celebrated swordsman Miyamoto Musashi fought a duel or two, right nearby. Perhaps over there.' She pointed at some trees.

I shot the woman a glance, straight after her words sank into my resistant skull. 'This sounds suspiciously like information you gleaned from Y, doesn't it?'

'So?'

'Don't you feel ashamed, using one man's romantic banter to butter up another?'

'Is that what you think I'm doing?'

'If the geta fits. You're the one who intimated a cosy relationship with my grandfather.'

'I was a geisha. My modus operandi was to beguile and sweet-talk the males I met, thereby gaining their favour—and, hopefully, their custom.' Kohana pouted. 'I thought you'd appreciate the effort. I was being courteous to a foreigner and trying to make him feel welcome. I wasn't some kind of exotic vulture.'

'Now I worry about what kind of welcome you're implying. He was married. He was too old for you. This is the father of my mother, for Heaven's sake!'

'He was only twenty-eight.'

Pop took that moment to kneel on one knee, for the entire world as if he were going to propose.

I think I swallowed my stomach.

Instead, the man ran his fingers along a worn floorboard. 'I reckon I can almost feel the history,' he murmured.

'The famous Tōshiya archery exhibition contests were held right here, from the late sixteenth century,' Kohana said. 'Have you heard tell of the Tōshiya?'

'Can't say I have.'

'People shot several arrows in rapid succession down the length of this verandah. Three hundred and ninety-three feet.'

Les peered along the decking. 'That long, eh?'

In spite of her restrictive wardrobe, Kohana somehow managed to squat beside the man, and did it with aplomb. She placed her palm on the floorboard beside his.

'You won't find very much proof of the competition here on the floor,' she said, with mischief, 'but if you look hard enough, you'll see some of the arrows' impressions in the wall.'

Les grinned. 'There's nothing like this in Australia. Back in Melbourne, I doubt we have a building any older than a hundred years.'

'Youth too has its attractions.'

He looked up at my guide with an above-board expression, nothing wolfish about it. 'I reckon there is that to be said.'

I don't know why, but I felt strangely annoyed. I paced around the two of them. 'Just how well did you know Pop?'

'I suppose you could say I was in love with him.'

'Good Lord—another one?' The growl I made was monumental.

20 | 二十

Surrounding us, on all sides, was a large tract of war-torn disarray, pockmarked with lagoons of dark, odorous water. I could make out methane gas in the air.

Someone, sight unseen, plucked at a guitar, and I heard mosquitoes buzzing about. At my feet was an abandoned, half-buried doll. Enclosing the open space were the shells of dozens of broken and shattered houses—in which life was starting to return.

I lifted the doll and shook it down. 'I wonder if the owner is still alive? Hopefully, she more simply grew out of it. All this reminds me of some Akira Kurosawa films I saw, from his gritty urban phase, post-World War Two.'

'Over fifty percent of Tokyo looked the same,' I heard Kohana pipe up, 'in 1946—levelled. All Kurosawa-san had to do was lug his camera crew outside the studio, and take some footage.'

In the middle of this eyesore, my grandfather was playing cricket.

Kohana had propped herself up on a broken wooden fruit crate, reclining back in the weak winter sun.

She had her hair tied back loosely, a single pink flower tucked behind the left ear, very little makeup, and she was wearing a short-sleeve white shirt tucked into beige, boyish shorts.

I thought she showed too much leg.

Her feet were tucked into brown American-style open-toe platform high heels, with ankle straps, that looked more dangerous than the geta wooden clogs she wore as a geisha.

Every now and then, she leaned forward to cheer and applaud some on-debris shenanigans.

Out there in the rubble, Pop ran about with a group of happily shouting children, dressed in rags. He had a prodigious smile plastered across his face.

He had donned an oversized white v-neck cricket jumper, turned grey from the dust and mud, as well as long khaki shorts, and shoes without socks. His army slouch hat was stuck on the back of his head.

After catching something in his bare hands, he cursed—it obviously hurt—and then, straight after, held up the object, and whooped.

It may have been a primitive version of cricket, but I did eventually recognize the game. For starters, the willow bat was real enough.

'He borrowed it from one of his mates,' disclosed Kohana.

The 'ball', however, was an endless supply of lumps of rock or concrete, each one replaced when it was accidentally knocked into a rancid pond. There was some hefty surface damage being done to the borrowed willow.

'The kids here loved it when Les dropped by. He had so much time for the children—sometimes he forgot all about me, to entertain them.'

Kohana put one elbow on her knee, and her chin in her hand. 'It's a terrible thing when you become jealous of people no higher than your hip bone.'

21 | 二十一

'My father's career choice, in his younger days, was a military vocation—he was captain of a navy vessel immediately before the outbreak of the Russo-Japanese War, in 1904. He was the first member of our family to take to the seas, and no doubt he hoped to elevate his status in the ensuing combat.'

Kohana was staring out of the window of her hovel, while I had a blanket over my lap and was sipping at a delightful cup of tea. I watched Kohana's reflection over in the glass. Her face was impassive.

'Things didn't go as planned. While most of his colleagues celebrated resounding victories against the Russians over the nineteen-month conflict, thereby nurturing often-brilliant careers, my father's calling careered in the opposite direction. His ship, the *Kobayashi Maru*, was sunk without a salvo being fired— thanks to poor navigation, he hit a shoal just outside the waters of the Liaodong Peninsula in China, and lost two hundred sailors on board. The fact that he was one of only thirteen survivors was all the more dishonourable.

'Forced into early retirement after the military enquiry, Oto-sama retreated to the anonymity of rural life in Tokorozawa, about thirty kilometres west of Tokyo. The residence was not far from a new air force base and air service academy, and he developed an enjoyment of watching airplanes. An arranged marriage, with a woman thirty years his junior, took place in 1928. I will never know if he loved her, but judging from the two photographs we had, and my aunt's glowing description, Noriko was a delicate, charming bride.

'Any effort Oto-sama put into the marriage bed must have paid dividends, because twelve months after they were wed, my sister and I entered the world—and Noriko passed out of it, aged just twenty-three.

'Once the funeral was finalized, my father found a live-in nursemaid, while he sat in his study, spending most of his days in the construction of model flying machines, made from matchsticks and glue—not for his children, but for his own gratification. We were never allowed to touch them, not even as we got older. They dangled from fishing wire, just out of reach—though a couple of times, when he wasn't about, I used to poke at them with a broom.

'The evenings were different. Oto-sama drank himself into oblivion, but on occasion—before that oblivion crept into his bloodshot eyes—he tried to hit both his daughters into the same state. Sometimes he used a leather belt, at other times one of his wooden geta. Often he'd surprise us with an improvised weapon that was neither strap nor shoe.

'The highlight of his retirement, however, appears to have been trainspotting the German airship *Graf Zeppelin* in its only flight over Tokyo, two months before we were born. He had a big-framed photograph of the airship, hanging on a wall beneath the trophy *katana* sword of my grandfather, a low-ranking samurai who had served in the household of Rokurota Makabe.

'The hired nursemaid we called Oba-chan, or Auntie, though she wasn't our real aunt—our mother's sister lived in Hachioji, and she only visited us twice that I remember. Oba-chan was a nice enough woman. She had her own large family an hour's walk away, and she gave us any leftover affection she had to spare.

'I remember ginkgo trees surrounding the ageing wooden house, and there was a huge camphor at the front. Oto-sama kept Jersey cows for milk, as well as a solitary brown goat. Our neighbours Aoki-san and Toyama-san were polite, diffident old men who grew sweet potatoes. There were no other children, for miles.'

I finished my tea and placed it quietly on the table. Time to interrupt the long-winded, disturbing monologue.

'There's something I wanted to ask you,' I said.

Kohana didn't turn around. 'Go on.'

'Your name, the one Oume-san recoiled at when she heard it.'

'Oh, that. Well, for his children, Oto-sama was very inventive: my elder twin was called Tomeko, using the kanji usually reserved by parents for a child they intend to be their last, while I was anointed Akuma. For anyone interested in video games— don't worry, Wolram, I know this won't include you—'

'Hold on a minute.' I sat forward at this last phrase. 'I'll have you know, I loved my TV games when I was younger. There was one, what was the name of it, the tennis one you played on the telly?'

'*Pong!*'

Kohana looked over at me and smiled, but I stared at her.

'I beg your pardon?'

'Not you. The game you're talking about—it was called *Pong*, since it simulated ping pong, not tennis.'

'I honestly don't remember. But I was also an absolute whiz at another game, *Space Invaders*.'

'Those games are a little... shall we say, old school? Single chip and 8-bit—plus the fact you call them "TV games". I was thinking more along the lines of their sophisticated 32-megabit brethren, about a decade later. Video games.'

'How in blazes do you know these things?'

'What can I say? I have a soft spot for new technology.'

'I thought you liked books.'

'I'm allowed to have more than one interest, aren't I?'

'Given your age, I thought you would have been far too archaic for TV, let alone video games.'

'Nice. I was lucky. In the 1970s, for a while, I dated Tomohiro Nishikado.'

'And this should matter to me because...?'

'He designed your precious *Space Invaders*.'

'I thought *Space Invaders* was an American game.'

'Are you kidding? The manufacturers, Taito, are as Japanese as my Toto toilet. You know, Nishikado-san was only in his mid-thirties when the game was released? He was an engaging man — he taught me how to use one of his earlier video games, *Speed Race*, and I was captivated.'

'Was all of this before, or after, your escapade with my grand-father?'

Kohana rolled her eyes. 'After, of course. Two decades later. I said already. Anyway. Where on earth was I? I think I need to consult cheat-notes when I'm chatting with you, we get so off-track.'

'Memory problems can be an issue for the extremely elderly.'

'Right. So, as I mentioned before we swerved off course, if you have an interest in video gaming — which I now appreciate you do — you might be aware of a hidden character called Akuma in *Super Street Fighter II*.'

'The same name as you.'

'Ah, but this Akuma — who's actually a chunky male and often referred to as just plain "Devil" — was defeated by Popeye in an episode of *South Park*. Have I mentioned that, in my time, I had a fond regard for *South Park*?'

This was getting to be too much. 'I'm assuming you rolled in the hay with one of the directors?'

'No. That's one acerbic tongue you have there, my sweet. Anyway, this name — Akuma — popped up often. *Akuma-kun*, or *Devil Boy*, was the name of a 1980s anime; the *shōjo* manga series *Akuma na Eros* tells the story of Satan in love; while *Gini Piggu: Akuma no Jikken* — in English, *Guinea Pig: Devil's Experiment* — was a horrible torture movie I would recommend to no one.'

'Duly noted.' I stifled a yawn. I was getting pins and needles in my leg, so I tried to give it a shake, once my lector wasn't looking.

I shouldn't have been concerned. She was preoccupied.

'What you may glean, from these admittedly obscure references, is that Akuma wears the reprobate's badge. Also known as Mara in India, this is the god that maliciously obstructs one's path to Nirvana. Akuma is also equated with a recurring character in Christianity, Islam and Judaism: you know Lucifer, I suppose?'

'I think I've heard tell of the name.'

'Akuma didn't originate from local Japanese mythology, but arrived on the boat from India, via Buddhism. Still, the name resonated with deep meaning in my country. Its mere mention encouraged people to conjure up images of wicked brutes and evil characters—the mere sight of whom is said to bring on bad luck.'

'I believe I do get the gist.'

'I thought as much. So Akuma is what my father called me, with the name listed on our *koseki*, or family registry.'

'Wait a moment. I thought this kind of business was illegal— an abuse of a parent's right to decide on a child's name, or some such guff. I'm fairly certain it was banned in Australia to call your child Beelzebub.'

'In Japan, we also ended up with similar legislation, but it arrived seventy years too late for me.'

'I'm guessing it wasn't retroactive.'

'I never asked.' Kohana got up from her place by the window. 'Another tea?'

'I thought you'd never ask.'

'You can make one yourself, you know.'

'Ahh, but your brews are superb.'

'Flatterer. No wonder you get pins and needles.' She picked up my cup and saucer and went over to the fireplace. 'By the way, there is a point to all this.'

'I should hope so.'

'Sometimes it gets difficult to sift through all the memories, and the different angles, at once. It's so easy to get distracted and end up someplace else entirely.'

'You started out rambling about your father.'

God knows why I was being helpful. Probably, I bothered because I knew the man was a subject she didn't relish.

'Oh—him.'

Bingo.

'I think I know which tack to take now. Back in Tokorozawa, we lived near a place called Takiyama-jō—the remains of Waterfall Mountain Castle. It was a stronghold that had been abandoned centuries before, and was now not recognizable as a structure, a wild place on a hill, with vague evidence of the fortifications, pathways chiselled into the rock, big boulders laid together, and a dried-up moat.'

'Then why was it called Waterfall Mountain?'

'There was also, obviously, a waterfall. I thought that went without saying. From the age of four, I used to go there by myself. On one of her visits, my real aunt had gifted me with a picture book of European fairy tales, illustrated by Arthur Rackham. The text was in Japanese, which I had just started to learn how to read.'

'I don't know Rackham. Was he American? Or was he Japanese with an odd-sounding name?'

'He was English.' She poked out her tongue. 'Don't ask me anything more about him, but I loved his artwork. Waterfall Castle reminded me of those pictures. It's all very Arthurian— you'd despise the style.'

'I'm sure.'

'One day, I met a boy at the site of the old castle. He was five years older than me, and there he was, swinging across the waterfall between two trees, dangling from an old rope. When he jumped down to the ground to confront me, the first thing I noticed was a mole on the tip of his nose. Behind the mole was a wiry boy with untidy clothes, short-cropped hair, and a dirty face.'

'Another love interest?'

'I was five.'

'I had a girlfriend at five. Also, a holiday girlfriend.'

'At the same time?'

'Yes, one was in Melbourne and the other up on the Gold Coast, where my grandmother—Pop's wife—lived.'

'Well, there was no hanky panky here. Straight away, he handed me the rope to take a swing. Which I did, after fearing for my life. He never told me his name, but we thereafter met every weekend and spent hours together, talking nonsense, playing make-belief, climbing trees, tossing stones into the waterfall. We built ourselves a secret fort, in a glade beneath the old castle foundations. All right, I'll admit I *was* in love with his mole. I wanted to show him off to Tomeko, so one day, just before our sixth birthday, I brought her along with me. I coerced her, actually—she was not interested in cavorting around the countryside in the middle of winter.'

'I think I know why,' I said, as I slowly looked around.

The landscape surrounding us was blanketed in deep snow, with only the skeletons of trees poking through. It was freezing, and the condensation billowed from my nostrils. I felt my ears were plugged with cotton wool.

Kohana had on a thick coat trimmed with sable fur, but I was clad only in my threadbare smoking jacket—an indoor garment, intended to spend company with a raging fire or a warm heater.

I wrapped arms around myself.

'This is just not fair. Couldn't I borrow something from you? I don't care if it's a woman's coat. And there's ice between my toes! For whatever reason it is that we're here, can we make it speedy? I don't want to catch my death.'

There was a skinny kid standing on a small hill nearby, like me inappropriately dressed for this weather. From our distance, I could see the black dot on the end of his nose.

Several metres from him, an equal measure away from us, were a pair of pretty, identical little girls with short, black, bowl-shaped hairstyles. They wore heavy jackets that looked too big for their tiny bodies and probably would have fit me far better.

There seemed to be some sort of standoff going on between one girl and the boy.

Neither moved. Their eyes were glued upon one another.

The other girl fidgeted, and hopped from leg to leg—as uncomfortable with the situation as I was with the climate.

'He was bewitched,' Kohana said softly beside me. 'He couldn't look away from her, and she felt the same way. I ceased to exist. From that day forward, he only wanted to spend time with Tomeko.'

The woman turned her attention from the children, and as she looked around at the frozen vista, they vanished entirely. 'I stopped coming here soon after that. Tomeko took my place.'

'Did you tell him how you felt—about his mole, I mean? Or did you let Tomeko know?'

'Of course not. That wasn't the done thing.'

'Why the Devil not?'

'Just part of my culture.'

'To be reticent.'

'To be discreet.'

'A trait you've since shed.'

'Having lived to a ripe old age, I realized some things need to be said. But that was later on—when I was five, I abided by the philosophy of my peers. Besides, I was bored of childish games.'

Kohana went over to a place that looked like it might have been the fort she had mentioned earlier, the one she and the boy had made together, and kicked at the snow-covered roof. Of course, she didn't leave the faintest impression. Without a further attempt, she strode back through the snow.

'I spent more time in my room in the house, safely out of sight of Oto-sama. I taught myself to read, so that I could pore over more of these brooding, moody books set on moors and in primal forests, a world away from Japan. It was from these that a fancy began—my own private shelter from the real world.'

Thank God, we'd switched scenes and now hovered by a thawing fire in a large room, and for once I could feel the heat. Kohana watched a girl on the floor, with several opened books.

I recognized folk-tale tomes with fairies on their pages, and others awash with knights, princesses, and other such nonsense, looking like bored Pre-Raphaelites had painted the lot.

'It was always the same daydream: a simple farmhouse atop a cliff on a wild northern European coast, the only abode for miles in each direction, and on the western side was a raging sea, several hundred metres below. The sky alternated between slate-grey clouds and sunshine, and there was a forbidding wind, but the farmhouse was inviting, and a fire warmed within. A woman stands at the edge of the cliff, waiting for the return of her knight-errant. There's a Jersey cow and a scarecrow, and the atmosphere, in spite of the weather, is—'

'Wait. Hold it right there. A knight-errant?'

'So I was a hopeless romantic. I was just about to start elementary school. My head was full of these books.'

'Clearly. But you're describing precisely this place,' I waved airily around us, for we were back inside Kohana's hovel. 'Looks to me like the motif has been a recurring one far longer than that.'

'It was a place where I could always hide. Waiting.'

'For this knight-errant.' I looked at her. 'You worry me sometimes.'

'I think I worry myself.' She smiled.

'So what happened to the boy?'

'I told you previously. We moved away from Tokorozawa, when we were six, taken to the okiya in Tokyo. Oto-sama then returned to Tokorozawa, to continue making his planes. I didn't cry for my father's ways when he sold us to the geisha house, but Tomeko did. She wept for days on end. It was pathetic.'

'And that was that?'

'Not quite. Years later, once Oto-sama died, I went back to settle up the property. Our neighbour Toyama-san was still alive, pushing ninety, but he came over to pay his respects. At some stage in the polite conversation, he informed me that the boy had got married, fathered two children, and been drafted into the army. He was killed in New Guinea. All before the age of nineteen.'

'New Guinea? That was the campaign my grandfather fought in.'

'I know. Les told me.'

Cue visual shift, this time like a page being torn out to reveal the one beneath. Thankfully, a Pre-Raphaelite artist hadn't been involved. The room was much smaller than Kohana's hovel or her father's house, but the floor was covered with tatami mats. There were simple, white sliding doors on two walls, and a window, with its own shōji screen—made from a lattice of wood and paper—allowed in a pale illumination. It would have to have been either early evening, or dawn.

Kohana and I stood in one corner, me longing for a chair.

Two other people lay on top of a mattress, in the middle of the floor. I recognized the young Kohana and Pop.

They were lying side by side, their bodies only just touching, and they were fully dressed.

'Would that we could exchange places,' I muttered. 'They look comfy.'

'Hush.'

My grandfather spoke straight after.

'There's rarely a case of black and white,' he said in a low voice. 'Only the grey, between both. Terrible people are capable of wonderful deeds, and good people can stoop to the lowest level.'

Kohana, the one over on the bed, seemed to be listening attentively as she gazed at his face.

'I saw it all, in the war—as I'm certain you did too. Nationality, culture... Neither matter when it comes down to the basics. Human nature prevails. I did things for which I will never, ever forgive myself.'

'He didn't talk much about it,' the Kohana beside me said. 'This was one of the few occasions he opened to me.'

Les turned onto his side and raised himself to an elbow. 'I was stationed in the Territory of Papua for a year, in the campaign to hold the Kokoda Track against the Japanese advance. Do you know about it?'

'No.'

'It's inconsequential, really—a tiny, narrow walking trail, about sixty miles long, that is used for transportation across the country. The track weaved through dense jungles and some of the most rugged terrain I've seen—remember, I'm from Australia, which has that aplenty. Along the route, from the middle of 1942, we fought some vicious battles with the Japanese army. Both sides had chronic supply problems, and we were forced to cope not only with the hunger, but also leaches, snakes, spiders, torrential rainfall, mud. Most of us ended up with malaria. Eventually, we somehow won the standoff; we pursued the enemy to the north, and by January were mopping up the leftovers. If victory is supposed to be sweet, I felt none of that. All we found were exhausted and starving soldiers who were too weak to put up much of a fight. Then we came across a field hospital.'

Les sat up. He rubbed his face, using the balls of his hands to push hard. That done, he sighed. It was a loud wheeze.

'Dozens of wounded men were scattered about a large clearing, on mouldy mats, or lying prone in the mud, covered by flies and mosquitoes.' He glanced at his partner. 'Most of this mob were in the last stages of starvation. Skeletal corpses were tossed in a pile, with chunks of the remaining flesh carved off. Streuth. Some of the chirpier ones tried to put up a commotion, but the rest, they barely moved a muscle. Couldn't. There was one young lad; he—I—'

My grandfather took a break and inclined his head. A silence prevailed, before he spoke again.

'Two days before, I would've shot at the bugger in an instant. Now, all I could think about was how I wanted to help him. It was too late. He had a sunken face, with hollow cheekbones, and a gaze that, thank God, looked like it'd vacated the madness of the world. Wouldn't be long before his life followed it. He had this dark mole on his nose that stood out above the desolation around it. It seemed to be the only thing alive there. I squatted beside him, to give him water from my canteen, which he couldn't swallow. His clawed hand passed me a damp, creased photograph that had a picture of a woman and child, and he said one word, over and over: *Jihi*. Only that.'

'*Jihi?*' The word rang some abstract bell.

'"Mercy",' uttered both the Kohana on the bed and the one beside me, in unison.

Les nodded.

'I was in the intelligence corps, so I knew a smattering of key Japanese phrases, most of them military-related stuff, but this word was beyond me. I assumed he was telling me the name of his wife. So, when I came to Japan after the war finished, I tried, in my own small way, to find "Jihi" — the woman in the picture — until I learned my mistake. He was asking for mercy; he wasn't telling me his wife's name. I never found her, of course. I wouldn't have known where to start.'

The other Kohana sat up too, and placed an arm around his shoulders. 'Thank you. For trying.'

He looked at her, and he smiled.

My Kohana looked away.

'Les never so much as kissed me,' she said. 'On the mouth, I mean. On the forehead, yes, and that was precious. He occasionally gave me a hug I never wanted to end. But that was all. When my hand or my lips strayed, he would gently maintain distance. "I can't. I'm so sorry. I'm married," he would remind me. He had a locket around his neck, and inside that, a tiny photograph of a beautiful golden child. "My daughter," he told me when I first saw her. "She was only two when I left for the war. Now she's nine. God, I miss her." And his face looked so sad in that moment.'

'My mother,' I mused.

'Yes. Did I mention that Les was a history buff?'

'You did.'

'Oh. Though he never studied history at university, he'd read up on all sorts of things related to the European medieval period. We ended up spouting so much, mostly about Arthurian legends and poems—the drivel you despise.'

'Kohana, I don't despise it.' I pecked her forehead, something bold for me. 'I just find it a wee bit disagreeable. I picture people running amuck with coconuts, pretending they're making the sounds of a horse.' I regarded her. 'Can we sit down now? My back is killing me.'

22 | 二十二

'Itai! — that means "ouch" in Japanese, by the way — *Itai! Itai!'*

The metaphysical carousel continued its merry twist, on this occasion depositing us in some kind of artists' studio.

It was an ill-lit, grubby place, with black-and-white and garishly coloured pictures on the walls, most of them flowers, fish, dragons, demons, women, and assorted *ukiyo-e* clichés. It was also over-heated in there.

'Why is it so damned hot, and why am I aware of that?'

'It adds to the ambience.'

Kohana was in the middle of the room, face down on some kind of hammock, with her top off. A wiry old man, with several needles, leaned against her, pottering over something I couldn't see from my chair against the wall. Whatever he was creating accounted for the repetitive 'itais' coming from my companion's mouth.

I glanced at a man seated next to me.

He was dressed in a dark suit, with a thin tie and American pilot's sunglasses, and he distractedly masticated on a toothpick. Sweat beaded around his buzz-cut hairline.

I noted that he'd misplaced the little finger on his left hand.

There was a bulge beneath the jacket, just under his left armpit, and I suspected what it might be. I'd had my full of firearms. I shook my head and looked away.

'What on earth are you having done?' I asked Kohana.

'I'm getting Orochi tattooed across my back.'

'Ahh, so this is the grand occasion. How silly of me.' I stared at her. 'Why?'

'I was sick and tired of being the identical twin of someone as stainless as Tomeko. I needed to stamp my own mark. I felt it best captured who and what I am, beneath the sham veneer.'

'What, that you have eight heads, or an uncontrollable

hankering for saké?'

'*Itai!*'

Kohana pulled a face, and then relaxed.

'I think I also needed to mark myself, in order that I'd not be tempted to play my sister—with a branding like this, I could hardly give consideration to any silly stunts.'

'Sounds to me like you don't trust yourself.'

'Would you trust me?'

'I don't know.'

I said the comment before I gave it any thought. When I did think it through, I came to the same conclusion.

Kohana chewed her lower lip. 'Precisely.'

23 | 二十三

In return for my honesty, I almost fell into a diabolical-looking, makeshift gutter.

Kohana's hand steadied me, and I clutched it gratefully.

When I turned to the girl, I saw she had on a long blue and white polka dot dress, boasting a revealing neckline, lapels, and a skirt that came down beneath the knee. The waist was cinched in, accentuated by a thin belt, while the sleeves of the dress sat at mid-length on her arms, rolled-up at the ends. She had a tight coral necklace, high-heeled pumps, and a flower—an orange lily—was tucked into the side of her hair. That hair was pulled back on the sides but heavily rollered at the front, with backswept curls.

'You look top-heavy,' I decided.

'It was the look. 1948.'

'Post-Orochi?'

'Pre. I'll be getting him done next week.'

'Are we here to meet Pop?'

'No. He left Japan the year before, in '47.'

'You don't seem so upset about it.'

'Life goes on—and as you continually reminded me, he was married.'

This time around, we were outside on a street that showed signs of war damage, yet on the mend. Basic construction and slapdash scaffolding could be seen in both directions.

There were still a lot of dilapidated, uneven wooden houses and shops, none of them taller than two storeys—save for the one before us, which appeared to be four. It was a huge hall, with a patched-up roof and a garish new sign that read 'Western Saloon' in English, and had a picture of a ten-gallon cowboy hat.

Somewhere nearby, I could hear a big band number, as a trio of rowdy GIs in uniform passed us by—but not before ogling my companion. One of them issued a wolf-whistle as he pushed his side cap to the side of his head.

Kohana ignored them. 'Americans,' she sighed. 'Time for a bop.'

She led me through the double doors, into the building, where I found an East/West collision that socked my senses.

The music, much louder inside, came across desperate and dissolute, a frenzied primeval dirge to which the young men and women here, dressed in copycat Hollywood gangster-and-moll style, shook their frames with reverence.

Their older, far more sensible peers sat at tables, drinking in civilized repose, and there was a band on a stage, comprising a dozen or so musicians, carrying a lot of brass.

The dancehall had two floors.

There was an upper level, with less space, that looked down onto the dance floor, and had a flimsy bamboo trellis to prevent inebriated patrons from toppling over the edge.

I looked back at Kohana. She had just finished speaking to a woman with bulging, frog-like eyes and a bizarre hat with fake fruit all over it, and now was swaying her head to the music. She looked tickled pink.

'You're in luck. Shizuko Kasagi sings tonight,' she said.

'Astounding! Really?'

'What, you know her?'

'Never heard of the woman. I, er, assume it's a woman?'

'She is. A little before your time, I s'pose. We christened her the Queen of Boogie, since she mastered American jazz straight after the Occupation, though I heard she sang opera before the war. When she performs, she has a tendency to gesticulate wildly, and acts a little mad—which drives the audience frantic. I mean *really* deranged.'

I looked around. There were a few hundred people squeezed into the venue, all of them a distorted version of garish, promiscuous, cinematic hoodlum culture. This was deranged enough.

'Surely the Japanese were not so enamoured with this ugly and absurd side of American popular culture that they renounced their own?'

'Most of these people are black marketeers—you know, yakuza. But this is the real economy in Japan now. The old structures, and the old formalities, have been ruptured.'

'The American influence again?'

'Well, we were occupied by them for seven years. At this point we'd been under the cusp for three. That, and our resounding defeat in the war, changed the way of thinking. Some people got depressed about it—we had a name for it: *kyodatsujoutai*—while others made a quick buck.'

'Human nature.'

'For many people, the black market was the only place to get basic goods. We were struggling to find a new identity. Things like that change society, for good and for bad. The conservative press had a field day. What did they soapbox about? ...That young people had become irresponsible, obsequious, listless? Other things too, mostly negative.'

'Ahh, the youth of today,' I breezed.

'In all honesty, Japan in 1948 was a dysfunctional state, in sore need of renovation, like the ceiling above our heads. After World War Two, jazz took off as something modern, an invitation to a new world, from the dustbin of the old. Plus, we got a Japanese Equal Rights Amendment in the new constitution, partially aimed at helping women escape household chores—penned by an American lady, of course.'

We weaved around people who were obviously inebriated, and stopped at a table next to the dance floor. There were three chairs, one taken.

Tomeko was in it.

She smiled at Kohana, and pushed a drink across the table as we sat down. If she uttered something, I couldn't make it out above the ruckus of the band.

I grabbed the tumbler intended for Kohana, and peered at the contents. It was apparently alcohol, but it smelled off.

'The rich clientele are drinking brand stuff,' Kohana said. 'The lackeys, the girls, and most of the others are getting liquored-up on *kasutori*, a kind of moonshine *shōchū*. Who knows what's in the recipe?'

I put the glass back on the table. 'You know how to cure a thirst.'

'Live a little.' She swiped it and took a large sip. 'Oh yes, I remember this taste. Oh boy.'

I heard a minor commotion above the music, as a diminutive gentleman, with an entourage of three taller minders, wandered in our direction.

The short man was clad in a striking white linen suit that would have cost more than the construction of the entire ramshackle club. He had slicked-back hair, a lime blossom in his lapel, and a winding scar that travelled all the way down his cheek, from brow to chin, riding roughshod over a self-satisfied mien.

'His name is Katsudo Shashin,' Kohana said discreetly, 'and the man is a turning point, of sorts.'

'He certainly turns heads.'

While Victor Laszlo in *Casablanca* had a facial scar that made him look dapper, Katsudo Shashin's scar was just that—a disfigurement. It possibly helps that Laszlo's was created from stage makeup and could be washed off in a jiffy, whereas the newcomer's was likely made from a razor and would zigzag there till the day he died.

He had dark rings and an unhealthy pallor that was visible indoors, intimating some kind of illness.

'Syphilis,' Kohana whispered.

Shashin had reached our table by this stage and stood close by, his gaze centred on my erstwhile companion.

The man was toying with a cigarette, affecting a pose by

continuing to hold the thing with all the fingers of his right hand as he inhaled and puffed out smoke.

The music ceased, and all I could make out was uncomfortable silence as everyone in the room looked this way.

'Kohana-chan,' Shashin purred, taking her hand and pressing it to his lips, at the same time that he affected a bow. 'As luscious as ever.'

'Shashin-san, what are you doing in these parts? I thought you were moving up in the world, and we'd be henceforth deprived of your company.'

This comment was said so sweetly and so politely that it was impossible to detect the lie. Yet there was something bogus that tainted the sentiments therein.

If he noticed, the man chose to ignore it.

'Oh, I am, I am. But I'm here for the women—you know what they say about hoodlums that can dance.'

'Actually, I don't.'

'Allow me to demonstrate. One Yokohama jitterbug, to go. Shall we dance?'

The band had just started up again, as a diminutive female waltzed up the stairs, onto the podium, and reached the microphone.

'Shizuko-chan,' Kohana said, and then she laughed as the song commenced. 'Oh, "Jungle Boogie"! Would you believe the timing? Perfect.'

It was hard to tell if the tag 'perfect' was meant with sincere, or sarcastic, intent.

Kohana gave her hand again to Shashin, who led her to the middle of the crowded dance floor, just as the singer on stage embarked in a frantic jazz work-out and some wild high-notes that the audience loved. I found myself ducking for cover whenever she hit a crescendo—until I looked on the floor.

Shashin could, indeed, dance.

He had a monstrous energy—menacing and sinister, yet at the

same time, the women round the room appeared to find his prancing magnetic. Knees bent, he roved across the dance floor, shaking his backside, like a grotesque Groucho Marx who had suddenly discovered how to live *la Vida Loca*.

For her part, Kohana was the consummate partner, adapting without any glitch to the man's footwork, as it weaved from tango to seemingly tangled. He spun her around on the dance floor—her dress lifted up and revealed a lining of red, to contrast with the navy blue and white polka dots—and they almost collected a couple of kids in the process.

Shashin then stormed up to the girl, face-to-face, and slapped his palms on each cheek of her derrière. They had their eyes latched, and I would swear the temperature of the place, clammy as it was, spiked a notch.

I felt myself stiffen. I picked the drink back up and downed it in one shot, though I felt no ill effect whatsoever, nothing to chase away the discomfort. Kohana eclipsed every other person in this place, and did it with flair—even while dragged down by an uncommon brute like Shashin.

Then I looked at Tomeko, opposite me at the table.

The girl also had a flower, a white lily, tucked behind the ear on the left side of her head. Yes, she had Kohana's glamour, to be sure—but there was something transparent about her, as if she lacked gumption. A passive, enduring temper occupied this space, but the artistry had strayed.

Likely, I did her an injustice.

It's possible that, were we allowed the opportunity to carouse, I'd debunk such talk once I realized otherwise. I had misjudged people's character traits before.

Which brought me to another point—if Kohana were here, with me, and this was her memory, where was the real Tomeko? Was she also dead, but elsewhere? If so, why were they separated?

Or was Tomeko alive, living up the real world, sans sister, at an age most people only dream of reaching?

Tomeko.

I looked harder at her. Either this girl lacked life because Kohana wasn't standing right here feeding it to her, or Kohana's memories faded, the further she stepped away from them.

Alternatively, it was my doing. If I were a flesh-and-blood person, Tomeko surely wouldn't stare through me like this. She'd bother to put in an effort, and there would be far more, I don't know—oomph? Why bother performing when you're alone at a table in a place like this? If I were Tomeko, I'd lay an egg too.

'Stop her.'

I think I jumped.

Tomeko's lips moved, while her gaze, following Kohana and Shashin, had not changed at all. The swing was too loud for me to be certain of what she said—but she had spoken.

I leaned forward, as puzzled as I was disturbed.

'What did you say?'

Right then, Kohana squeezed in between her sister and me.

'Oh my gosh, I'd forgotten how much he takes out of me,' she said, as she sat down to my right. I could feel the heat radiating from her. 'The man can move. He's the Devil on the dance floor.' She took up another drink, sipped, and stared into space. 'And elsewhere,' she muttered.

'Another cad you fell in love with?'

'Not at all. I couldn't stand him. But Tomeko…'

Kohana held out a hand and touched her sister's impassive face. The sister didn't notice. All of her attention was focused on Shashin, who had found a new, less able-footed partner with whom to tread the boards.

'Tomeko what?' I asked.

'Tomeko was infatuated. Just like all the other women here. You can see that. She was nineteen, and she still hadn't lost her virginity.' Kohana polished off her drink in a flash. 'Tonight, Shashin will take advantage. He has a charming concept of seduction, very smooth—you'd like him. He dances a girl off her feet, gets her drunk with the cheapest of kasutori, whisks her home to play some records, and then he tends to beat them up.'

I started. 'You're joking?'

'I wish I were.' Kohana's voice sounded sad, but I was horrified. 'It's all a part of his foreplay,' she pasted.

'Good Lord, then we have to stop him!'

'How?'

'How? You appear to be interactive in this memory—tell your sister. Just damned well warn her.'

'You really think she'll listen to me? Look at her face, Wolram. Right now, she'd let him tear off her dress. Which he does do, by the way, though at a latter point in the evening, when Tomeko is no longer willing.'

'He rapes her…?'

'Mm-hmm.'

'But his illness. It's infectious. You're not going to—Wait.'

The words froze in my throat as I glared at the woman. What was it I believed I'd heard Tomeko utter? 'Stop her'? This was insane.

'All of this has happened before, and you're going to sit back and allow it to happen again. Aren't you?'

'P'raps.'

Kohana lit herself a cigarette, crossed her legs, and leaned back.

'Do you despise your sister that much?'

'Oh, Wolram.' I never thought to hear a patronizing tone swing back my way. 'It's just a memory. We can't change anything—what happens, happens. Deshō?'

I almost punched her on the nose. 'You could at least try. You could do that much.'

Kohana smiled. A bitter, hateful, offensive-looking thing it was. I never thought I'd be so disgusted in her.

'This is *Tomeko* we're talking about. What do I care? Or you?

Since when did you sprout a conscience? Martyrdom is out of style.'

24 | 二十四

Not that I was in a blind rush to forgive Kohana her sins, but she shoved us into the next scene without so much as a by-your-leave, or at the very least a tea break between adventures—stuff guaranteed to make me more ticked off.

We were in a small, tidy room, with paper-lined shōji screens surrounding us. It looked like it might be the same place that I'd seen Pop in bed with Kohana, but this time someone was lying on the floor, outside the sheets.

Also belying the tidiness was something spilled from a one-litre bottle, without a label. I could smell the fumes of rotgut liquor a mile off.

'Tomeko, you stupid idiot.'

Kohana rushed over and lifted the other girl up, into a sitting position. There was bruising around her face, she had a swollen eye, and smeared makeup framed the damage.

'Is she all right?' I asked, kneeling next to them. I wasn't sure what exactly I should do, let alone could.

'I don't know,' Kohana said as she looked her sister over.

'What do you mean, you don't know? This is your memory—correct?'

'I don't know! *Baka*—stupid, stupid girl.'

'Shashin's handiwork?'

'Yes.'

'Then I'm not sure we should be blaming her. You could have stopped this.'

'I know that.'

'Just saying.'

Kohana pulled open the torn gown, presumably to check the other girl's body for injuries, so I quickly looked aside. The bottle on the floor gave me something to mull over.

'There's so much bruising, and she's bleeding from the

vagina,' I heard her sum up. 'No, not that time of the month. Tomeko needs a doctor. I know someone. We have to take her there.'

'Why are you so interested in saving her now?'

Kohana wavered. 'I went through a moment of absolute madness last night, Wolram. Forgive me.'

'Forgiven. Now, let's get help.'

Before I knew what was happening, we were rushing with Tomeko through crowded streets. Well, to be honest, I did a lot of that rushing. It was up to Kohana to carry along her swooning sister.

'*Doke*—Get out of my way!' Kohana yelled at a sleazy-looking man, who had started pestering her.

I placed myself between them, just as the man lost interest.

'You know, at one point I thought we were supposed to be incorporeal beings,' I spoke up, as we zigzagged through pedestrians, bikes, rickshaws, trams, and heavily laden carts.

Having passed over an arched, classical Japanese bridge, we struggled past a theatre marquee that had big bold kanji letters and a hand-painted picture of a samurai.

'But I have two questions for you: number one, why am I so damned afraid of passing straight through someone? And secondly—how is it that you're able to physically hold your sister?'

'Wolram, you pick your fine moments for a quiz,' Kohana muttered, her breath labouring. 'Question one doesn't deserve my time—you answer it. Number two, well, these are my memories, so I suppose they're occasionally interactive.'

'Convenient,' I said suspiciously.

'Whatever. I'm kind of busy right now. Why didn't you ask me this when you saw me dance with Shashin?'

Tomeko's head lolled. The unswollen eye, caked with mascara and specks of dried blood, opened. Her head rolled forward, and she peered straight at me. It was like looking back at a broken

Kohana—and yet also not.

'She can see me.'

'She's delirious.'

We passed a woman in a brown cotton kimono, lugging along a small mountain of rice in a circular wooden bucket. There were dozens of bamboo poles on either side of the street, leaning under the weight of gaudy banners. A performing monkey in a sailor suit swung between the poles above various stalls that sold things I couldn't begin to fathom.

The loud sounds of a familiar jazz song drowned out everything—'Yes, that's "Tokyo Boogie Woogie" by Shizuko Kasagi; you heard it last night,' Kohana shot at me before I could think to ask—and we weaved around a big, vulgar-looking building in ruins, that Kohana said had been the Asukusa Opera—and where opera had rarely been performed. On the other side of the road, beyond low buildings, I made out a five-storey pagoda.

Constantly in our way were raffish men, rowdy children, destitute beggars, and glossed-over women in polished coiffure. Parasols, straw hats, boaters, wigs and shoulders were everywhere.

Idiotic as it sounds, I felt like we were being followed—so I told Kohana.

'That's ludicrous,' she replied, vocalizing my own doubt in eloquent fashion.

Finally, on a corner where there was a sandal-maker's shop and a grocery with snapping turtles in a pool out the front, we turned into a quieter alley and arrived on the doorstep of one Dr Hirayama. It said so, on the little wooden plaque outside his house. I don't know when I picked up the talent, but apparently I could now not only comprehend the spoken version of the language, but had learned how to read Japanese as well.

'He's a provincial man, from Onomichi in Hiroshima,' Kohana advised, right before he knocked. 'A stuffed-shirt, but he expressed—in his own way—a certain degree of affection for

Tomeko, so he should be able to help.'

'Why does it feel like we're playing this by ear? Don't you know?'

The door partially opened, and a tall, handsome man examined the two women on his doorstep—from top to bottom. Then he opened the door wider.

'Kohana-chan. What happened to you? What are you doing here?'

'Hirayama-sama, I need your assistance.'

The man looked both ways, up and down the street, as if afraid his visitors' presence might unsettle the neighbours. Heaven help him if he knew there was a ghost.

'I'm afraid I can't help you at all. I'm a paediatrician,' he said. 'I specialize in children, not adults.'

Tomeko is basically a child, I found myself thinking.

Someone whispered on the other side of the door, and Hirayama looked annoyed. 'Get back inside, Fumiko. This is none of your business. Go!'

'Charming fellow, isn't he?' I muttered.

'I'm very sorry. As I say, I can't help—you must leave.' Then he slammed the door.

'I have a mind to go through and give this place a good haunting. He strikes me as the kind of arse that would refuse hospitality to his own mother.'

Kohana stared at some point on the other side of the alley, and then she brightened. 'There's always O-tee-san.'

'Whom?'

'O-tee-san. He's an artist.'

'Wouldn't we be in too much of a rush to go look at pictures?'

'No, no, he's a good friend of mine, very diplomatic and caring—and he's studying to be a doctor, while drawing comics on the side.'

'A medical student?'

'He can help, I'm sure.'

'How about a real hospital, with a bona fide doctor?'

'I thought you didn't like them?'

A valid point. 'Even so.'

'I can't. If I go to a hospital, they'll report the matter to the police, it will leak out to the press, and our geisha career will be over. This is my life, Wolram, as restrictive as it can be. We wouldn't survive outside it.'

So it was we took up trudging again, back out on the main, busy street. Tomeko was pushing unconscious, but at least she walked. We detoured down another alley and entered the large space of a shrine, or temple. It ended up being both.

'Sensō-ji,' Kohana said, as she paused to catch her breath. 'It's the most famous temple in Tokyo, but as you can see, most of the place is in ruins. Asakusa Shrine, over there, was lucky. Remember? It survived the blitz. Who knows how?'

In the shade of the pagoda, which I could now make out to be heavily damaged, we passed a few stickers, slapped willy-nilly on the walls of a half-burned hall.

'What are those things? Some kind of local business propaganda, or is there a more profound intention?'

Kohana was preoccupied, looking this way and that. If I didn't know better, I'd say she was lost. Still, she found the time to glance at the *objets d'art* I was pointing out.

'Those? They're votive stickers.'

'And my question remains unscathed.'

'Votive stickers are stuck up in sacred places, like this temple, for religious purposes.'

'Fair enough. So what about that one? It says *moshi*—"if"— followed by a Roman alphabet question mark. What kind of religious message does this impart?'

'If?' Kohana closer inspected the sticker I pointed out. 'I'm not really sure. Then again, I don't pretend to be an authority.'

'There's a refreshing change.'

Kohana again turned a circle, holding Tomeko up. I'll give her full marks for energy and persistence.

'This is off. It's like my memories of Asakusa have started to collide—much of this area is the rowdy, risqué place I first encountered before the war, when I was a child. It took years to recover from the 1945 bombing, and in all honesty, never really recovered at all. It was nowhere near this hectic in 1948. The whole area was redesigned in the post-war period—so I'm getting confused as to which way is which.'

'But this is just a flashback. The Kohana in the memory—the one you're playing now—would not have had the same concerns, surely.'

'Makes you wonder how honest these memories truly are.'

We left the grounds of the shrine, where things became compacted again. Sandwiched amid music halls, snack vendors, and the occasional movie house, were what I took to be vaguely concealed brothels—and business looked brisk. Between these retailers, plastered on the remaining inches of wall space, hung peeling posters of erotic, more often grotesque, nonsense.

'Shouldn't you get a taxi, or a rickshaw?' I suggested.

'And where do we get the money to pay for it? I left my bag at our house.'

'I have a gun.' I flashed the Webley-Fosbery.

'Put that away!'

To my mind, it appeared as if Kohana were now soaking up the atmosphere of the place, not pursuing any purpose of getting her sister to help. She breezed along at a lethargic pace, taking in the sights, with a vague smile. I was about to lob a cantankerous remark her way, when that smile reworked itself into a furrowed brow.

The reason for the frown had just walked by us—a man in a dark kimono and baggy pants, with a small ponytail folded up on top of a head that was closely shaved. He had a sword tied around his waist.

'That's odd,' Kohana murmured. 'I don't remember seeing

him at the time. A samurai would have stuck out like the proverbial sore thumb, since the wearing of a katana in public was outlawed by the Haitōrei ruling, fifty years before I was born.'

'The Haitōrei ruling?'

'Similar to the eighteenth-century Act of Proscription in the UK, forbidding Highlanders the right to carry swords or wear their tartans.'

'I can't say I know that one either—but I get the gist.'

I also felt a chill. There was a massive shadow that progressively covered the street, and something blotted out the sun.

We both peered up to see a dirigible, some two hundred metres in length, passing overhead. It narrowly missed the pagoda.

Around it buzzed clumsy, blocky airplanes that looked like they were made out of logs. When I squinted to see them better, I realized their building materials were giant matchsticks.

'Interesting,' I remarked. 'I say, they wouldn't want to venture too close to any naked flame, would they?'

'Look at the name of the airship,' Kohana cut in, bypassing my jest. 'It's written up there, see, right there, on the fuselage.'

I followed her directions. With my dubious vision, I could make out tall capital letters that read 'GRAF ZEPPELIN'.

'Still more interesting.'

'P'raps, but this is all wrong. The *Graf Zeppelin* came to Japan on only one occasion—before I came out of my mother's interior, kicking. Sure, just a few months prior, but I never saw the thing. I have no idea what it's doing here. This is not my memory.'

'Wait—conceivably it is. Remember the big photograph at your father's house?'

'So?'

'Think, Kohana.'

'I don't have time to think.'

'You've been blocking your father out of everything we've

seen and done thus far. Possibly your memories of him are beginning to seep into proceedings. Take a closer look at the airplanes up there.'

Kohana sighed loudly. 'Oh, I see. His models. Well, this is getting inventive. They can fly, but are as out of reach as when they dangled from the ceiling.'

'When do I get to meet the old terror?'

'Hopefully? Never.'

She scanned about, as if making sure. My attention was on the blimp.

25 | 二十五

We ended up hailing a cab.

It was a primitive taxi-cycle that took us from Asakusa—'O-tee-san will pay for it,' Kohana decided—as Tomeko had turned worse and was unable to walk.

The three of us crowded into the dilapidated back seat, behind the driver.

'I don't like this,' I muttered, a feeling of panic in my veins. 'Is it safe?'

'Safer than flying.'

'In 1948? I thinks planes were safer than you suppose.'

As we sped along over bumpy streets, Kohana gazed at the reconstruction going on around us. 'I first met O-tee-san last year,' she said, 'when I was dressed as a man.'

'I see.'

She glanced over. 'You do? I was expecting some kind of flippant remark. This isn't surprising?'

'If I expressed surprise at all your yarns, I doubt we could make room for regular conversation.'

'Oh.' The girl turned her head and watched the road ahead. 'There was a reason I was dressed in men's clothes—I was trying to entice a visiting German stage actor, named Franz.'

'And were you successful in this enterprise?'

'Sadly, not at all. Franz was a strikingly handsome man, but he preferred other strikingly handsome men. Probably, I was too short and too skinny.'

'How was your German?'

'Worse.'

'So, instead, you caught the notice of this O-tee-san character? He likes his cross-dressing women?'

'Actually, he does. O-tee-san is a big fan of the Takarazuka Revue, a famous all-female musical theatre troupe. I was waiting for Franz in a café in the Ginza, dolled up in a grey suit and hat, with a pencil-thin moustache that I'd perfected, using my eyeliner. The customer at the next table kept on stealing peeks, and scribbled something into a sketchbook. Franz never showed up, so I asked to join this other man. He was sheepish, at first, about the undercover pet project he'd been doing, but I was charmed when I finally saw the picture he'd drawn—a caricature of me, dressed as a Renaissance European male aristocrat. The big, ribboned hat was particularly striking.'

We hit a pothole, and the taxi lurched—along with my stomach.

'God, I hate this,' I mumbled.

'The story, or the ride?'

I hadn't intended Kohana to hear. 'The ride, my dear. I'm not at my best inside any wheeled contraptions.'

'Car sickness? You should talk to O-tee-san about it; he can probably recommend some medicine. He acts like my doctor, always telling me to get proper bed rest and take a regular dose of vitamin C. Though he's a year older than me, he feels like an overactive younger brother sometimes. But he's a sweetheart.'

'I don't think he'll hear my complaints,' I reminded her.

'I'll mention it to him anyway. No harm.'

I looked for a long time at Tomeko, seated between us. I could feel the girl's hip poking into my side. So, I could touch her? I raised my hand to her face.

'Don't, Wolram. Let her sleep.'

The drive finally came to a stop in a dead-end street, where makeshift wooden apartment blocks loomed around us. There were some children nearby—the girls skipping rope, the boys playing baseball, and never the twain shall meet. The light here had an amber, dusty hue.

Kohana waved at two grubby boys of about ten or eleven. 'Shotaro-kun, Fujio-kun, could you come over here?'

They walked to the cab and stared at the two girls on the seat.

I noticed that the younger lad carried with him a blue bucket, in which oversized beetles were crawling.

'Kohana-chan, what happened?' asked the oldest boy in a slow, deliberate voice.

'A long story, Fujio-kun, not necessary now. Is O-tee-san about?'

'He's upstairs, working.'

'Fetch him for me?'

'He won't be happy. He doesn't like to be interrupted.'

'I'll take that risk. Tell him Kohana needs him—quickly now.'

The boy raced straight into the entrance of a flat, his legs faster than his tongue. While we waited, our cab driver lit himself a foul-smelling cigarette.

'What kind of tobacco is that?'

'I doubt it's tobacco.'

The other boy—what was his name? Shotaro?—stood motionless nearby, with that pail full of creepy crawlies. His mouth was wide open, and I wondered if he used that pose to catch unsuspecting flying insects.

'Shotaro-kun loves his bugs as much as his comics,' Kohana said. 'O-tee-san thinks he'll either become an entomologist or will one day create a superhero team of insect people.'

'How is Tomeko? Is she all right?'

Kohana didn't answer.

I saw someone approaching with the other boy Fujio-kun. This man somewhat comically resembled a Frenchman, with a beret, heavy-framed glasses, and a horizontally striped T-shirt. He was carrying a half-chewed baguette.

'What's happened?' he asked, as he leaned over the taxi-cycle.

'Rape.'

'I can see that.' The man mixed and matched concern with anger. He tossed the breadstick aside. 'Who did this? Who is responsible? I'll kill them.'

'I can't tell you.'

I leaned close. 'Why not?'

'Either he'll follow through with his threat—and get himself hurt—or he'll call the police. Shashin-san is my responsibility. It's the way it was then, and the way it will be now.'

'We need to go straight to a hospital,' the man said. 'I'm not qualified for this.'

Kohana shook her head. 'No hospital. Please.'

'Kohana, I am not a doctor.'

'Please.'

Without further argument, and with surprising vigour, O-tee-san lifted Tomeko and carried her toward the same building the boy had entered earlier. We followed him, past a wooden plaque with 'Tokiwa-sō' on it, and went upstairs to the second floor.

'Fujio, the door.'

The boy opened it for him, and O-tee-san hauled Tomeko to a couch, setting her down in gentle fashion. She didn't stir. The man then cautiously started to investigate the damage.

I looked around a small living area, packed with books and boxes. Pictures completely covered the walls, mostly kids' comic puff like robots and humanized animals, but also darker, more striking images.

'Gekiga,' Kohana said. 'Dramatic pictures. A lot of the manga-ka did them—they weren't only interested in cuteness. The cute ones, however, paid the bills.'

'Fujio,' O-tee-san called out, 'be a good boy: go get Fujimoto and Abiko next door. Tell them to bring boiling hot water and clean cloths. Clean, I say! And tell them to leave their stupid cat at home this time.'

He started to unravel Tomeko's kimono, but then produced a pair of scissors to cut off the material he couldn't undo without overly moving the girl.

The taxi driver was hovering in the open doorway, his hand out. He noisily cleared his throat.

'I think the man wants to be paid his fare,' I said.

'Get out!' O-tee-san shouted, as he jumped up, slammed the door, and whizzed back to his patient. 'I'm begging you, let me work!'

I stood back as far as I could in that cramped space. 'So, Kohana, what's the plan?'

My companion looked at me with an icy expression. 'You'll find out. But you have to remember—you're a spectator here. That's all.'

'I understand. What about Tomeko? Will she be all right?'

'No.' Kohana stared down at her hands. 'She dies tonight.'

'What? Just like that?'

'Sometimes death is a cheap and nasty creature. Haven't you noticed?'

26 | 二十六

Ten days passed.

At least, this is what Kohana told me when we arrived. For all I knew, it could have been ten years, although the war-damaged street was a recurring clue.

We were standing at the base of a rickety wooden staircase that looked like it ought to be condemned, post-haste, and we were waiting for a man. Katsudo Shashin, the gangster.

Kohana had gotten her tattoo four days before, and she inferred it still hadn't healed properly. The girl was fitted out in a long black coat, with gloves. Her hair hung loose, trailing down past her waist, and it slightly veiled one eye. Most striking was her wide-brimmed hat.

'Les gave it to me, before he left Japan, as a kind of present,' she had said earlier. 'Told his superiors he lost the thing.'

'Pop's army slouch hat?'

'Mmm. I reshaped it—gave it a good beating with one of my okobo—and dyed it black. Part of my disguise, you see, just for this occasion.'

Otherwise, Kohana had on geisha makeup, and beneath the coat her kimono and the other familiar courtesan's trappings. It was a warm evening—she must have been overheated, wrapped up in all that baggage.

Two cigarettes came out and were lit. 'Here you go.'

'Thank you.'

'You're okay with this?'

'After what this monster did to your sister, I'd be up for anything.'

'Remember, tonight I *am* Tomeko. Promise you won't try to interfere?'

'Could I?'

'I strongly doubt it.' Kohana exhaled one of her virtuoso

smoke-rings. 'But I do have your word?'

'I believe I gave it to you earlier.' The ring dissolved.

'Tomeko!'

It was Shashin, striding with his short legs along the footpath, dressed in another pale linen suit, and there were dark sweat-marks around the armpits. No bodyguards were with him.

My companion flicked away her cigarette, and a folding fan replaced it.

Like before, the man took Kohana's hand and swept it to his lips. His stare, however, remained glued on her face. 'Wonderful to see you—I never expected a return visit, but I am happy. Why the geisha paint tonight?'

'I needed to cover some of the prizes from our last encounter.'

'Ahh, yes. A glutton for punishment perhaps?'

'Oh no, it's all your doing. You have such effervescent charms,' Kohana said coyly, in a childish tone, the fan fluttering.

'I always wanted to have you as a geisha, but you were a class above me—another elusive trophy.'

I took a long puff from my cigarette. I had been incorrect. I was not okay with this.

'I have something, Tomeko. A gift.' From inside his jacket, Shashin produced a small bottle, in a brown paper bag. 'Much better than last time. American bourbon. To celebrate the reunion.'

'Are we going to stand out here all night? I'd prefer somewhere quieter, where you can relax. And a geisha has her reputation to uphold.' The fan fluttered. She peered upward. 'Your apartment, perhaps?'

'Of course, of course. Follow me.'

Kohana followed Shashin up the stairs, with me on her tail, all of us silent.

At a door numbered 17, the gangster took out a key, unlocked it, and—in an ill-mannered gesture—went through first, allowing the door to swing back in his guest's face.

Kohana didn't care.

She gave the door a discreet shove, and we entered a humid, boxy-looking abode, with very little in the way of furnishings. It was a dreary, untidy place in which a steel-framed bed took precedence. Kohana stepped out of her okobo shoes, but I resolved to leave my slippers on. My tiny protest.

A lamp clicked into use, just as we heard the crackle, pop, and hiss of vinyl, on a turntable in a cabinet by the entrance.

When I checked the black label in the middle of the rotating record, I could only decipher the bold, white words 'Nippon Columbia', and 'Made in Kawasaki'. The rest escaped me, it was spinning so quickly.

'Shizuko Kasagi,' Kohana informed me, as she slipped off her outer clothes. 'You remember her.'

'How could I forget?'

'This one is "*Rappa To Musume*", "Trumpet and a Girl". Written by a famous composer, Ryōichi Hattori, and restrained for Kasagi-san. I revered the song—up till this very moment.'

Once the music kicked in, it reminded me of Billie Holiday messing around with Desi Arnaz. Not bad at all.

Shashin had his back to us. He was busy pouring drinks, into dirty glasses.

'Don't do this,' I whispered. 'I have the gun.'

'Not now. Trust me, I know what I'm doing. I've been here before.'

After giving a sofa-chair a careful wipe, Kohana placed her coat, gloves, and hat there. She remained clad in kimono, obi, and white socks.

Perhaps conscious of the tattoo of the dragon Orochi that now distinguished her from Tomeko, Kohana extinguished the lamp. A streetlight outside cast through the grubby window, giving enough luminance to see by.

When Kohana put her arms around the man from behind, I could feel my hands curl up into fists.

When she pulled him around, kissed his chin, and then unwrapped her obi and dropped it to the floor, I felt the need to scream. She drew him down to the bed on top of her, with her gown slipping open around the knees. His hand darted in and pushed right up over her hips.

I wanted to dash the man's brains out, to choke a confession and an apology from his good-for-nothing lungs.

But in my impotent state, I could do none of these things—were I still breathing, I doubt I would have been any more persuasive. Shashin may have been short, but he was a third of my age and twice my width. There was no doubt he'd know a thing or two about the Marquess of Queensberry rules, and could probably juggle razors if provided—which would account for the scar.

My lasting aptitude was for a two-step of chicanery and commerce.

I fingered the gun in my pocket. I remembered the feel of Tomeko's hip in the taxi-cycle. Perhaps I wasn't as impotent as I thought. Was it possible I could make a difference?

Right then, a knife came into play.

It was a long kitchen number that caught the light—with the brand name 'Béroul' etched into the surface of the blade. In absolute silence, Kohana had acquired the tool from some place—God knows where—beneath her slip.

The man was rutting her, making animal noises as he did so. I could hear them above Kasagi's crooning. I covered my ears with my hands to try to blot them both out. This was awful. It was the worst sound I'd heard in seventy-one years of life, plus the lukewarm existence eked out since.

Kohana's face had no expression whatsoever.

I'd seen her hone a sphinx-like demeanour, in combination with the mask the makeup offered, but this rang different. This was bloody-minded focus.

'I've never had a lover as rough as you,' she groaned.

The hand with the knife rose into the air, and then lashed sideways into the man's throat.

Seconds passed before Shashin noticed.

When he did, he slowly arched back, his hands around his neck, dark liquid gushing out of somewhere. His body rutted in reverse now—he was gasping and shrieking—and then he fell off the bed. Kohana, however, hadn't finished. She wiped a rose-red streak across her pale cheek, lifted herself up, stood above him, and leaned over with the knife.

'*Shinde moraimasu,*' she said. 'You will do me the favour of dying.'

From my vantage point, I could not properly see her follow-through, but I have my suspicions—the man wailed like a castrato, until he ceased about ten seconds later.

Kohana got up and took out the packet of cigarettes from her coat pocket.

I sat down on the bed, astonished.

The woman eased herself next to me, wiping away blood. She removed one of the cigarettes with her mouth, taking care not to touch it with her hands. 'Light me up, will you?'

'Certainly.' I found some matches and flicked one across the sole of my slipper. It lit straight away—I'd always wanted to try non-safety matches. I held it out to her. 'He's dead?' I asked, more for the sake of making conversation.

'As a doornail.' A plume of smoke spiralled heavenward.

'So. What shall we do now?'

'I don't know about you, but I'm enjoying the song and this cigarette.'

'You don't mind sharing them with a man you just murdered?'

'Well, I'd say he's far more functional in this state.' She took off her socks and placed her bare feet on the corpse's back, wriggling her toes, and then leaned back to relax. 'That's better. Who needs a footstool?'

'We're not going to bump into him back in the land of the lost, are we?'

'God, I hope not.'

The apartment dissolved.

Next up, we were on our feet, wandering a narrow, quiet street as the occasional person passed by.

Kohana had scrubbed herself clean.

For starters, the red smudge on her cheek was gone, as was most of the makeup, and her hair was tied into a bun. She wore a conservative-looking brown cotton kimono, and had a newspaper tucked under one arm.

A sticky, summer evening surrounded us.

'The same night?' I inquired, doubtful.

'No, it's a few days later.'

'What happened regarding Shashin?'

'That was interesting.'

'Fill me in.'

'Of course, the major dailies didn't touch it, but the second-rate newspapers went into a tailspin, splashing about the murder in lurid detail—and, to make things more exciting, there was an eyewitness.'

'What?'

'Oh, fear not. He saw only me enter the apartment—you were lucky!—and he missed the actual murder. A twelve-year-old boy, identified as "Shinohara-kun", described a woman dressed in a black Fedora and cloak. He dubbed her the Scorpion Lady.'

'A catchy name.'

'I liked it too.' Kohana unfolded the newspaper as she walked, to show me a black-and-white caricature that took precedence on the front page. 'Now they're printing up wild stories about a female yakuza assassin, one who's on the prowl for rival gangsters.'

Her tone was more matter-of-fact than concerned, and the drawing didn't look at all like the woman.

'Did this boy see your face?'

'It would seem, well, not so clearly — or he has a fertile imagination. Either way, I was lucky.'

'You said this is a few days later. What did you do afterward?'

'I went up to Lake Nasu for two days with my writer friend Kawabata-san, but he was in a peevish mood and hardly fun. I remember when I woke up at dawn, there he stood at the window of the inn, staring at a white-tipped Mt Fuji. "Can you hear the sound of the mountain?" he asked me. "I can't hear a thing," I said. "Even the crows are asleep." It was true. "I must be getting old," was his verdict. That was the kind of disagreeable getaway we had. Not surprisingly, I was glad to return to Tokyo. Today.'

When we arrived at Kohana's housing block, there was a middle-aged man lingering on the steps. He had on a tired-looking kimono, baggy trousers, and an inappropriate derby hat.

He stamped out a cigarette, and after a brief introduction, bowed and handed my accomplice a card.

'It is with tremendous regret that I am disturbing you, m-m-madam,' he stuttered. As he did so, he removed the derby and scratched at tousled hair. 'I realize the impertinence of my visit, but —'

'A private detective,' Kohana cut him off, holding the business card up closer to me, in order that I could view the single name 'Kindaichi' printed on its surface. 'Wanting information about the night of the murder. I don't think he had been commissioned to investigate, but he was curious.'

I refocused on the man.

'Doesn't look like a competent individual,' I muttered.

'Did you ever watch the TV series *Columbo*? Peter Falk passed himself off as ineffectual, but he always got his man or woman. Kindaichi-san struck me as the same stock. He looked unkempt, but there was a clever glint behind the façade.'

'Another look I have to master.'

'Are you forgetting the state of your smoking jacket?'

'Not by any means.'

Kohana rejoined the conversation, and after more head scratching and an impish smile, the man shuffled off.

We watched him go.

'Did he question you any more about the murder, after today?' I asked.

'Twice. To be honest, I got the impression he suspected me, but he didn't follow through or report any suspicions to the police. I don't know why. I was grateful. I never had the opportunity to thank him—besides, doing so would have confirmed my guilt.'

When I finished rubbing my face with the palms of my hands, I looked up.

We'd switched venues. Surprise.

All this hopping about was making me feel like I was on a bargain-basement, all-stops package tour through pandemonium.

I chose to close up shop. 'God, I'm so tired of this. Can we take time out?'

'Don't be like that,' I could hear Kohana whisper. 'This one's fun.'

'Why?'

'Just because.'

'You really have to work on your powers of persuasion,' I said, determined not to give in to the girl.

'Oh, be a devil. Look around!'

So I did. Apparently, determination had fled its post.

I don't know that I would call it fun. Around me was a huge, crowded arena, full of Japanese people dressed as if they'd stepped out of the old 1960s American TV comedy *Bewitched* — which was one of my family's favourite shows as a kid, but it had dated. Still, some of the men did have on thin, snazzy ties.

We were positioned in hard wooden alcoves—seats?—a few rows from a raised ring, which was made from a combination of clay and straw.

I was in a closer row, three back from the ring's sandy edge. Kohana was seated directly behind me, in the next row, looking very Audrey Hepburn in a simple black dress and pearls, her hair up in a beehive. She was sandwiched between two gentlemen, poles apart.

On her left was a man in his late fifties.

He had short-cropped, white hair and a moustache, with

remarkably large lips. He was smoking, and I noted that once he butted out one cigarette, he straight away lit up another.

On the other side of Kohana, to her right, was a beefy-looking forty-year-old, with thick, scowling brows and a head of wavy black hair.

I could tell both men were with Kohana, since each had a hand discreetly touching the thigh closest to them. As I leaned over the back of my chair, seeing that sight, I felt—I don't know—vexed?

Kohana was oblivious. She leaned over to speak softly in my ear.

'It's December 1963.'

'Well, now. I was almost born.'

'There you go.'

'How come we're skipping ahead fifteen years?'

'Nothing much happened in between. We introduced television, the US occupation ended, our Crown Prince got married, and we built Tokyo Tower—but that was a cheeky copy of the Eiffel Tower anyway. Oh, and I quit being a geisha.'

'No prison term for you?'

'Nah. I spent this time on the loose.'

'You got away with murder?'

'I did. Can we drop the subject now?'

'Very well. I have to say, you don't look the part of someone who's careered forward fifteen years.'

'Why, thank you. The benefits of a good makeover and soft lighting.'

'Possibly they help.'

'Would you like to know where you are?'

'I'm sure you'll tell me.'

'We're in the Kuramae Kokugikan in Tokyo—later closed and replaced by a bigger sumo stadium, in Ryogoku. But you may be pleased to know that this is the same one Sean Connery visited a few years later, in *You Only Live Twice*. There is something about the spectacle of two exceptionally fat *rikishi*—in a nation of skinny people—clad only in loincloths, shaped like a sexy G-string, that is, well, hilarious.'

Kohana applauded, after one of the behemoths stumbled out of the ring.

'Don't you think?' she added.

'Astounding.' I'm unaware if I meant the comment. It really didn't seem to matter what I thought. 'I see you've dragged along two boyfriends. One isn't enough these days?'

'Oh, they're just companions.'

'Does either man know that? Or realize you have *two* playmates?'

'Don't be like that.'

'Like what? They're looking territorial, though my money would be on the younger fellow. He's a genuine gorilla, Kohana. I'm surprised he's able to sit down for any length of time. The gent on your left looks too civilized and a dash seasoned—he'd likely end up with his neck wrung.'

Kohana unfurled a grape-coloured fan and pretended to be shy. Her eyes, somewhat heavily marked with black eyeliner, said otherwise.

'You'd be surprised. Shimada is a more powerful man than he appears, and R has his vulnerabilities. R is a recent acquaintance, a famous wrestler who, sadly, will be stabbed in a club this very night and will die in a week from peritonitis—since he won't bother going to hospital to get the wound examined properly.'

Kohana closed her fan.

'Shimada I've known ten years.'

A spotlight came out of the ceiling high above, straight onto the older man on Kohana's left.

The rest of the auditorium quietened, at the same time that the lights went down.

'I should tell you that "Shimada" wasn't his real name,' Kohana disclosed, through the transition. 'It was a nickname we shared between us, a souvenir from a movie he was shooting when we first met. At that time, he was a famous actor, and worked with Akira Kurosawa. But he'd also just volunteered his services for the first *Godzilla* romp in 1954—something he would soon repent, becoming a habitual player in *kaiju* monster movies.'

The surrounding blackness and the spotlight remained the same, but we back-pedalled about a decade, judging from the years peeling away from Shimada's face, his devolution in fashion, the darkening and thickening of hair, and the loss of his midriff paunch.

Kohana looked virtually the same, aside from a change in wardrobe, from Hepburn (Audrey) to Hepburn (Katharine)—she was now wearing a baggy pants-suit, all wide shoulders, and her hair long and straight with a curled fringe.

We were standing on a golf course, in bright sunlight.

'I met him here.'

'Is that so?' I looked around. Aside from Shimada and Kohana, there were a group of strangers, mostly older men, milling near the green. 'I didn't pick you as a golfing aficionado.'

'Oh, I can't stand the sport. But I played occasionally, to be sociable. Shimada shared my abhorrence, which is one reason we got to talking. I also loved his performance in a recent movie I'd seen, in which he played a dying bureaucrat. I just had to tell him that. He looked much younger and far more handsome in the flesh—and he was *funny*! In a gloriously self-deprecating way.'

The scene did its flip-flopping thing, and the golf course became a bedroom, with Shimada dressed-down in a singlet and shorts and Kohana, well, in nothing whatsoever, flaunting a shocking peroxide hairdo.

'I say, what's with the—'

'Hair? Your questions are getting predictable, Wolram.'

'Even so.'

'All right, all right. A few months before, I'd seen *The Three Musketeers*—you know, the one with Gene Kelly? It was finally released in Japan about four years after being made in

Hollywood. What can I say? Lana Turner turned my eye.'

'Head. She turned your head. I believe you're mixing your idioms.'

'Oh yes, with the blind eye one, right? Funny. Well, the next day, after I saw the movie, I went into a drugstore and bought bleach. It took several attempts to get my hair white, but it was strong and survived the process for a year or so, when I moved on to the next fad. My scalp, however, itched horrendously for months afterward.'

She and the man Shimada were sitting up in bed together. At least he was partially dressed, but I had to avert my attention from the girl's nakedness.

'Kohana, could you please at least pull up the blanket and show a modicum of discretion?'

'My, aren't you upright? I never thought you had it in you.' Thankfully, she did as requested. 'Happy?'

I peered over at the two people in bed together. They looked as excited about their proximity to one another as a husband and wife after thirty years of marriage.

'Relatively,' I said.

Shimada had a cigarette dangling from his lips, which Kohana borrowed, off and on, to take a puff.

'I'm glad the shoot is over,' the man was saying, in a gravelly voice. 'I mean, it's worrying that he's grabbed so much of Kurosawa's attention, but he does make me smile with those wild ways and the sense of humour. What did you make of him, Nora Inu?'

'I like him,' the woman said, as she coiled peroxide-white hair around two fingers. 'He's dangerous—but you're right, he's also funny. And together that makes him sexy.'

'The boy has it all over me there.'

Kohana extracted the fingers from her hair to reach over and caress the man's face. 'No. It's just different.'

He grinned in lopsided fashion.

'Nora Inu?' I piped up.

Kohana turned her attention fractionally my way. 'Stray Dog. Shimada-san is the only person in the world I would allow to call me something so ribald—don't get any ideas, okay?'

'Roger.' I gave her a mock salute. It was past time she got one back.

The left corner of the girl's mouth rose as she returned her focus to the man in the bed.

'You know, some people have doubts, because he grew up in China,' Shimada was saying, 'but the man proved he had enough balls to be Japanese during the war, and I haven't seen an actor better skilled to alternate between gangster, *rōnin*, salaryman. He's talented and fastidious—but he also has a self-destructive tendency.'

Kohana took his dying cigarette, stamped it out, and lit a new one. 'Tell me more about this big-lizard film you're doing.'

'Ah-hah, that. I took the man-in-the-rubber-monster-suit movie for the money,' he muttered as he flicked through a book. 'There's not much to tell. That schlock has no future anyway. They'll never make another one.'

'What are you reading?'

'Kurosawa recommended it to me. Do you know Dashiell Hammett?'

'The name isn't familiar.'

'An American writer. The one who created those movies with William Powell and Myrna Loy, *The Thin Man*. Do you remember?'

'Seems to me, I only recall chubby people in American movies.'

'Perhaps you're a little young.'

Kohana took another drag on his cigarette. 'What's the title of the book?'

'That's what disturbs me. This is a collection of short stories, about a San Francisco detective, the Continental Op, and it's called *Dead Yellow Women*.' Shimada glanced at his bed partner. 'Americans seem to believe that we have yellow skin. Do you think we have yellow skin?'

Kohana placed the cigarette between her teeth so that she could hold both her bare arms straight up in the air. In doing so, the quilt tumbled down.

'They look pale to me. Bordering on chalky. Perhaps most Americans have only met malnourished Asians, or Japanese suffering from jaundice?' She returned the smoke to the man.

'Hammett also seems to think all Asians are opium smugglers and gun runners.'

'Are these particular people Chinese?'

'Yes.'

'Perhaps he has a point.'

'Nora Inu—really.' He shook his head.

The bed vanished as we fast-forwarded back to 1963, to the older, somewhat sadder Shimada. The spotlight diminished, and the crowd returned around us.

Two excessively large men were facing each other in the nearby ring.

'Well, I'll give them this much,' Shimada was saying, 'ogling sumo wrestlers is easy, since the practitioners of the sport aren't the waif-like types you geisha tend to be. I usually wear glasses—but who needs spectacles here?'

'Former geisha,' Kohana spoke up. 'And are you implying sumo will put optometrists out of a job?'

'Only the optometrists whose client base is made up of sumo-wrestling fans.'

'Oh, I see.' Kohana briefly laid a hand on the man's arm. 'What are you doing next week? Are you free for dinner?'

'Actually, I'm going to be busy—did I mention we start shooting tomorrow? It's for a film due to be released in a few months. In the year that Japan introduces its world-beating bullet train service, and hosts the Olympic Games for the very first time, I get to star in one more of those silly kaiju movies.'

He flicked his lighter at another cigarette.

'I was wrong—men in rubber suits, playing monsters, do have a career future. This one is about a giant, three-headed beast called King Ghidorah, indulging in fisticuffs with Godzilla, Rodan, and Mothra. Where they dig up the sophisticated scripts and the silly names, I have no clue. I've worked with Kurosawa, Mizoguchi, and Kobayashi, yet here I am spending my time with quarter-star directors barely out of high school, who care more about the placement of an overturned Tokyo Tower prop than the live actors in front of the camera.'

'You told me the director is Honda-san—wasn't he Kurosawa's assistant? And isn't he much older than you?'

'Pushing sixty-three, I believe.'

'Yet barely out of high school.'

Shimada chuckled. 'Yes, you're right, I exaggerate.'

'I also think you enjoy the roles.'

'I could play them in my sleep. This time, I'm a psychiatrist, but my guess is I'll be holding up an office desk somewhere, and asked to look serious.'

'Or the desk will be holding up you,' Kohana giggled.

'There's a point—perhaps I can drink my way through proceedings. I could always sneak in a hip flask of shōchū. By the way, have you spoken lately to Mifune? There are troubles in matrimonial paradise, and I hear his relationship with Kurosawa is under some strain. Finances and whatnot. I'm sure he could use a friend.'

We hit the accelerator again, the crowd vanished, the lights faded, and the stadium shrunk into a tiny, poorly lit bar.

Did I mention the queasy sensation I get when we hurdle locations?

Probably, it has as much to do with the suddenly switched depths of vision and the abrupt changes in light. This time, however, the queasiness was minor. I think I was getting blasé about the experience.

Like the illumination and the surroundings, Shimada diminished before us.

He was hunched over the bar, with almost no hair, knobby fingers clenched around a ceramic cup, while Kohana sat up straight beside him, an affectionate arm around his shoulders.

For once, I didn't wait around to be spoon-fed information by my tour guide—I jumped up and played detective.

Not that there was much room in there to move. Behind a bored bartender with a receding hairline, a waistcoat, and a fat, burgundy-coloured velvet bowtie, was a calendar. I leaned on the bar to gain a better view.

Beneath an ukiyo-e picture of an eight-headed dragon, standing out amid the kanji, were the numerals '1-9-7-8'.

'He's seventy-three. I'm forty-nine,' Kohana said from her stool.

I'd like to say she looked half her age, but would have shaved off ten years. An elegant late-thirties, with minor laugh lines around her mouth and eyes. The Farrah Fawcett-Majors hairstyle she sported—feathered, wavy, and voluminous, much like the roof of that temple we'd seen in Kyoto—wasn't so flattering.

'It was the '70s,' Kohana complained, having once again picked my brain.

Shimada was, then, only a year or so older than me when I kicked the bucket, but he seemed twenty years beyond that. He was struggling for breath and wheezing, and the cigarettes were nowhere to be seen.

'I'm too old for Kurosawa, and I've stooped to playing bit-parts in domestic comedies like *Tora-san*,' Shimada said in a weak, husky tone. 'But it beats playing it straight in rubber-suited monster yarns.'

'Oh, shhh. We both know how you really feel about the monster yarns.'

He laughed, but the sound came across more like a punctured

tyre tube. 'I do miss them. A thing of the distant past, Kohana-chan, just like that sexual drive I misplaced between movies — and the ability to breathe easily, like anybody else.'

Kohana smiled and kissed his forehead. Then she looked straight at me. 'Shimada died in 1982, just before his seventy-seventh birthday. I miss him.'

'As much as you will miss me?'

'Miss you? I'm stuck with you. Remember what they say about absence and fondness? In your case, we're miles from that.'

And, bang, we were back in the sports arena in 1963, with the crowd shouting encouragement to two bulls of men pushing each other toward the ring's cordoned edge.

The healthier, middle-aged Shimada was seated beside Kohana, and she was back to her Audrey Hepburn shindig.

'So, here we are again at the sumo,' she said as she leaned over to me. 'Aren't you excited? I remember you saying this was one of the things you loved in the James Bond movie. Take a good look. We probably won't again see many two hundred kilogram men throwing themselves at one other.'

The bout ended quickly, and after much meaningless speech-making and a crooning by the referee, a couple more mostly naked men lined up against one another.

'What most spectators don't realize is that there's so much more to the sport than its remarkably hefty wrestlers,' Kohana whispered in my ear. 'Behind the cataclysmic grappling that goes on are centuries-old traditions like the Shintō-related throwing of salt — see?' She pointed her fan as one of the wrestlers lobbed a handful of white. 'That one's for purification.'

'I remember my grandmother lobbing salt over her left shoulder, although I believe in her case it was to dispel demons hovering there.'

Kohana wasn't listening.

'See that remarkably revealing loincloth they're wearing?'

'Shimada was right — how could I miss anything about these

people?'

'Well, it's known as the *mawashi*, and has a story too: it's made of silk, is approximately thirty feet long, weighs up to eleven pounds, and sometimes bears the name of a sponsor.'

I pictured one of the sumo boasting a logo of an H-in-a-circle on their nether regions, and pined for my grandmother's salt.

'Oh, and the competitors' hair, which you can see is precision-slicked into topknots, is coiffed using a waxy substance called *bintsuke abura*, the main ingredient of which comes from the berries of the Japanese wax tree—a member of the same family as poison ivy.' Kohana wasn't even pushing breathless. 'It's been used in hairdressing in Japan for around a thousand years, and is also used by geisha as a waxy base for our makeup.'

Straight after she finished her speech, one of the sumo competitors toppled out of the ring, down the slope, and onto a person sitting in the front row.

'*Itai*—imagine two hundred kilograms in your lap!'

'Rather brutal,' I agreed.

Shimada stood up, applauding. 'Encore!'

28 | 二十八

I found myself alone. In a crowd.

What I mean to say is that Kohana wasn't with me—there was a surprise—but this didn't mean I had time to sit and twiddle my thumbs.

I was forced to dodge waves of pedestrians on a very busy main street, definitely still in Japan.

Judging from the walking wardrobes, the advertising, neons, and signage, I'd say I had again been deposited in the '60s, but also going by these surroundings and the hive of activity, you'd never have guessed only twenty years had passed since the Second World War hobbled the place.

'Wolram!'

I turned on my slippered heel.

Kohana was seated in a white, convertible sports car, with sleek lines, that she had idling at the curb. She was dressed in a powder blue one-piece, with a matching silk scarf over her hair that lightly held it back.

'Don't dawdle,' she called, as she leaned over and opened the passenger door. 'Hop in.'

'And why would I do that?'

'I'm going to take you to see my elite ninja training school.'

'I'm in no mood for juvenile quips. The one thing my esteemed mother taught me long ago was never to get into a car with a strange girl.'

'Suit yourself—but Tokyo, in 1964, wasn't the cleanest city in the world. You'll find the pollution is aromatic.'

'In case you haven't noticed, you're driving a vehicle that doesn't have a roof. I'm sure I would suffer either way.'

'What is your problem with cars?'

'None to write about. I think the Jaguar E-Type is a most stunningly designed mechanical gizmo—and, by the way, that's a charming Toyota 2000GT you have there. But sitting in the things, driving about on dangerous, overcrowded thorough-fares, is another kettle of fish.'

'Relax. I won't kill you,' she laughed.

'This is my second life. I'd like to hang on to it.'

Kohana tapped the open door. 'You only live twice, deshō? Come on, Wolram. Trust me. I have something special awaiting—lip-smacking martinis.'

My left leg moved forward, in spite of better judgment, but I kept its right-hand partner in check. 'What kind of martini?'

'A Vesper.'

'Ah.' My right leg started to give.

'C'mon.' She had a twinkle that suggested more high jinks were afoot.

Damned woman.

I finally did as instructed, and got in.

Once I was seated, Kohana hit the accelerator and we shot out into the traffic, weaving past several cars. I clenched the door handle.

The car flew past massive construction taking place over a river.

'One of the new expressways they're finishing, in preparation for the Olympic Games,' Kohana said. 'It seems part of their mission to modernize is to make the city hideous.'

'That's progress.'

'So they claim. By the way, you might want to brush up on your Japanese with this.'

The woman casually tossed a small book onto my lap.

Turning over the tome, I read the title aloud. '*Instant Japanese: A Pocketful of Useful Phrases*, by Masahiro Watanabe and Kei Nagashima. Do I really need it? I thought I had this God-given gift of international gab.'

We cut a corner, and in the process very nearly collected a street sign. 'For Heaven's sake, keep to the road!'

'Loosen up, dearie. Here we are.'

With no finesse whatsoever, Kohana stuck her foot on the brake pedal and I came close to careering through the windscreen. The English–Japanese dictionary ended up on the bonnet, pages dancing in the breeze.

'I am never, ever, setting foot in a car again,' I decided.

'Come on. We're late—for a very important date.'

I followed her, grudgingly I must confess, from the automobile. 'You never learned the art of parking in a straight line, flush with the footpath?'

'No need.'

'I'm inclined to think a police officer, or two, might argue the point.'

'Why?'

'It's against the law.'

'When you're gorgeous like me, you don't need to concern yourself with petty things like the law.'

'Well, now. You have tabs on yourself.'

'I'm ribbing you. Boy—you sure take the bait.' Kohana pulled open a big wooden door. 'After you, my dear fellow.'

'It seems you are always holding doors for me, ushering me into places I don't want to be.'

'The martini…?'

'Oh well, that's another matter.' I promptly pushed past her. We entered a large, cavernous space filled with chatter, and people drinking and smoking far too much. Compared with the dancehall where we had met the gangster Shashin, however, this was a more upmarket establishment. Now, the only crystal-clear crooks were the framed ones on the wall, from Japanese movies.

From out of the crowd, the actor Shimada sidled straight up and kissed Kohana on the cheek.

'You're just in time to see two more refugees from the kaiju classics,' he said, as he motioned to a small stage on which two pretty vocalists, who looked like twins, were singing a duet that sounded like it was affected with reverb.

'Ahh, Emi-chan and Yumi-chan,' Kohana spoke up. 'The Peanuts. They were in *Mothra* and sang the theme song. A giant butterfly tale. Mothra also battled Godzilla. Did you ever see it?'

'No, I can't say I have.'

'You should watch. 'Tis fun. Now—that Vesper martini I promised you?'

'Never thought you'd ask.'

'That was stirred, not shaken?'

'Ahem. The other way round.'

'Excuse me a moment, Shimada-san.' Kohana lightly touched the man's shoulder, and he blushed.

I followed her through the crush.

'I expect Shimada is enamoured with you.'

'Nonsense. Are you referring to his scarlet complexion just now? That's just the alcohol talking—I've seen it before.'

'When you're present.'

'Well, obviously. Otherwise I wouldn't be able to see it.' Kohana stopped at the counter and caught a bartender's attention. 'A Piranha, and a dry martini,' she told the man, 'in a deep champagne goblet.'

'*Hai.*'

'Just a moment.' She leaned over in order to be closer to his ear. 'Three measures of Gordon's, one of shōchū, half a measure of Kina Lillet. Shake it very well until it's ice-cold, then add a large thin slice of lemon peel. Got it?'

'*Hai.*' Dispatched, the man set about his task.

'That was very professionally done,' I admitted.

'I must've read it somewhere in a book.'

'Strikes me as something Ian Fleming would have appreciated.'

After a minute, two drinks presented themselves for our approval.

I lifted the martini and took a long sip. 'Excellent,' I said after, 'but if you can get a vodka made with grain instead of rice, you will find it better.'

'We are in Japan. Rice is a popular ingredient.'

'Indeed. But isn't this around the same time they were faking the rice in the saké? Anyhow—what are you having?'

Kohana held up her drink. It had a blood-coloured cocktail in it, with shards of ice arranged like sharp teeth around the top.

'It's a house speciality: The Piranha.'

'Ahh, of course. Well, *bon appétit!*'

'*Kanpai.*'

We clicked glasses.

29 | 二十九

'I was stabbed in February 1972.'

We were standing on a snow-covered field, on the cusp of a shallow irrigation gully in which lay the twisted corpse of a woman, when Kohana uttered these memorable words.

I was so shocked, I didn't know what to say, and therefore settled for a callow kind of commiseration. 'Kohana—good Lord, I'm sorry...'

'Um, Wolram, that's not me. I didn't say I died. In case it slipped your mind, I lived to be a hundred. But I *was* stabbed in the back, in the metaphoric sense as much as the literal.'

It took me a few shakes of a lamb's tail to process what she implied, and as my tardy grey matter refined it, Kohana rested on her haunches, using a stick to poke at the body in the ditch.

'Not a time I'm proud of. This is Michiko. Michiko, this is Wolram.'

Michiko remained speechless, and I did not have a thing to say.

The woman's face was difficult to see because of the way in which she lay, but I presumed she'd been dead a few hours. I'm hardly an expert. She was young, perhaps in her early twenties, and looked relatively pretty.

'She was beaten to death for being too negative,' Kohana said. 'One person's negativity is another man's realism. Michiko cottoned on early that we were going about things the wrong way.'

'Do you mind if I ask which things?'

'All of it.'

Not the kind of answer I was counting on. 'Then who did this?'

'Very stupid people. Friends of mine and hers.'

I waited, in vain, for an expanded response. 'Why?' I pressed on.

Kohana stood up straight, and flung away the stick. For my part, I shifted from one foot to the other. It was bitterly cold here. The extremes in temperature really were going to be the death of me.

'Seriously? I don't understand the whys. Michiko didn't deserve to die like this. She was a decent woman.'

'That word "decent" always concerns me.'

'Well, yes, she had her flaws—and who doesn't? For one thing, she was overly naïve and trusting.'

'Something neither of us has to worry about.'

'Undoubtedly.'

'Anyway, back to you—you said you were attacked too.'

'Mmm.'

She was keeping a million things close to her chest this time. I felt like I was deep-sea fishing without the proper tackle. 'And so your infraction was…?'

'Not negativity—I kept mine hidden, but I wasn't cautious elsewhere.'

'Go on.'

'My crime was getting caught kissing a boy.'

'Oh, that old one.' I was perilously close to laughter. 'One of your jealous lovers, I expect?'

Insofar as Kohana was concerned, this was bound to happen sooner or later.

'Actually, no. It was another woman—and no, she wasn't in love with me.'

'Of course, you slept with her husband, then?'

'Wolram, what kind of awful opinion do you have of me? God.'

Kohana looked up for a time, at a slate-grey sky. An apology was on my lips, but she spoke first.

'More snow is on its way.'

'You remember that?'

'No, I can tell. Can't you? Look at those clouds.'

'I'm an Australian. It rarely snowed there, and never where I lived. When I look up, all I see are clouds; no special messages.'

'That's a shame. It's one of the few things my father taught me.'

'I'm chuffed to hear the old geezer came in useful for something.'

'Surprising, isn't it? I'm not sure why it mattered to him.'

I rubbed my hands together. They were stiff, chilled to the bone.

'I swear I'm going to end up with frostbite. Might we get back to the reason we're here, if there is one—apart from showing me corpses and intimating at a dangerous romantic interlude?'

'Okay.' Kohana fiddled with her sleeve. 'Ten other members of our group, not counting Michiko and me, were killed for equally trivial reasons. Cleaning a gun incorrectly, wearing too much makeup, that kind of nonsense.'

'Your group? What group?'

'I'll get to that. You think it's cold today? The temperature drops below zero in the evening. Most of the people I talked about were tied to trees and froze to death overnight. It was all part of a power play by our hypocritical, increasingly paranoid leaders, Seibei and Ushitora. Within days, they reduced the membership by half.'

There was an astringent taste in my mouth. I felt like spitting it straight out, but refrained.

'Seriously disturbed men, I take it.'

'Actually, a seriously disturbed man and woman. Ushitora Hiroko was nicknamed "Oni-babaa"—Devil Bitch. Rumour had it she was barren, and she had the foetus torn out of one of her peers because she was jealous.'

'This insane woman was your leader? What kind of group are we discussing here? Some bizarre off-campus club? A cult?'

'No, don't fuss; it wasn't a club or a cult. And to be honest, this might have been scuttlebutt about the pregnancy, like I said. I have no idea if it's true. Aside from that, Hiroko is the one who knifed me, straight after she discovered me in the middle of the smooch I mentioned. I wasn't devoting equal ardour to the revolution.'

Kohana pointed across the frozen farmland, and I followed her index finger.

'There I am, over there,' she said, 'scurrying for help.' I saw a distant figure, staggering along a narrow road. 'I'd been stabbed in the back, right between one of my dragon's eyes, and left for dead too.'

'Ahh—so that explains the split head on your tattoo.'

'On the dot. I told you I'd get around to the telling of the tale.'

'Well. Let's look at the positives. You move spritely for someone so recently employed as a pin-cushion.'

'Yep, I'm impressed too—though, let me tell you, the experience is far more enjoyable from this perspective. It was either run for help, or lie down, feel sorry for myself, bleed to death or die from exposure. I was lucky the knife bounced off my shoulder blade, but there was enough blood to make Hiroko think she'd done a good job.'

'Where are we?'

'In the southern Japanese Alps, not far from a secretive training camp for the newly formed and short-lived Rengō Sekigun—known as the United Red Army.'

'Red Army?' I stared at her. 'Communists?'

'Communists.'

'You?'

'I know, I know—it sounds passé now, and you can laugh if you want to, but our passions ran high in the late '60s. Not just here, but in Europe. In three former fascist countries—Japan, Germany and Italy—communism was a captivating backlash against the psychotic right-wing antics of our parents.'

'You joined the Communist Party? I thought only quixotic

dimwits joined those outfits. It's just like co-opting oneself to a cult.'

'This wasn't a cult.'

'Split the difference.'

Kohana blew out a cloud of condensation. 'You're from a different generation. You don't understand what we went through, or what we saw around us, and I'm not going to stand here in the cold, arguing politics. How old were you in 1972?'

'Seven.'

'I think a seven-year-old might find it difficult to relate.'

'You were old enough to know better, Kohana.'

'I was—I'll give you that. And while our German and Italian brethren rallied against the imperialist state, which we hoped to do, here in Japan we killed our comrades. It wasn't the ideals that went astray; the people we'd elected as our leaders went mad. I sometimes think the "United" part of the group's name was a facetious addition.'

'Why on earth did you hook up with these people?'

'What can I say? I was infatuated with a man.'

Again, I felt like laughing, only it was getting beyond the joke. 'What a surprising turn of events. Well, you did warn me—you mentioned you were stabbed for kissing someone.'

'Don't be angry.'

'I'm not angry. "Depressed" would be a better word for it. What about the person on the receiving end of the peck? Who the Devil was it this time?'

'Kunio Yamadera.'

'Oh, how many infatuations do we have now? I swear I've lost count.'

'This was different.'

'Of course it was.'

Kohana hadn't cottoned on to my impatience.

'He was like the Japanese Che Guevara,' she said in a breathy voice, as if I cared, 'except he wasn't caught, and there's no iconic image of him to screen-print onto T-shirts. But he was such a charismatic man for his age! He was outspoken and reactionary, and after we started sleeping together, he convinced me to join him as a member of the Red Army Faction, which later became the United Red Army.'

'How old was this man?'

'Twenty-three when we first met.'

'And you?'

The lady lost some of her sentimental sparkle, just as I intended.

'Forty.'

'How long did the fling last?'

'For two years—up until I received the nip in the back.'

I'll tell you, often I felt like throwing up my arms, to leave all this idiocy behind me. Yet every time I looked at my companion, and those eyes, I gave it one more shot. 'All right. You say this mad woman punished you by stabbing you in the back. What was Yamadera's punishment?'

'He was far too important to "The Cause". Hiroko let him off scot-free.'

'But he jumped to your defence, of course, endangering himself in the process.' Yes, I was baiting, but could not reel myself in.

'Not at all. He walked away and left me to her.'

'You do pick them,' I muttered.

We wandered across the field, watching the distant figure stagger to a farmhouse and begin pounding on the door.

'Quite a fist she has there,' I said.

'The same fist I would have used on Kunio's skull if I'd ever seen him again.'

'You said this Yamadera fellow was never captured?'

'Yes—and no.'

'Well, which is it?'

'In actual fact, he was caught later this same month, after

holding a woman hostage for ten days at a resort near Mount Asama. He even shot a police officer. But a couple of years later, his mates in the Japanese Red Army—a different faction—took more than fifty hostages from the American and Swedish embassies in Malaysia, and Kunio was released as part of an exchange.'

'Be serious.'

'Then? He vanished. Hearsay popped up in the media that he'd been spotted in Russia, Thailand, China, the Philippines. But he was never captured again.'

'Well, what happened to your two mad tyrants?—What were their names?'

'Seibei and Ushitora.'

'Seibei and Ushitora.'

'Some justice there. They both died in jail.'

The farmhouse door had opened and closed, and this world's Kohana was obviously inside. They would be calling an ambulance, or the police. Probably both. I would.

'What about you? If you were so involved with these killers, a member of the club so to speak, wouldn't the police have had an interest in you as well?'

Kohana looked at me with an expression so blastedly sweet and innocent, I actually lost my train of thought.

'I played dumb,' she said, and then she winked. 'Shhh, say nothing. Not really all that difficult for me, I know.'

'I wasn't—'

'It's far better for me to get in first than to leave the door wide open for your cruel barbs.'

The angelic façade dropped in an instant, and she poked me in the ribs.

I tried not to squirm.

'So I was all tears, sugar-sweet smiles, and silly, when they interviewed me. I gave the police the information they wanted, they took pity, and left me to recover in the hospital—no charges laid.'

'How do you get away with it?'

'Well, in this case, I didn't actually do anything wrong.'

'You were socializing with terrorists.'

'It was an error of judgment.'

'I don't think judgment entered into the equation.'

'See what I mean? Cruel.' Kohana shook her head. 'When I was recovering in the hospital, I had a visitor who brought me flowers every day. Plumerias, better known as frangipanis.'

'Oh God,' I groaned, 'not another Romeo.'

Finally, we were thrust indoors, in the middle of a whitewashed ward, where Kohana's bed was separated from the five others by plastic curtains. She didn't look at all poorly for a woman who had been stabbed.

A small young man, with bad posture, wearing a forgettable black suit and a characterless dark tie, had just finished bowing to her, and handed over a bunch of white flowers—each one with a ring of rich yellow towards the centre.

The fellow was timid, bespectacled, and a couple of centimetres shorter than me. So much for a potential inamorato. I could warm to this walkover.

'His name was Toshiro,' Kohana said from over on the hospital bed, just as she sniffed the flowers. 'He was Kunio's younger brother. Toshiro was twenty-two then, and he would become the head of a famous Japanese electronics firm by the age of thirty-eight. You would never have known he was a Yamadera, if you compared him to his infamous sibling. Toshiro hated Kunio. He blamed him for their father's suicide.'

She smiled faintly.

'I never thought I'd end up marrying the man.'

30 | 三十

There was a rap on the door, so polite I almost didn't hear the patter.

I removed my head from the bar-fridge to double-check. There was no decent food there anyway, aside from the plastic sushi.

After several seconds, the soft knock-knock repeated itself.

'Are you expecting company?' I called to Kohana, since she evidently hadn't noticed—she was busy vacuuming tatami mats. Where the hovel's electricity came from, I declined to ask.

The woman ceased her housework and switched off the machine.

'Sorry? I couldn't hear a thing.'

'I said, are you expecting company?'

'Why?' Further tapping answered the question on my behalf. Kohana behaved genuinely puzzled. 'Can't say there's anyone I invited. You?'

'None that I remember.'

There was a fourth knock.

'We're forgetting our manners, aren't we?' Kohana went over, opened the door—and then slammed it shut. 'Gatecrasher,' she said, her face suddenly pale.

'Eh?'

That was when we were treated to a shriek outside the hovel. This started relatively low, but reared into a shrill, piercing high note. 'Ko-ha-na!' the voice wailed. 'Ko-ha-na!'

'Good Lord... that sounds like an ailing version of Stanley Kowalski in *A Streetcar Named Desire*. Who the Devil is it?'

'You do not want to know. Hardly a devil, but the next best thing?'

The delicate cuff on the door had become a ruffian's pounding. 'I'll huff,' that eerie, cacophonous voice called, 'and

I'll puff, and I'll blo-ow your house down!'

And here I'd been thinking I was meant to play Big Bad Wolf.

The door shook violently one more time, before it crashed aside, and a man blundered in. His stature might have been a disappointment, but I recognized the scar straight off the bat—it was the gangster Shashin, that shortish fellow Kohana had used as an ottoman.

'Crap,' I heard the woman exhale.

Our visitor waltzed further into the house, wrapped in a dirty, ragged-looking old army greatcoat, though I noticed he'd bothered to remove his shoes. His face, pallid before, looked chalky and irate as he examined us both.

'Kohana—I say, Kohana, I think the man can see me,' I opined as I backed away. More disturbing was the fact that his head rested at a thirty-degree angle.

'Fascinating,' Kohana said. 'I thought only women in Japan sought vengeance from beyond the grave.'

'Your point being?'

'I misunderstood my own culture?'

The man was in no rush to converse. Either he was pausing for dramatic effect, or he was willing to give us a few extra seconds' idle banter.

This suited me. 'I thought I had your guarantee we wouldn't be troubled here by the bugger.'

'I don't recall any such thing.'

'Well, that's why I let you make use of him as a hassock.'

Possibly the chatter was so idle it bored him senseless, or mention of his previous status as a footstool stirred Shashin. He veritably flew into action and chucked off his coat, whereafter the illumination in the room changed—as if some lighting man, sight unseen, had flicked a switch.

When my sight adjusted, I saw he'd assumed a more confident stance, clutching a katana sword and clad in a kimono, with a loose obi sash. Detracting from the warrior image was a cream-coloured silk scarf, gift-wrapping his throat.

'Wolram, I think he's been taking fashion pointers from you,' Kohana whispered.

'No, that shade doesn't suit his complexion.'

'Shut up!' the man roared.

He raised the sword in two hands, presumably to punctuate showmanship, but the pose was cheapened when his head lazily bounced around. Shashin was forced to loosen one hand from the sword's hilt and straighten up his skull.

'Shashin-sama,' Kohana said from her side of the room, 'we can talk.'

'Talk?!'

'Or we can stay mum and enjoy the silence,' I suggested.

'Who are you?' Shashin was drifting my way, the sword outstretched.

'Nobody at all.'

'Coward,' I heard Kohana say.

I glared over. 'Haven't you caused enough trouble? I stick my neck out for nobody. Sorry, no offence.'

'None taken,' the man tried very desperately to growl. It came out all wrong, a rasping treble that bordered on a soprano.

'That's right, blame me.' Kohana blew out loudly, annoyed.

This thoughtless gust reminded our guest of whom he'd come to visit, and he turned accordingly.

His face, however, stayed in the same place, looking at me, so he had to again use his fingers to swing it round. I noticed there was a patch of red soaking through the scarf.

'Kohana,' I called out, as the man advanced on her, 'did you see his neck?'

'I did. *Ew.*' Kohana held up her hands as Shashin placed the sword-blade next to her throat.

'Now—Now!—it's my turn to slice and dice.'

'You'll never do as pretty a job as me.'

I'll give her chips for bravery, but I'm certain Kohana was

wondering whether, in this place, she could be injured, or forced to give up the ghost. We had our doubts.

Shashin was ready to give the concept a whirl.

This did not mean I relished standing by, since I'd be the next sacrificial lamb on the block. What was it I conjured up, earlier in the piece? 'I recognized the scar straight off the bat'?

The cricket bat.

I edged toward the suit of armour. There was always the axe, but that was too messy. No, willow would do fine.

Seconds later, I crowned Shashin with the same bat Pop had used to entertain kids, in the neighbourhood where this crook had probably started up protection rackets and was smuggling liquor.

'I always figured that would again come in handy,' Kohana appraised, as she came over to inspect the body at my feet. 'Can you help me? He's getting blood all over the floor.'

'You weren't overly concerned about that when you killed the man.'

'Because it was at his place, not mine. Come on, Wolram—let's stick him on the sofa. At least we can wipe that down afterwards.'

So it was that I helped Kohana haul our caller to the couch.

We eased him down and he rolled back, his head swinging so wildly, I fretted it might detach. The head stayed in place, but he groaned.

'And now?' Kohana said. 'What's next?'

'We could always feed him that sushi you have in the refrigerator.'

'Be serious. Do you think we should drive a stake through his heart just in case?'

'He's not Bela Lugosi. What is this fixation you have with vampires?' I didn't wait for an answer, since I had other concerns. 'Say, my head repaired itself when I ended up here, while you appear to have been guzzling from the fountain of youth—why is his throat still mangled like that?' I looked down several inches.

'I don't like to think what's afoot in his private parts.'

The man groaned again, and then leaned forward to place his wobbly head in his hands. He sat there like that for some time. Meanwhile, Kohana and I stood awkwardly, waiting for a sign.

'Are you all right?' I finally asked.

'Look what you did to my neck!' he cried out between his fingers. 'You... you bungled it! You and your stupid attempt to kill me!'

'Not I.'

At that, the gangster really did cry. Yes, he bawled. My friend and I looked at each other. Aside from his blubbering there was another ungainly silence.

Kohana broke it first. 'Well, this is comical. What should we do?'

'Are there any tissues?'

'Only toilet paper.'

'Well. You should apologize.'

'Apologize?'

'You could try. I'm not sure I can stand much more of this. It's all a bit pathetic really.'

'I'm not going to apologize—don't you remember what he did to me?' She frowned. 'And to Tomeko?'

'That's in the past. My God, it all happened before I was born. Besides, do you want that knight-errant of yours to stop by? I think atoning to this fellow might be part-and-parcel of the deal.'

'You don't know that. You're guessing.'

'I'll admit it—of course I'm guessing. But what if I'm right? It's time to move on.'

'Easy for you to say. I'm beginning to wonder who really is playing the Ghost of Christmas Past.' Kohana sighed. 'All right.' She knelt before Shashin, with a hand behind her on the fallen sword.

'Be casual. Don't frighten him. Smile.'

The woman gave me a diabolical look from beneath her

fringe, before turning back. 'Shashin-san. I'm sorry I stabbed you in the throat,' she said, in a measured tone, 'and I'm sorry I cut off your… you know.'

'And the other thing,' I urged.

'I think I just mentioned it.'

'Not *that*. The other thing.'

'The tissues?'

'No.'

'Oh—yes, sorry. I apologize for using you as a footrest. I was angry. You deserved it.'

'A polished piece of work, my girl. One would think you've been doing this all your life.'

'Shut up, Wolram.'

'Absolutely.'

Shashin dropped his hands to his lap and slowly raised his head. He peered from Kohana, to me, and back again.

'I'm parched,' he decided.

'I'm happy for you.'

'Do we have any of that saké?' I asked.

In return, the woman bristled. 'We? Whose place is this, again?—okay. Yes. You'll find a fresh batch on the stove.'

I went over, poured a cup almost to the brim, and brought it over to our houseguest. 'Here you go. Try this.'

'Thank you.'

The man gulped it down so fast, I doubted he would taste the fine drop. Straight after, I noticed a clear liquid stain growing around the red patch on the scarf.

'Not bad,' Shashin said, as he took his lips from the cup.

'Served at the correct temperature as well.'

'There is one?'

'Please,' Kohana cut in, 'don't get him started.'

That comment put a dampener on things. The three of us fidgeted in silence.

'Well, it's been pleasant,' Shashin abruptly announced, 'but I won't impose on the two of you any longer.'

We took the man to the broken door and showed him outside.

'Run along now,' I said. 'There's a good boy.'

'May I please have my sword now?'

'Don't push it,' Kohana muttered.

'You're absolutely right.'

He tried to take Kohana's hand, but she pulled it away from him and scowled. The man bowed deeply, and his head momentarily lolled around in that position, before he stood straight again.

'You despise me, don't you?'

'If I gave you any more thought, I probably would—but I think Wolram's on the ball. We've shifted somewhere beyond that. There's no point in holding a grudge or whatever you call it.'

'True. You know, Kohana-chan, I had many a friend in Asakusa, but somehow, just because you despised me, you were the only one I trusted.'

'You have an odd way of showing it.'

'I was conflicted.'

'No, you're a sociopath. Anyway,' Kohana said, 'I would say it's been nice to catch up, but I'm not in the mood for fiction.'

Shashin looked out over the dreary landscape. 'Do I have to leave? I don't see any native girls, hungry for affection.'

'Go,' Kohana said, in a sterner voice.

'Yes—of course.'

'And be careful out there,' I added. 'Don't go losing your head again.'

With another gruff bow, Shashin had one more thing to add: '*Nagaremono ni onna wa iranai, onna ga icha arukenai.*' Then he left.

I glanced at Kohana. 'I didn't catch that. What did he say?'

'A drifter doesn't need a woman. If a woman's around, he can't walk.'

'An interesting deduction.' As the man traipsed away, with his head at an odd angle, I sighed. 'He doesn't look the part of a bad guy.'

'Neither do you.'

'Cheers. I think. You know, I am exceptionally proud of you.'

'Why? Because I didn't cut off any more body parts?'

'There is that.'

'It was difficult.'

'But mostly, I'm impressed you moved up a notch, from the petty depths of revenge.'

'You didn't think I had it in me?'

'You, I wasn't sure. As for myself, I know I don't.' Feeling a little daring, I placed my arm around her shoulders. 'Have you given any consideration to the notion that I might be your knight? In casual-wear, I mean.'

Kohana tried to suppress her amusement—to a minor degree.

'You?' she laughed. At least she didn't remove my arm.

'I seem to recall rescuing you in there. I usually run away.'

'A splendid principle.'

'Thank you.'

'The role of saviour makes you happy, huh?'

'It does indeed.'

'Yes, yes, all right, you do have your moments, but a real knight would have grabbed the axe.'

31 | 三十一

'Kyoto—shit a brick.'

Kohana screwed up her eyes.

'I'm still only in Kyoto. Every time I think I'm going to wake up, back in the okiya in Asakusa. The first time I went through these flashbacks, it was worse—I'd wake up, and there'd be nothing.'

'You mean, you were wading through these memories before you deigned to drag me along?'

'For a while, yes.'

'The same ones?'

'Some of them. Others too that you'd likely find more boring.'

'You look older.'

'Thanks for the vote of confidence.'

'Older, but far more beautiful.'

'Can I trust you or are you on the prowl in the afterlife?'

'A smidgeon of both perchance.'

'Peachy. This was my fourth trip to Kyoto, in January 1975. I'd recently celebrated my forty-fifth birthday. The city was under a blanket of snow, and I'd never previously seen it so splendid. Go on, Wolram—take a peek.'

I put my face to the nearby window. Whiteness was everywhere, like someone had spread out a pristine sheet across the scene. 'It's pretty, I will give you that.'

'What an earth-shattering visit this one was. You're about to meet the father of my child.'

'Didn't you mention marrying that nondescript salaryman? I've already met the fellow—in passing, of course.'

'Toshiro? No, he's not the father. And we had no plans to get married, at this point in time.'

Kohana was wearing a dark blue kimono that had a steel-grey sheen. It was decorated with plum blossoms that rubbed shoulders with either hyenas or jackals—I was not strong with my mammalogy. She had her hair tied back and braided, and wore very little greasepaint. Just a bit of mascara and lipstick.

The look was lovely.

'I met Yukinojo Nakamura VIII at a function in Tokyo the week before. I'd been star-struck—his interpretation of the dance of the *Fuji Musume*, the Wisteria Maiden, was sublime. Everyone who saw the show hailed his performance. I would have sworn he was a real woman.'

Kohana's eyes went straight to mine.

'Don't look surprised, Wolram. Often the feminine side is superior to the masculine—remember the saké?'

'I am not arguing.'

'Yukinojo Nakamura VIII, or Hachi-sama as he preferred to be called by those close to him, was the greatest living *kabuki* actor of our generation. He was also an *onnagata*: the male actors who portray women in kabuki. In the flesh, off stage, he was manlier. Hachi-sama had a bearing that dominated those around him. Including me. One thing led to another at this party, he swept me off my feet, and two hours later I was in his bed.'

I walked away from the window and wandered around a large, Japanese-style hotel living space.

'I miss carpets,' I decided. 'Especially with bare feet.'

'Actually, I'm not the biggest fan of tatami mats or carpets. You know they have mites? We call them *dani*. That's why I always vacuum mine.'

'I did wonder. Kohana, can I ask you something?'

'Have I stopped you before?'

'No. But this is, I would say, rather personal. Why all the men?'

'I was wondering when you'd get around to that.'

'I wasn't so direct, but I've hinted at the matter a few times—sometimes without subtlety.'

'I noticed.'

I went to the kitchenette, located some green tea bags, and put on the kettle. 'I'm not judging you, not really. I'm the last person who should be allowed to do so. As you noted once before, my romantic history is a skewed mess. But you—you're an incredible woman.'

'Thank you. Really.'

'Then why?'

'I don't know. Can you tell me why?'

'No.' I laughed as I poured hot water into two cups. 'Perhaps it's all James Bond's fault? He's a ruffian's role model.'

'In your case or mine?'

'Both?' I brought her one of the cups. 'Service, m'dear, with a smile.'

'That's the first cup of tea you've made for me, did you know that?'

'I'm becoming domesticated in my dotage.' I sat on the cane chair next to hers. 'Now, where were we with this Hacky chap?'

'Hachi.'

'Exactly.' I sipped my tea. Not bad.

'This visit to Kyoto was the first chance I had to see him, since that heady night I mentioned. After settling in at this hotel, I joined his new manager, and two of his associates, at a famous Kyoto *fugu* restaurant. I presume you know blowfish?'

'I do.'

'I was the only woman there. The four men proceeded to get very drunk on rounds of saké. I can imagine this is one memory you're keen to sit in on.'

Just like that, I was invited to a fugu banquet.

When I say 'invited', however, I feel I may mislead you. In actual fact, I was the in absentia plus one, the nobody who doesn't warrant a chair.

I got stuck on a cushion, with no drink, while the other five people wined, dined, and caroused. Then again, they were sitting on thin cushions too, so perhaps I was not so badly off.

The lack of liquid refreshment was punishment enough.

'You certainly know how to torment your guests,' I voiced above the rowdy dialogue of the party, the only one in the restaurant.

Kohana, who was sitting on the opposite side of the table, in full view from my vantage point, angled her head to one side. 'Can you guess which one is Hachi-sama?' she asked, in a tone colder than the dreamy abandonment of someone who'd been swept off her feet.

On cue, I studied the quartet of men.

They had red, sweaty faces, thanks in all likelihood to the alcohol, and in my book were far too old—aged between sixty and senior to me. I do find it difficult to accurately gauge people's ages, yet I was repulsed to think a member of these hoary, perspiring men had bedded the far younger woman.

As quickly became clear, one of the old-timers dictated proceedings, lording it over the others. I presumed this had to be Hachi, or whatever his real name was—I'd forgotten it already.

The fellow wore a kimono, casually opened at the chest to reveal a few stray silver hairs, while his chums were dressed in business suits. Not a particularly handsome man, he had jowls spilling over the collar. He was also losing his hair up on top, and vain enough to apply a comb-over to shelter the fact—a none-too-successful ruse.

Still, there was something striking about him, a kind of powerful magnetism.

'Good work, Sherlock. That's our man.'

Hachi had his head back and was roaring a laugh, or laughing a roar—I am unaware which description best applies. Then he took out his wallet and placed it on the dinner table.

'I'm now going to show you all something I keep for very special occasions—such as this,' he growled.

'Let me guess,' I said. 'Pictures of his grandchildren.'

'And I was beginning to have faith in you as a detective.'

Having unfastened the catch on his wallet, Hachi-sama opened it with a show of great ceremony.

He removed a strip of photographs, perhaps a dozen in all. Just when I thought I'd reclaimed Holmes' deerstalker, I leaned forward to see what the others were looking at, and understood why they had collectively gone quiet.

Instead of showing cute kids, with baby teeth missing and a little league trophy or two, they displayed children without hands, without feet—trophies of the soldiers that stood grinning at their corpses.

I stared, and then averted my eyes. I felt numb. Some fool had surely shot me with a stray anaesthetic.

'His Nanjing keepsakes. Hachi-sama was one of the soldiers that seized the city in 1937. Our troops massacred hundreds of thousands of people in six weeks.'

Kohana leaned forward to me, ignoring the party.

'I don't want to listen to this again. I hate this. I can't stand any of it. What this evil man said tonight changed everything for me, especially my skewed opinion of history and race. I would never again drop thoughtless asides about the Chinese, or wallow so much over my personal losses in World War Two. One evening spent in the company of this man and his wartime reminisces was akin to having bamboo splints gradually hammered beneath one's nails.'

Kohana stared at her fingertips.

'The splints remain. I'd never, ever met such a depraved, unrepentant soul.'

I shook my head. 'Kohana, I can't comment—not in all honesty. Someone will toss the blackened kettle-cum-pot in my direction. And it was war. People did grotesque things. Remember what Pop said to you.'

'I do remember, but don't sell yourself short. You aren't a completely lost cause. This man, however,' she nodded at our balding host, 'was malevolence, pure and simple. Hachi-sama flashed those pictures to us, recounting the story of the massacre behind them, and he laughed. He laughed. This was his handiwork. All these children.'

My gaze fell.

'Perhaps he has his own Kohana right now,' I mulled, 'sharing her memories, forgiving him his sins?'

'Perhaps. I don't think it likely. In any case, her name would need to be Xiao Hua—Little Flower in Chinese.'

After my first inspection, I was not keen to further peruse the pictures. 'What did these other men do when he flung about the wealth of wartime atrocities? Surely somebody voiced a contrary opinion?'

'You can't be bothered watching the action, right here in front of you?'

'I'd prefer to skimp on the details. "Traumatized" comes to mind.'

'Well, they were in awe of him. You cannot dispute the opinion of someone you consider your superior.'

'What? That's utter nonsense.'

'In your culture, perhaps it is different—there was no one here, with a pistol in his pocket, to hammer home the moral point.'

Floyd jumped to mind. I hadn't thought of him in an age. 'Now, we are getting personal.' I looked at her again. 'How about you? What did you say? Anything in defence of these victims?'

'No.'

I squeezed between two of the men and laid the Webley-Fosbery on the table, right next to a plate of pickles.

'There's someone here, now, with a pistol in his pocket, to hammer home the moral point.'

That was when Hachi picked up the gun by the barrel and started to bang on the wood in an irritated fashion, using the grip to create a ruckus. 'Fugu! I want fugu!' he shouted at a worriedly bowing staff member.

I was flabbergasted. 'That is not quite the outcome I was looking for.'

Kohana casually removed the gun from her older boyfriend's fingers and passed it back to me.

'We don't need that now; put it away,' she said softly. In a louder voice, after waving over the apoplectic staff member, she ordered fugu *sashimi*, milt, deep-fried *karaage*, and stewed *fugu-chiri*, to be served with *hire-zake*—saké, with dried and baked fugu fin.

'Now I remember why we invited you along,' Hachi-sama announced in an abrasive, self-satisfied voice. 'As we know, very few people die from eating fugu.' The man gathered his photos together and placed them inside the wallet. His captive audience listened with baited breath. 'The trouble is that when anyone does get poisoned, the media swarms all over the news and makes it a national drama of truly epic proportions.'

'Come with me,' Kohana whispered.

'Why? I'm riveted by the man's hyperbole.'

'I have to go to the bathroom.'

'And you need my help with that...?'

'No—I just need to show you something else. Don't argue.'

'Yes, *memsahib*.'

With that, we got up and vacated the party.

Kohana took the lead, past shōji screens and up over a raised platform until we reached the door to the kitchen and lingered there. I spied the chef, a fine-looking man, perhaps in his forties, with an intense look as he sliced and diced blowfish. He was singing, something about an Osaka sparrow.

Kohana whipped out a compact, powdered her nose, added scent and a little lipstick, and appraised the result in a tiny mirror.

'How do I look? Not too shabby for a woman of forty-five?'

'Ravishing—why?'

'This is where you and I need to part company, just for a short time. Another man. I hope you don't mind, Wolram. The chef and I have an appointment in one of the stalls—and I was not mistaken about his virility.'

I drew back from her, admittedly aghast. 'By God, that is far too much information.'

'Knew you'd understand.' Kohana leaned so close, I could smell the perfume she wore, a floral, green-citrus fragrance. 'I need to get Hachi-sama out of my skin. I need to expunge all trace of his bodily fluids.'

So I stood there in the passageway next to a rubbish bin, whistling 'Waltzing Matilda' as I gazed at a sequence of ukiyo-e woodblock prints on the wall. These looked like they told Kohana's story of the eight-headed dragon and his suicidal saké binge.

At least the woman didn't take long, given circumstances.

When she returned, Kohana adjusted her makeup. She looked flushed, but satisfied and in better spirits.

'Diverting enough entertainment?'

'I forgot just how much,' she muttered.

It was a full half hour before we rejoined the kabuki tyrant and his cronies—who, sad to say, had apparently not missed our absence at all. They were in the midst of trying to order more fugu and saké, but were drunk and confused.

Kohana had settled herself on her cushion next to Hachi-sama. 'What about the liver?' she piped up, in a charming way, as if it were nothing at all.

Hachi-sama stared at her, his smirk sagging. 'Of course not. Are you mad? I'm not interested in playing dice with death.'

'But you're the great Yukinojo Nakamura VIII —you're no average mortal!' Kohana leaned into him, her head on his shoulder, and their faces close. 'Not like those inferior Chinese pigs at Nanjing. You're a *real* Japanese man. Only someone as courageous as you would dare eating the liver of the fugu—and, of course, survive to pass on the story at future dinner parties.

Imagine the reverence that would surround the telling of this incredible tale, the people that would swoon and kiss your feet.' She had her eyes on his, working their magic. 'Imagine it, Hachi-sama.'

'What are you doing?' I hissed.

'Appealing to his egoistic sensibilities,' Kohana said under her breath. 'A fairly easy thing to accomplish.'

'But aren't blowfish livers the dangerous cut?'

'Are they?'

'You have a very, very valid point,' Hachi-sama announced, as he got to his feet and tottered. He summoned the staff and added four fugu livers to the order. The woman looked aghast, and she in turn summoned the chef—who paid more deference to Kohana, until Hachi bailed him out and demanded his fugu liver.

Kohana leaned over to the chef.

'You can't refuse any request from such a prestigious artist as Hachi-sama,' she said.

Both chef and staff headed into the kitchen, and several minutes later they returned with the rest of the banquet.

The four fugu livers had pride of place in the centre, enthroned upon a black and red lacquer dish, adorned simply with a sprinkling of grated white radish and one single black poppy.

Three of the men looked horrified by the sight, but Hachi-sama swept up the fugu livers, one after the other, and dropped them down his throat. Then he ate the radish and the poppy, and licked the plate clean.

He declared to all that he felt fantastic, like he was floating on air. To my mind the likelier culprit was the vat of saké he had consumed over the course of the evening.

He didn't up and die—he merely looked drunk.

After the Nanjing slide show, I seriously doubted Kohana wanted more than dinner and drinks in return for her trip to

Kyoto.

If she had desired the kabuki star beforehand—which I surmised—the woman had miscalculated his intentions.

Hachi dropped her off (with me) outside the hotel, and announced that he was going home to his wife. He then said we would rendezvous for tea and sweets the following afternoon.

When the black Mercedes slid away into the traffic, I looked at my companion. Relief was written all over her face.

'He's mistaken,' she said. 'We won't meet tomorrow. He'll die tonight, from paralysis, convulsions, and respiratory arrest.'

'Jesus,' I responded. 'Remind me to steer clear of blowfish the next time we step out for a bite to eat. So, you killed him too.'

'I prefer to think his vanity was responsible.'

'I'm sure you do. Are there any other murders I should be aware of in this wayward back catalogue?'

'Just one.'

'Which is—?'

'My own.'

I looked at her. 'Give me a cigarette, would you? I think I need one.' She had it lit and in my hand in a blur. 'By the way, whatever happened to the restaurant chef?'

'He lost his job and his license, and he hanged himself. Every action has a human cost, even deserved retribution. You should know that.'

'I'm beginning to appreciate the concept.'

Kohana eyed the hotel before us, as if it housed something reprehensible.

'I don't know if the chef was the father of my child, or I have Hachi-sama's semen to thank.'

32 | 三十二

Beneath a vacant Hills Hoist rotary clothesline, a child of ten lay on his belly, parked in the middle of a browning lawn.

He was perusing a comic book.

On one side of him leaned a shed made of asbestos plasterboard, and on the other rested a tiny, panting Silky Terrier that was asleep.

When we approached, however, the dog peered straight at me.

I eased myself onto my haunches and squatted there to look back at her for a few seconds. 'Hello, old girl,' I mumbled, as I stroked her under the chin. 'It's been a long, long time.' If the dog had been a cat, she would have purred.

It was a hot summer day. Little white clouds danced willy-nilly in the azure-blue sky. I shook my head. It seemed I was getting poetic in my old age. I'd expect to read nonsense like that, inscribed on the back of a cheap cornflakes packet.

'Where are we?' I heard Kohana ask.

'It's still January 1975. But we've shifted about eight thousand kilometres.'

Somewhere nearby, perhaps two houses over, I could hear a Sherbet song I recognized: 'Silvery Moon'.

I noticed Kohana was staring at the boy.

'His hair is so golden, it radiates,' she marvelled as she circled him.

'Needs a good haircut,' I grumbled. 'The 1970s, as you know, had a lot to answer for.'

'What's that he's reading?' The woman knelt on the grass to take a better look, something I had no need to do.

'*The Fantastic Four*, issue 25—Part One of the Thing versus the Hulk.'

She eased over the cover, though the boy didn't notice. 'Spot on. Number 25. I'm impressed. An Australian comic?'

'Hardly. American. 1960s stuff, by Jack Kirby and Stan Lee.'

'How do you know this?'

I didn't answer. I sat down next to the boy and tousled his hair. He kept reading, oblivious.

'God, I loved this issue—I read it multiple times. A couple of years passed before I found issue 26, to see what happened in their big brawl. I preferred the Thing to the Hulk, and though he kind of lost this bout, he did have some wonderful moments. Oh, by the way,' I flipped a lazy thumb at the boy, 'as you're possibly well aware, this is I.'

'You? Then we're in your memory?'

'Looks that way, doesn't it?'

'This is odd. What's the dog's name? I'm sure she senses we're here.'

'I don't know.'

'Say again?'

'I don't remember. Sad, you agree? I vividly recall the name of the song on AM radio that's playing right now'—which I did; it was 'Ego Is Not a Dirty Word' by Skyhooks, but they kept reminding me of the title in the repetitive chorus—'yet I don't remember what we called this little dog. I adored her.'

I found myself peering underneath the canine.

'You know, I'm no longer certain it was a girl. I could be wrong.' At that, I recoiled. 'I'm scared to look—in case the dog has become a hermaphrodite because I can't recollect its sex. This is supposed to be my memory, and it's defective.'

I shook my head and gazed around the small enclosure, first from the humble, beige-coloured weatherboard house to the greying, wooden back fence and the outdoor loo with its septic tank. You could almost trainspot the enormous Nylex clock from here.

Skyhooks had given way to 'January' by Pilot. I remembered only too well this inane, catchy song. The neighbours must have had their radio dial set to 3XY.

'My grandparents' backyard, in Duke Street, Richmond.'

'Les?'

'No, my dad's parents. The shed here was like a goldmine—it was full of comics that belonged to my half-brother. My dad had married another woman, before my mother, you see. My half-brother was a few years old than me, and he lived here with my grandparents.'

'You liked reading comic books?'

'As much as you did,' I reminded her. 'Yes, I'll admit it now—I cherished them. At first I started out on *Casper the Friendly Ghost*, then moved on to DC, the usual fodder like *Batman*, *The Flash* and *Superman*. But when I found my brother's decade-old Marvel stash, I was hooked. The 1960s was a superb time for comics. *Captain America*, first as he was drawn by Kirby, then later a few precious issues by Jim Steranko.'

I picked up one of the comics that lay beside the boy. It didn't have a cover. *The Avengers*, issue 21. I remembered that one too. I flicked through it. The part where the Avengers disband had rocked the pre-adolescent me.

'My dream job at school was to become a comic artist. I was always drawing superheroes and barbarians and scantily clad, buxom women. That was the style. I had capes down pat, but musculature was a challenge. I'll tell you a quick story. Frustrated with the fact that there was no Aussie superhero at Marvel back in the '80s, I created one for them—a fellow from Melbourne, of course—called "Southern Cross". I sent the idea to Stan Lee at Marvel, and he actually wrote back, via his secretary, that he loved the idea and recommended it to the then-Editor-in-Chief... who shot the idea down in flames.' I sighed. 'Then again, Southern Cross was a patently silly name.'

A thought came to me.

I flicked through the pages, hoping it would be here. Not all '60s Marvel comics had the ad, but a lot of them did, going by my dubious memories.

'Ah-hah. Found it!'

I opened the comic wide and showed Kohana a one-page advertisement.

'The Insult that Made a Man out of "Mac"—see how this skinny kid is accosted on the beach by the local bully, humiliated in front of his girlfriend? He then does a Charles Atlas body-building course, and goes back to the beach to sock the bully, win friends, and influence people.'

'Your role-model perhaps?'

'Don't laugh too much. You'd be surprised what kind of impact on me this tall tale had.'

'So, you gambled a stamp for the free body-building book?'

'I'm not talking about that kind of influence. The stamp trick was only available to Americans. We would have had to pay far more in Australia—and anyway the comics were almost ten years old when I was reading them. I doubt the offer would have held.'

'Obviously, you've thought this through before now.'

I pondered that. 'Mmm. Obviously, I have.'

'Who was Charles Atlas?'

'He was awarded the title of "The World's Most Perfectly Developed Man", haven't you heard?'

'Yes, that's what it says here.' Kohana was checking through the fine print on the page. 'Really?'

'I have no idea.'

'Well then. Peas in a pod.'

She sat back on the grass too.

As I mentioned, it was a beautiful day, dry and sunny and about thirty-two degrees in the old Melbourne—why not? We soaked it up. The boy had no idea he was positioned between two contemplative ghosts, tanning themselves.

Kohana leaned back with her face in the sunlight. 'You seem happy here.'

'I was. My grandparents left me to my own devices. Nanny

Deaps is probably cooking right now, and Paddy would be in the loungeroom, in his favourite threadbare recliner, multi-tasking — he liked to listen to the footy on his transistor radio while watching the horse racing on the telly. Me? I had these comics and I enjoyed exploring the area. Richmond was an interesting place to grow up, in the '70s.'

'Is this the grandmother who liked making doilies?'

'No,' I said, impressed she knew, yet not surprised she did. 'That was Nan. My mother's mum. Les's wife.'

33 | 三十三

'I went home from Kyoto, and once I found out I was pregnant, cut my wrists with a razor. It was my intention to destroy both myself and the devil inside me.'

There were no Technicolor images.

Kohana huddled on the tiles, next to the hovel's fireplace, with her chin on her knees. There were bits of ash and charcoal stuck to her skirt, and I'd never observed her face this beaten down.

I dragged closer a blue plastic milk crate and placed it next to her, flipped it over, and then sat. I placed a hand on her arm.

'Patently, you weren't successful.'

'Deshō?' She ran her fingers through her hair. 'I believed I'd lost enough blood by the time my maid found me, damn her eyes, but she was a bossy woman and bundled me off to O-tee-san's house. He stitched me up, and the two of them conspired to nurse me back to health.'

'The baby?'

'I didn't miscarry.'

Kohana stared at the fire for a time.

'As my stomach grew, I cursed it. I loathed it. At the beginning of autumn 1975, a week before my birthday, I gave birth to a healthy girl, weight six pounds.'

'That must have changed your mind.'

'Why?' Kohana's response was flat, lacking any spark whatsoever.

'It often does—or so I've heard.'

'In my case, not at all. Once the baby was out of my womb, I pushed the thing into my maid's welcoming arms. If I could have coerced the woman to be the mother, I would have, but she had three children of her own and, as I say, she was stubborn.'

I stared at Kohana's profile. Without wanting to make any noise, I carefully shifted my weight on the crate. 'So you raised her?'

'I had no choice! This child was the reason I bound myself to Toshiro, in a marriage all wrong—so she would have wedded parents listed on the government koseki.'

'The man knew the child was not his.'

'I didn't love him, but I would never have misled Toshiro. Funnily enough, he proved to be the better parent, workaholic that he was. What's the expression? "The flower falls close to the branch on which it grew"? Is that how it goes?'

'I have no idea. I'm not good at idioms and homilies—they wear me out.'

'Well, the naming of the child I left up to O-tee-san. "Kaede" was a poor choice, in light of Kurosawa's later movie *Ran*. The Lady Kaede in that film is a coquettish bitch who lays waste to all around her. My Kaeda was a spiteful, mean-spirited child, qualities she likely inherited from me, but I sensed Hachi-sama lurking in there as well.'

'Not the chef?'

'I wished.'

Kohana threw back her head, scrutinized the ceiling, and let out a grunt of exasperation.

'I wish I could have been a fitter mother, but I don't know if it would have changed things. This augured sadly for Kaede's daughter, many years later. My grandchild was a godsend, a girl with a heart and a beautiful nature. Kaede had a field day despoiling these, and there was very little I could do to stop her—until she killed herself, again an action provoked out of spite. That saved Nina. Is it terrible I feel nothing but relief that Kaede died?'

'You had a daughter, and wanted to give her away,' I said slowly, fighting against an overwhelming pain in my chest. 'I had a daughter, and was robbed of her.'

34 | 三十四

We disembarked in a wide, cream-coloured, empty corridor, the most striking feature of which was a disinfectant smell, masked by something artificial—reminiscent of strawberries.

I shuddered. 'A classic stench I never could abide. Where are we?'

Standing beside me, my travelling companion was dressed in a simple black dress and wearing little makeup. Her expression told me she was struggling with inner demons, but the aroma of the place less mortified her.

'Looks like a hospital.'

'Oh, surprise,' I muttered.

'I don't have any recollection of being here.'

'Aren't we getting absent-minded in our old age?'

I smirked indulgently at my minor league put-down. At the same time, I leaned over to read a poster on the wall.

My initial attraction to this public notice was that it was pasted up at an angle, not straight, something guaranteed to annoy me. English dominated the thing, warning women of breast cancer. In the bottom right-hand corner, the poster was branded with a purple, not entirely legible hospital stamp, about the size of a twenty-cent coin.

While I couldn't read all these details, I didn't need to. I recognized the hospital's name.

'I know this place.'

'You do?'

I nodded my head. 'Yes. Why are we—?'

Comprehension didn't just dawdle up to me; it cudgelled my senses. This in turn caused a loss of balance, and Kohana put a confoundedly reassuring arm around me. 'What is it?'

'Christ, it's another bloody flash from *my* past.'

'Well, that explains things.'

'This is wrong. I do not wish to be here. Take me away, immediately.'

'Um... Not that easy, Wolram.'

'Not so long ago, you intimated it was. End this. Now.'

'I'm sorry, I can't. This is your memory, like you say. You brought us here—it stands to reason only you can wind it up.'

'How on earth do I do that? This is ridiculous. Wrong. I would never again inflict this on myself.'

I decided to act on my own—stuff the woman—and peeped both ways down the corridor. Perhaps I could stroll out of the fix? Manageable. No need to run. I could retain some dignity.

Just as I made up my mind to do this, I noticed the closed door.

It's possible I hadn't marked the entrance because the door was the same colour as the walls and the ceiling and the linoleum floor, but it was distinct enough now. I really needed to have my eyesight retested.

The number there—42—clutched all my attention. Oh yes, I knew it well, and what life on the other side implied.

Mostly pain, anguish. Memorable things like these.

'Also joy,' Kohana broached softly.

'Bullshit.'

'Look again. You need balance to remember this correctly. It's not how you convinced yourself to see it.'

'Rehashing existentialist hogwash, like you?—No bloody way. I recall exactly what happened. Right here.'

I tapped my temple. By chance, I did so on the same stretch of skin where Floyd's bullet had ostensibly entered my skull.

'And let me tell you, once was enough. I never volunteered for this—we were only ever supposed to visit your memories.'

'Not particularly fair, stalking my seedy past while you get to remain aloof. What kind of business arrangement is that?'

Kohana gripped my hand, and with force laid it on the stainless steel door handle. She allowed her fingers to remain there, holding mine.

'It *is* your choice, but don't play the coward.'

'I'll have you know, I'm no coward. Let go.'

'If you're not afraid, it shouldn't be any trouble to step through this door—a piece of cake, right? Easie peasie?'

'I refuse to listen to these inane clichés. I have nothing to prove.'

'Only that your bravado is not mere blustering.'

'It isn't.'

'Then why vacillate?'

'I'm not. I am considering options. Let's go someplace else.'

'Where?'

'Madagascar.'

'Obscure. You have other important business there?'

'Yes, that's right.'

'Liar. Madagascar is definitely out. Let's focus closer, on the next room. I'll come with you. I won't vanish, I promise. I owe you.'

'You owe me nothing.'

'If you think I'm persistent now, just wait till I get going.'

I pressed my lips together so hard it hurt. 'For goodness' sake, will it stop you playing the harpy?'

'Possibly.'

'And you're coming with me?'

'Didn't I say as much?'

'I'll hold you to that.'

'Hallelujah for small mercies.'

'Bah.'

In spite of better judgment to hotfoot it away, I had a yen to prove the woman wrong, swallowed my distress, and opened the door.

On the other side was a bright, relatively spacious private hospital room, just like I recalled: an electrocardiograph machine in one corner, a huge bouquet of irises in another.

The centrepiece display was a woman on her back on top of a hospital bed, stomach huge. I couldn't see her face, but I could clearly hear the shrieking.

There was a midwife hovering nearby, and a man who sat on the edge of the bed next to the pregnant woman, holding her hand. He leaned over to wipe the woman's face with a damp cloth, and whispered sweet nothings in her ear.

Me, at fifty. I was already an old fool.

Right then, the door slammed in our faces.

'Did you lose your nerve?' Kohana wondered aloud.

'Of course not! I had nothing to do with that. Although, come to think of it, this may be the opportune moment I stepped out to indulge in a Cuban cigar.'

'Well.'

'Well, what? It was the done thing in traditional Western culture. I'm not going to apologize for smoking it.'

'Not the cigar—I could care less. I mean the door.'

'Ah.' I again pushed it open. The scene, and its furnishings, had changed.

There was a pretty woman sitting up in bed, face drawn and pale, her expression jubilant.

Dozens of red and yellow roses occupied every available space.

And again there was me, this time in an armchair alongside the woman, holding a bundle at which we both gazed. A priceless combination of wonder and elation was stamped upon my face. If it had been at all possible, I'd have strode right up to me and torn the expression off my cheeks.

'The best of times, the worst of times,' I mused, as the room folded up on itself, and other memories assembled before me.

I had no idea if Kohana caught these.

'I never thought to quote Dickens—what's the world coming to? Hackneyed stuff. I suppose, however, if you write twenty tomes, like him, you're bound to hit poignant at some stage.'

There was a longer vignette, a memory of the baby, now aged about fourteen months, asleep on top of a bed.

'Corinne.' I threw myself into the sight. 'God, I adored this little girl. More than anything you could begin to imagine.'

'I see that.'

'From my memory here, or from the stupid look on my face?'

'Both?'

Kohana nudged me, in a playful way. I wasn't in the mood.

'What was it?' I mused. 'What changed me? A combination of the small things?—I guess that's what you call it. The feeling of warm, tiny hands enclosed in mine, the way she started seeing everything around, as she grew and developed. I remember hours, lying in warm sunlight from the window, staring at the miniature person sleeping so soundly beside me. It was a miracle. A goddamned miracle. When she started to walk—the ambles we had together, observing the world with brand new eyes. Insects, rocks, flowers, junk, all fresh. As she got older, the infectious smile on her face once I set foot through the door after a long day's work. I never told Corinne how I used to rush from the office, push through people, and race to our house, just to be gifted with that smile at the end of the sprint.'

I stared at a younger me, standing on a landing near some stairs, painting pink a wooden bedroom door. Calm, patient, content. Happy.

I loathed the fool.

'Think again, Kohana, if this makes you conjure up some idealized childhood you never had, or never gave. There were times the stress of parenting became too much. Josephine and I constantly fought over petty differences and, frankly, I was over-absorbed in my job. Still, there were incredible times—till we turned the page.'

The flow of snug, chipper memories ended. Everything changed in a wink.

A dark shadow settled itself over the preceding colours.

Hospital, again.

Doctors. Machines. Fluorescent lighting. A sour smell, masked by something vaguely reminiscent of strawberries.

We stood before a steel cot in which a five-year-old child lay unconscious, pinioned in the midst of wires and tubes.

'She got sick,' I said. Stating the obvious was somehow appealing.

'What was wrong?'

'Polio—it was polio. For God's sake.'

I leaned over to stroke the girl's wet, troubled forehead. She mumbled in her sleep and the lids fluttered.

'There, there,' I cooed—and then I yanked my hand away. I took a long step back.

'Are you all right?'

It was my turn to ignore Kohana. Too many things battered me. I believed I'd put all this behind me—but I was in error.

'At first, we thought Corinne had the flu, worrying enough at her age. Our GP told us so. When the symptoms persisted and in fact she got worse, the doctor struck me as panicky. He referred us to over-qualified "specialists"—that's what the certificates proclaimed on their office walls. Specialists... hah! One by one, each was at a loss to explain the illness.'

I was back to hovering, close by the little girl. I wanted to touch her hair, hold her hand, remember her warmth. More than anything, I wanted to help her through this confounded horror.

Instead, I suffered the same debilitation I remembered from the first time round: I was powerless to do anything. I was useless. I could barely breathe.

'Finally, one of the bastards did some proper research and found the truth. He told us it was a dead disease. Said they hadn't come across a single case in years and that ninety percent of people who came in contact with the virus never suffered any symptoms. Of the unlucky ten percent that did react, a single percentage point had the virus enter their central nervous system, and only one in two hundred infections led to irreversible paralysis. The quack that stumbled across this pot of gold gave us the figures in a monotone speech, and handed me poorly photocopied notes straight after.'

I shook my head; all the old frustrations, disbelief and anger running riot. I wanted to scream.

'What the blazes was the point of the waffling? Our child knocked on death's door—one percent, or one hundred, the numbers didn't matter, not when they proved how absurdly unlucky we were. One in ten, or a hundred—what did this mean? The bogus sympathy, the hands thrown in the air in defeat... What kind of answers were these? I wanted to stuff the man's paperwork down his half-witted throat.'

'But... Aren't children immunized against polio?'

Even as I trampled atop the spiralling memories, and the doctors' faces, I could not make out my companion. Vision had become hazy.

'Corinne fell through some absurd gap. A medical bureaucrat must have neglected to add her name to a list, or clean forgot to add that vaccine to her inoculations. The doctors couldn't explain it. I don't want to try.'

It was Kohana's round to hold my arm. 'I can't imagine what you and your wife went through. I'm so sorry.'

I pulled myself free of her. I wasn't patrolling for sympathy. 'Josephine wasn't my wife. Not that it matters. Nothing matters.'

'What happened from here? Your daughter recovered?'

'Eventually, she was again able to walk, but with one leg significantly shorter and scrawnier than the other. She was lucky. The doctors made sure to let us know about another percentage— this time, ten—of the likelihood of her dying while she was at her worst.'

I had been unconsciously pacing the room, chewing my lower lip, so I diverted myself back to the cot and leaned on the railing. I was cleft in two. Love and affection, anger and rejection. A fury was percolating deep inside my gut.

'If I heard any more percentage possibilities, there was a ninety percent likelihood I'd sock someone in the jaw! All my life, I had this strange feeling that behind the medical profession lurked something sinister. This experience confirmed it. I mean, what do you think of doctors? You think they're saints? Hah! They're foxy beasts! They say, "We've got no medicine, we've no cure. We've got nothing!" But they have! They have everything! Dig under the floors! Or search the clinics! You'll find plenty! ...They pose as saints, but are full of lies! If they smell a battle, they hunt the defeated! They're nothing but stingy, greedy, blubbering, foxy, and mean! Goddamn it all! But then who made them such beasts? We did!'

'Wolram.' I felt fingers on my cheek.

'Take that away,' I hissed. 'I don't need it.'

I forced down my batty grievances, smothered the lot, and stretched out a tentative hand toward the fevered child—but the world flipped.

Now, I was on a street. Walking with an absurd spring in my step.

I turned into a small, overgrown front garden, hopped up to the solid front door of an old brick terrace house. I took a bronze key from my pocket, slid this into the lock, turned it, and entered the building.

It was daylight outside, dim within. I switched on a light.

Here was a long, high-ceilinged passageway, with stained wooden closets on the left, and to the right Victorian-style, William Morris-designed wallpaper, depicting white and purple lilacs. My ludicrous home improvements.

'Kohana?'

'Behind you,' I heard.

I wanted to check, but couldn't control my movements. I bent over to pick up, then sort through, a wad of junk mail that had gained access via the slot in the door—assorted brochures courtesy of Zoroaster, Henkel and Ambroise, an electricity bill, and a catalogue from Trillian's. An excessive waste of precious paper banned a decade before I died.

The sorting done, I walked along the passage. At the end was a staircase; I paused momentarily, and then I started to go up.

On the landing, I faced two doors, both closed.

One, to my right, was a pink door that had a wooden picture of an angel done in a childish hand. The other door was a plain light green.

'Take the door on the right,' my head counselled, but I gravitated in the direction of the green one. No, I warned. Stop.

I opened this door wide.

On the other side of a sizeable master bedroom, on top of a queen-size bed, two people were caught in the middle of noisy coitus. Josephine, sweaty and raptured, and an athletic younger man with whom I'd never before had the pleasure.

Bile ripped through my stomach and tore through my throat.

I staggered from the room, howling, back down the way I'd come—past wallpaper decorated with marigolds, and furniture I no longer recognized. Just as I was about to spill my lack of lunch, I recovered myself.

I was back in Kohana's shack, on the sofa, with my head between my knees.

I knew this because I recognized the rice straw that surrounded my feet. I was too ashamed to look up—blubbering is rarely a pretty sight.

'Twenty-two years her senior,' I choked. 'Stupid, stupid old man. How could I have expected her to remain faithful to an ancient fool? I should have known there was a reason she refused to marry me.'

I beat the sides of my head with fists, watched the mucus from my nose dangle and jiggle just above the tatami matting.

'I think I'm going to despoil your floor,' I muttered.

'Who decided on the paternity test?'

Ah.

I haltingly raised my head, wiped my nose on my sleeve, and peered at Kohana.

She was seated on the floor next to the couch, looking my way. While I found concern aplenty, there was a serenity there I appreciated. I couldn't have stood more sympathy.

'Me.'

'Why?'

'I had to know.' I breathed out loudly, and my body shuddered. 'Judy, my secretary, put the notion into my head—she made the suggestion as she passed me my morning tea, like it was just part of our day-to-day business routine, but once there inside my head, the thing sprouted. I *had* to know.'

'And the child wasn't yours.'

It took a while for me to answer the question.

'No.' I cleared my throat, and then coughed several times. 'So I'd lost her. But I couldn't let her go.'

'How old was she?'

'Six when this happened. Until that time, Corinne was my entire world, through good times and bad, everything to me. Everything. Afterward, she became my ball and chain. The more her mother begged and pleaded for me to give Corinne up, the more I dug in my heels. There was a principle to uphold.'

'Your revenge?'

'Something along those lines.'

'I now understand why you prefer Shakespeare.'

'I couldn't—couldn't—let her go.'

'That's just sad, Wolram.'

I again wiped my leathery old face, and scrutinized the collection of shiny moisture and other stains on the sleeve. It really did need a hearty cleaning.

'You know, it could be found amusing.'

'What could?'

'The hospital room number, 42. It's the ultimate answer to the

223

ultimate question of life, the universe, and everything else.'

'Says who?'

'Douglas Adams. *The Hitchhiker's Guide to the Galaxy,* a book I cherished in my university days.'

'So you did read, then.'

I almost smiled. The expression withered.

'When Corinne was born, I deluded myself that having a child was the meaning of everything—her arrival, in a room numbered 42, added to this certainty. In my middle age, I was a born-again Walter Mitty. Even her illness made no dent in the fool's paradise.'

I rolled up my sleeve to examine the sagging, discoloured skin on the inside of my elbow. How many doctors' needles had been carelessly poked there?

'This brainless theory was culled once I saw the result of the paternity test, and—after the anger and the humiliation and the madness and the despair had settled—I had an epiphany, of sorts. It dawned on me that something was fundamentally wrong with society. It was a botched bauble that needed repair work.'

I glanced at Kohana to see if she was listening. She nodded.

'At the self-same time, I could cast a spotlight on the medical profession for the inhumane, distorted, quack organization it truly was.'

'In other words, you took revenge against the entire world? The insult that made a man out of Mac?'

'Something of the sort.'

'Tell me, are you proud of what you did thereafter?'

'No. No. I was never proud. Obsessed, with a fiercely blinkered vision I honed over two decades, fighting for something. But what was it?—pride didn't figure into it. I thought I was right. I was convinced I was right. Everything I did was done for the greater good. The "greater good"—listen to me preach. Yes, I've had a lot of time to think about this. The insult didn't make a man out of me. It made a monster.'

I coughed a little more, and rubbed my eyes. Everything ached.

'Ultimate answer, my arse—and, quite bluntly, I never thought I'd end up beating about in Arthur Dent's pyjamas.'

35 | 三十五

We were in a crowded bar I'd never seen before, yet I knew it was my Melbourne, the city I lorded it over when I died.

Probably, the people with cosmetic enhancements were the giveaway, along with a predilection of the ladies for little black dresses.

It would be raining outside. Of course.

I recognized a young man waltzing through the crowd, past the vulgar-looking barman, whom he gifted with a thumbs-up on his way to the toilet.

Straight away, I knew what I had to do.

After waiting about half a minute, I followed the fellow in.

Where Kohana had got to, I didn't care. Better she wasn't here. My first impression, upon entering the bathroom, was that no one was present, and the aroma distracted me: a heady combination of vomit, sweat and excretion. I expected to find a rotting carcass, and I have to say I almost gagged.

Pulling my senses together, I saw the door to one of the cubicles was shut.

I fished in my pocket for the Webley-Fosbery.

Kohana hadn't allowed me to get any practice up to this point, and I'd never before used a pistol, but it was deceptively simple to work out. I'd seen enough films in my time to comprehend the basics.

I cocked the gun, with a click.

That was when I spied my man through a narrow gap in the doorframe, could see the misery and anguish inscribed across his harried face. Not all, it would seem, was caused by the bathroom stench.

'Do you think this is the answer?' Curse her—she was here, after all.

'It's answer enough, my girl, to see him in more pain after I insert a bullet into his stomach.'

'I don't think this is the point of our being here.'

'Isn't it? Looks fine to me.'

'Wolram, stop.'

'Again?' I glared at her over my shoulder. 'Why?'

'You're angry. And this isn't why we're here.'

'Then what is the point?'

'I'm not sure.'

'You got the fun of reliving your pointless murders. Let me have mine.'

'Those were memories. They happened. This didn't.'

'So I'm improvising.'

'Will it make everything rosy again?'

I breathed out loudly. 'Damn you, Kohana. Leave me be. I need to do this. Now.' I raised the gun and poked it through the small gap in the doorway.

'The man is already tormented—don't you agree?'

'So am I, Kohana. He's the one who murdered my daughter, then killed me.'

'Also, the one whose wife you killed first.'

'I had nothing to do with that!'

'You still believe the lie?'

The gun lowered of its own compulsion. 'I don't know.'

'After everything you've experienced since you fell from the perch, can you honestly say you think the world would be a better place if you knocked off your own assassin?'

'A degree of retaliation never, ever went astray.'

'That's where you're wrong.'

'I seem to remember you indulging yourself on a number of occasions.'

'I did some terrible things. I was wrong.'

'I thought you didn't know why we're here.'

'I said I wasn't sure. That doesn't stop me taking pot shots, and possibly coming to grips with a minuscule amount of it.

You've done the same, and I'm grateful.'

'Am I ever going to get to fire this gun? I'm sick of carrying it around.'

'There's a rubbish bin right there.'

'Convenient.'

I lobbed the firearm into a plastic bin pressed against the wall. It had a faded Hylax H-in-a-circle logo on it. Fitting. After that, I rinsed my hands in the grubby-looking sink. The woman was busy looking at herself in the mirror.

'So, you are here to play Jacob Marley's ghost, and rattle some chains.'

'I don't think so,' Kohana mused. 'But I am surprised to learn you remember the name of a supporting character from Dickens.'

'Whatever. Can we go now? Someone might get the impression I like to lurk in men's toilets and forgive people I loathe.'

The lights went out. Visions stretched before me, lopsided and ethereal—the first one of my mother crooning 'It's Raining, It's Pouring' as I, aged four, huddled (afraid) in the house and the rain hailed mightily without. The last was a recountal of my father, sitting on the sand at the beach, relaxed, jobless, strumming 'The House of the Rising Sun' on his guitar.

I awoke spread out, on top of a bed rather than the shore.

Kohana was perched close by, mopping my brow with that damned Scottish tartan tea towel.

'What was that about?' I asked, trying to rise.

'Stay put.' Kohana pushed me back.

'Not my memory or one of yours. Was I dreaming? Since when do dreams involve such abominable smells?'

'I'm not sure—if you were dreaming, I got to freeload. Are you feeling all right? You passed out on me.'

'How did I get here?'

'I carried you. You're not exactly a heavyweight, Wolram.'

I noticed I wasn't wearing my robe or shirt, so I pulled up the quilt around my neck. I didn't feel comfortable having this woman view my seasoned flesh.

Then an idea came to me.

'Could you please hand me the smoking jacket?'

Kohana stood up, leaned over to a dresser, scooped something up, and laid the robe before me. I poked one arm from under the covers and checked the pocket.

'As I suspected—the gun is gone.'

'Interesting,' Kohana said.

'Meaning what?'

'Interesting?' She shrugged.

'You didn't remove it?'

'Why would I?' She looked around her hovel. 'I hate guns, and I have enough baggage here to dust.'

'But how is it possible for me to physically leave something lying about, like the gun in the rubbish bin? If I leave a glass slipper behind, will some prince come buzzing after me?'

'P'raps it depends on the time of night.'

36 | 三十六

We took our constitutional through a large nineteenth-century park—Fitzroy Gardens in East Melbourne.

The place might have been right next to the CBD, but it was gloriously restful and quiet. There was no rain. The sun shone, and two mudlarks hopped about beneath a sprinkler.

Our walking route took us close by a building, partially covered with ivy. 'Do you know Captain Cook?' I asked Kohana.

'The pirate?'

'The famous English navigator. Cook, not Hook.'

'I know, I know. I was only having a bit of fun.'

'That joke's old hat, my girl. This is supposed to be his house. It was purchased for eight hundred quid, shipped out from the Old Country in the 1930s, and then set up here to celebrate Melbourne's centenary. The thing is, while it was definitely owned by Cook's parents, no one's sure if James lived there.'

Two blonde boys, aged about four or five, were running around the house. They had on corduroys and matching *Banana Splits* T-shirts.

'Must be the early '70s. I remember that show.' I scanned the place again. 'Which would make this around the time that I used to come to visit Pop before he died. That was in 1970 or '71. His hospital is right over there.'

'So you were, what, five years old?'

'Mmm. I don't remember the details so well, but he was a brave man. Always put on a smile when we came to visit. I knew he was in pain, but he never let on.'

We continued along the wide, paved path, before stopping near a tree stump that had carvings of cavorting sprites.

'The Fairies Tree, made around the same time Cook's cottage arrived in pieces,' I said, 'carved on the stump of a three hundred-year-old river red gum. That tree, right there, is older than Melbourne.'

'You know a lot about this place.'

'In actual fact, I'm trying to compete with Y, that pilot friend of yours, the one who liked flying into stationary objects. I don't know that the park stands up to Kyoto, but it has its own story to tell. We came here often while Pop was in the hospital. I think I learned all the tidings from my grandmother.'

'She was a good woman?'

'That sounds... odd. I never gave it much thought. She was good to me.'

'And to Les?'

'I have a feeling she wouldn't have been the easiest person to get along with, in terms of marriage—one probable reason he stayed in the army so long after the war.'

'I was never sure what he died from,' Kohana ventured.

'Leukaemia.'

'Leukaemia—*hakketsubyou*? That's our name for it. Oh.'

'You learn something new every day.'

I wandered ahead, my hands in the pockets of my smoking jacket, grateful the gun was gone. I had more space.

'Pop stuck it out in the army until the late 1950s, and he spent some time stationed in South Australia where the British were conducting nuclear tests. He and his unit got to be spectators for Operation Buffalo in 1956 and the detonation of a thirteen-kiloton weapon called "One Tree"—I seem to remember it was about the same strength as the bomb they dropped on Hiroshima, but I could be wrong.'

The rich green lawns in the park faded away, becoming an ocean of red sand with tufts of spinifex grass, and the introduced English elm trees disappeared.

In front of us was a line of soldiers dressed in khaki, and beyond them, as far as the eye could see, a flat, wild, dry place blessed with the occasional mallee gum.

The horizon flickered. A huge cloud spiralled up, and then

ballooned outwards.

I wasn't aware if Kohana would glimpse the vision too, but really should have known better.

'I see it,' she sighed. 'Perhaps we can recreate the things we thought long and hard about in life. Whether they're real or not is another matter.'

'Rings true. I suppose we both would have seen footage, at some stage of our childhood, of A-bombs or kamikaze attacks. They must have left a subliminal impression. Coupled with our imaginations, I'm not surprised. But most of that footage would have been in black-and-white. The colours here impress me.'

'You're impressed?' Kohana sounded like she was appalled.

'No, not by the thing itself—the colours. The rest of this vision has bothered me ever since we visited Pop in the hospital. For sixty-six years, with spare change.'

'I actually had no idea they tested nuclear weapons in Australia.'

'I think most people outside the country didn't know. The British detonated seven of the beasts, but it wasn't big news at the time. Later on, domestically, things got more interesting. Not only military personnel were exposed to the radiation—there were also the local Aborigines, and fallout from this particular bomb was detected as far as Queensland.'

'You believe Les's illness was related?'

'Honestly? I don't know, but it does make you think.'

The cloud bobbed about like a tethered balloon, one that chose to loom thousands of feet above our heads.

'We had no family history of leukaemia. When I was studying law at Melbourne University, I obtained part-time work helping out solicitors involved with the government's Royal Commission into nuclear tests. This would have been in—oh—1985?'

'Sorry, I have no idea what a "royal commission" is.'

'Before your time.'

I winked at her, and she reddened. Wolram—3, Kohana—0.

'A public inquiry. Generally, these things were set up to examine some controversial issue—police corruption, departmental mismanagement, whatever. This one was established to scour the British government's conduct during the testing, along with the complicity of our home-grown authorities. Leading up to the inquiry, there was talk of British and Australian servicemen being deliberately exposed to fallout from the blasts in order to gauge results.'

I kicked up orange sand, and straight after regretted it—I had to take off my slipper and pour out a bunch of warm pebbles.

'I kept tabs on events after that. In 1999, a British study found a third of the participants had died in middle age from cancer-related illness. Leukaemia was a popular one. A couple of years later, they unveiled evidence of troops being forced to, well, do this.'

I pointed to the soldiers, who first ran in twos, and then walked, jumped, skipped, and now were crawling across the sand.

'Nothing like a spot of calisthenics for a few days after a nuclear explosion, only a few kilometres from the blast site.'

The desert, and the soldiers, vanished.

We were standing by a hospital bed on which lay a middle-aged man. The haggard, creaky Pop I truly remembered from childhood. He slept peacefully, so far as I could tell. On the small, sterile bedside table were two objects: a framed photograph of me and my mother, and a timeworn corncob pipe.

Kohana was transfixed, tears threatening, as she stood closer to stare at a man she hadn't met in over eighty-four years.

'Thank you. For letting me see him.'

'You're welcome, but I really am being selfish.' I could not resist throwing back one of her favourite expressions. 'Deshō?'

'Deshō.'

'And it's funny. At the age of four, I realized the doctors in the hospital were goddamned useless. They weren't helping him.

They were keeping him barely alive, via a lot of tubes and contraptions.'

I noticed Kohana's hand was resting on Pop's.

'Are you all right to go now?'

'Yes.' She produced a nice smile. 'I've said my goodbyes.'

Once again, we were all aboard that supermundane carousel. When we disembarked, I found another place that rang distant bells.

A sparsely populated, typically Melbourne pub—the Victoria Bitter signage was a giveaway—but which one?

I could hear muffled music from the next room, and every time the door opened, it came through louder.

'Depeche Mode?' I realized. 'Well, well.'

'You know where we are?'

'Melbourne again. A pub called the Sarah Sands, on the corner of Sydney and Brunswick Roads. I think this may be 1989? If so, that's a goth/post-punk club next door.'

I went over to the counter—and was surprised when the bartender, an old gent younger than me, grinned and asked what I wanted.

'Two pots of VB—um, thanks.'

The barkeep walked away to pour glasses from a tap vividly marked with green, red, white and black. A tad screwy, I thought.

That was the same second I spied myself in the looking-glass, behind bottles of liqueur.

'Curiouser and curiouser,' I heard Kohana remark.

Staring back was a twenty-three-year-old, in a black suit and shirt, with spiky black hair and a pale face. It took a little longer to recognize the kid.

'No,' I said, stunned.

'Actually, I think, yes.' That was Kohana, in my ear as always.

'No. No way. Me? I'm young again?'

'Either that or you've been renting out your mirror-image.'

'Not that I recall. Bloody Nora.'

'Well, now, stovepipe trousers—stylish. And I'm digging the narrow, dark wine and black jacquard tie. I never thought you had it in you, my sweet. The minimalist, geometric design is a nice flourish.'

'My favourite at the time. I later lost it. I think.' It's fair to say, I was bamboozled. 'Vintage 1960s. Silk.'

'Let me see.' The woman took the tie partway out from under my jacket and flipped it over. 'Dior.'

I tore myself away from the mirror and looked at the tag. 'Dior? Oh, crap. That is just plain sad.' I then checked myself. I'd definitely shelved the smoking jacket. 'What the Hell is going on, Kohana?'

'It's not real, but enjoy it.'

'Just like that.'

'Why not? Live a little.'

Kohana was again the teenage hangyoku, in the pitch-black kimono, this time gift-wrapped with a scarlet obi.

'Well, now, your colours are appropriate for this place,' I noted, 'but aren't you going to change for this age?'

'Easy to fit in here.' The girl conjured up a compact out of thin air. 'I already have the deathly pallored greasepaint—all I have to do is add some Nefertiti-like eyeliner, and ta-dah.'

When she looked up, I burst out laughing.

'Not quite the image I was looking for?'

'No, no. I love it.'

The beers were in front of us, drooling, so I paid with a new-found wallet from my trousers, and we went to an empty table. My head was buzzing. I was sure I was taller.

Kohana had turned her attention to the drinks.

'I'll never, ever get used to the tiny beer heads in Australia. The froth in Japan took up over a third of the glass.'

'Sacrilege.'

'So. 1989, huh?'

'Yeah, I believe so.' I blew out as I looked around. 'Bloody

Hell.'

'The first year of the Heisei era. I moved to Melbourne in 1989.'

'You're joking?'

'No, no. It was the year that O-tee-san, singer Hibari Misora, and Emperor Hirohito all died, and my place with them. Time for change. I moved to a country where the incumbent prime minister wept on TV as he admitted to marital infidelity. That was… fascinating. I was used to men shedding crocodile tears on national television—in Japan, a common occurrence when company execs screwed up—but doing so over an affair was new to me.'

'You came over with your husband?'

'Oh, no. He stayed on in Tokyo, running his empire. He only came after the world fell to pieces. But my daughter Kaede tagged along. She was thirteen at the time.'

'How old were you?'

'Fifty-nine.'

I raised my beer in her direction. 'You look good for your age.'

'As do you.'

'I suppose—yes. Strange. Cheers.'

'I always liked "cin cin".' We clicked glasses. 'You know what "cin cin" means in Japanese? Penis.'

I almost snorted my drink. 'Damn. Now that's news to me.'

Kohana laughed, and then she leaned closer. 'So, your turn to play Y—our Kyoto tour guide, remember? Tell me about this place.'

'The Sarah Sands? Or about Melbourne?'

'Both would be nice.'

'Combination stuff, eh? Well, not far from here, in 1835, an unscrupulous fellow named John Batman made a deal with the local Aboriginal people for over a million hectares of land. He paid for it with a few dozen blankets, axes, knives, scissors, handkerchiefs, and some tubs of flour. A very good businessman, if you ask me. Twenty years later, this place, and many others like it, were built. The Aborigines regretted their part of the bargain ever after.'

'That's it?'

'That's all I remember. Australian history isn't as exciting as other places.'

'Well, time for a lark. Follow me.'

Kohana picked up her glass, and took small steps in her perilous clogs to a tabletop videogame. I plopped myself down on the other side of it.

'Do you have twenty cents?'

'It's that cheap?' I hardly remembered prices like this. I slid a coin across. Kohana slotted it, and beamed as the screen came to life.

'Show me your stuff,' she said, settling in.

I lost—Kohana was a demon on the thing. I never thought to see a geisha playing *Galaxian*. When she finally finished and had her initials at the top of the list, she asked for another coin, and ventured over to a decrepit Musicola jukebox.

Chris Isaak's 'Wicked Game' started up.

She returned and stood over me, towering in those thirteen-centimetre geta.

'Not my style,' I said. 'At this time, I was more into Front 242.'

'Will you shut up for one moment?'

Right then and there, she seated herself on my lap. Her face was close to mine, and I discovered I was intoxicated with her Nefertiti'd eyes. She pressed her mouth against mine. God help me, of course I wilted. Then I pulled free.

'Stop,' I said.

'Why?'

'It's not right.'

'Says who? Come on. This is probably the only time our ages are in sync and we get to have a good time. Don't ruin it.'

'You're not thinking of Pop, are you?'

'Just a teensy bit.'

Kohana kissed me again, and I thought my head would split. God. She finally detached herself and leaned back.

'There.'

'There what?'

'There nothing. It's the only thought that crossed my mind. It's been a while. I worried I might be out of practice.'

'No,' was about all I could manage.

She ran her fingers along my cheek, into my hair. 'You don't mind?'

'I'll live. Come on, I'll take you next door. They have the best *souvlaki*.'

37 | 三十七

I was an old man again, and went there alone.

I swear I could taste garlic sauce and was nursing a headache. All those beers had been effective after all. A ghost with a hangover would be a new, shameful entry in the annals of haunting.

It was daytime, but there were very few people on the narrow street. The place was pretty enough when you could see it. Much nicer than in the dark. The okiya with the round window was just behind me, and I saw the alleyway to my left, easy enough to miss.

Without Kohana to stop me, I sauntered down there.

It was past time to sort out the mystery of this thoroughly innocuous thoroughfare.

The first thing I heard was a loud, objectionable crow. It scared me half to death—an oxymoron if ever I've caroused with one. Stupid bird. Straight after, I made out laughter.

I wondered when I'd banish the impulse to move surreptitiously, though my jitters in this case had to do with the fact I was malingering in a place Kohana had done her best to stop me from entering.

So I stepped quietly, and hesitated next to a sagging wooden wall.

A girl and boy were sheltering further down, in the shadow of a great tree. It took me but a moment to identify Kohana. Her kimono was pristine and perfectly tailored, whereas the stripling with her had on an outfit that looked like a worn-in tradesman's.

I didn't recognize him at all, a handsome teenage boy whom she plainly liked.

He was entertaining her with a warm, familiar charm and wit. I liked him as well, straight away. One of those people you can place stock in, who aspires to better things and will—in probability—go places.

For her part, Kohana played the ingénue, giggling in a joyful manner, and after a while I realized that, this time around, it wasn't an act. The absurd behaviour was real.

'So, we're settled,' the boy was saying as I edged closer. 'I'll be waiting for you tonight, and we'll make our escape then.' With that, he grinned.

'But I have a booking in the evening.'

'Afterward, then. Come snow, sleet, hail or high water—I'll be here, don't you worry. Oh, unless of course I have a booking too.'

'You'd break your leg straight away, trying to wear our okobo!'

I saw Kohana roll her eyes as she turned my way, watched as a big smile rose across her face and her cheeks glowed, and then she swung straight back to plant a kiss on the boy's surprised mouth.

'I'll come,' she said, straight after.

In our time together, I had observed plenty of Kohana's moods, had witnessed her mirth and merriment, but never before had I caught sight of such honest happiness. This, it seemed to me, was a close relative of rapture. I felt a knot tighten deep inside me.

'I promise it,' she sang.

For a brief moment, the boy showed a more realistic sense of gumption. 'Wait. Seriously. Are you sure this is what you want?'

'Far more than just plain sure.'

'You'll be happy?'

'We'll be *so* happy.'

The boy crowed at the clear, cloudless spring sky. Certainly, it was an adolescent carry-on—but, for the life of me, I couldn't conceive of a single better way to react.

'I'd say I was the king of the world, but right now I'm located on its bottom rung,' the boy said. 'Even so, I have plans, Kohana. We will be happy, I swear it. You inspire me. More than that—you trust and believe in me. For these things alone, I adore you far more than any pot of gold.'

'Oh, gold is overrated.'

'My point exactly.' He poked his tongue at her, and she laughed.

All of us then heard a coarse voice from a few houses away. 'Kohana,' it was shouting. 'Kohana! Come inside, now!' Oume-san. I'd know those rough, smoky vocal cords anywhere.

'I have to go,' the girl sighed. 'Duty calls.'

'Kohana, don't forget—tonight. As soon as you get back.'

'As if I could ever forget.' She granted him that sweeping smile with the disappearing eyes, and then she held his tunic with both hands and pressed her head against his chest. 'You don't have to call me Kohana any more. From now on I'm just Tomeko.' Tomeko? 'My geisha days are over. Tonight.'

She ran away, and straight after, the boy retreated into the shadows and vanished.

I was alone in the alley, where silence prevailed.

Dusk settled at an exaggerated pace, followed by night.

I don't know when I first noticed the little fireflies dancing in the night air, slowly growing in number. I was beginning to also hear their hum.

Having never before encountered a firefly in my lifetime, I poked a finger at one of the nearest ones—and was burned.

How—?

The hum was louder, and the wall behind me began to vibrate.

Burning cinders and ash, not fireflies, were everywhere. Above the whir, I made out a new sound, a howl like a wild animal pinioned in a trap. It was coming from just around a dogleg in the alley.

I left my parking space and moved in that direction, carefully avoiding the floating debris that had already seared me. Impossible, I know, but I wasn't keen to experiment further.

On the ground, there was a dismembered fence and scattered bricks, smouldering woodwork and a fallen, naked tree with all the leaves ripped off. Something was huddling beside the toppled trunk.

As I edged closer I could see a black-and-white chequered silk kimono. The wailing sound was coming from inside the gown— from the person there.

It was petrifying. I'd never, ever heard anything like this.

'Kohana?'

The girl was hunched over a small thing I couldn't make out.

There was too much junk bobbing about in the air, and plumes of smoke obscured the view. I was about ten feet away when I recognized what she was holding to her chest.

It was a torso with one arm.

The other arm was mostly missing, and the lower half of the body, from the waist down, was gone. The head was there, and the face—though scorched—recognizable. It was the boy. Kohana was clutching him to her chest and bawling in a long, flat, breathless way.

God. God. I blinked quickly. This was abominable. A nightmare.

'What are you doing here?'

I swung around.

An older Kohana, about fortyish, was stepping over from the main part of the alley. I realized I was between her and sight of the couple.

'I told you not to come here,' my Kohana bristled, at the very same time that she tried to peer around me.

I went straight up, encircled her with an arm, and turned her about.

'I asked you a question. What are you doing?'

'Nothing,' I said. 'Come on. Let's go.'

'Wait. What is that sound?'

I attempted to distract her, by pulling her, really I did.

Perhaps I should have tried harder, because the woman pushed back against me and saw what I'd seen.

She fell away from my arm, and then trudged slowly towards the one-and-a-half people crouched next to the fallen tree.

Kohana stopped moving and stood there, her back to me.

I didn't know what I ought to do. This was far too much, I felt overwhelmed, and as I rubbed my face I peered around at the destruction of the street, such a familiar sight by now.

The bottom line was, I couldn't simply hover here any more, playing pedestrian. I had to accomplish something, anything.

I went straight over to Kohana, took in the spectacle of the sobbing, howling child one final time, and grabbed her hand. I pulled her away, off into the darker parts of the alley, and the world folded in on itself.

We were back. In Kohana's hovel—me on the leather sofa, and she deposited in her Egg chair.

I leaned forward to get a better look. The woman's face may have been expressionless, but there were tears coursing down hollowed-out cheeks.

'Are you all right? Kohana?'

Nothing.

She stared straight past me, without any focus at all.

38 | 三十八

Kohana aged quickly.

I slid open all the shōji screens of the bedroom, next to the living area, and propped her up in bed next to a lamp. She was wrapped in a white nightdress, snug, with a book in her lap.

The woman had shrunk in size, much smaller than me. Kohana's hair was white, thick still, and it hung down over her right shoulder in a ponytail that I had made myself.

I'm not going to sit here and paint a picture of a centenarian who miraculously looks like a teenager, let alone a middle-aged woman. This was genuine age before me. I was back to the place I would have been in the real world before we died—much younger than her, even at seventy-one.

When I looked closely, I could see the features I knew and those expressions I revered. They were right there.

'Age is a different kind of geisha makeup,' Kohana laughed, in a soft way that sparkled to my ear. 'I just can't wash it off.'

I walked across the room, to go make a cup of tea, paused next to the suit of armour, and inspected Pop's cricket bat. There was an extra dent in it where I had struck Shashin on the noggin, and I chuckled.

The only round of cricket I'd ever played well.

Putting down the bat, I carefully crossed it with the axe, as before. Then I reached up and felt the silk of that splendid, hanging kimono.

At the very least, I had learned the difference between a stork and an ibis.

Kohana looked over at me, mischief dancing on her face despite the frailty. 'What are you thinking, my sweet?'

As an afterthought, she held up a hand. I walked over to hold it, the tea forgotten. Her fingers felt brittle.

'Nothing.'

'Don't be afraid.'

'Impossible.'

I inclined my head away from her, in order that she wouldn't see the running of feckless tears. I should have known otherwise. Kohana's other hand pushed up my chin, and a modicum of strength had entered her expression.

'I mean what I say. It's not over.'

'I love you.' Out gushed the silly comment before I could bar its passage.

'And here I was, thinking you were enamoured with my good-looks.'

'They help. But I'm more in love with you, than your looks.'

No gushing this time. Honesty instead. A brand new sensation.

'You're an incredible lady, Kohana.'

'You embarrass me,' she grouched. 'You're overestimating me.'

'Rubbish.'

'No, listen here, I'm not a woman with any special skill, but I've had plenty of experiences in battles; losing battles, all of them. In short, that's all I am. Drop such an idea for your own good.'

'All right, all right.'

'By the way, that was my gruff samurai tone, gleaned from watching a few too many period dramas on TV. Was I intimidating?'

'Can I lie?'

'Hmpf.'

'Did you ever like magic?'

Kohana clasped her hands together. 'How did you guess? I loved it.'

'Allow me to show you some hocus pocus.'

I brought over a small blanket, very carefully unfurled it across the floor, and placed the Godzilla statuette beneath, at the centre of the spread.

'Deceptively simple,' Kohana mused.

'Hang in there. Abracadabra, alakazam—*voilà!*'

I yanked off the blanket and the Godzilla statue was gone.

Kohana's eyes opened wide with wonder for a few seconds, the reaction I was after. She couldn't see the blighter cleverly hidden behind me.

'This is what you used to do for your daughter, isn't it?'

For a while after this comment, I contemplated the smokeless fire.

'Yes. Well—without Godzilla. I used Corinne's doll Mimi as my assistant. Corinne loved it too, although she sussed out the method in the end. She turned the tables on me by making my mobile phone disappear. For good.'

'Oh, before I forget, when I disappear—'

'Stop that. You're going nowhere.'

'Be what may, there's something hanging up in the bathroom wardrobe that I'd like you to have. You'll know when you see it, but no peeking till then. Promise?'

'Whatever.'

'I'll hold you to that.'

'I expect you to do so.' I packed up my blanket and replaced Godzilla on his shelf. As I did, I thought of Shimada and his monster movies. I looked at Kohana on the bed. 'Can I ask something?'

'Anything.'

'Isn't life disappointing?'

'No,' she smiled, with warmth, 'it isn't.'

We fell asleep, not long later. I woke up kneeling on the floor beside the bed, with my arms spread out on the futon. I raised myself to my elbows.

The hovel around me was empty. All the furnishings and bric-à-brac had been looted while we slept.

I knew, the moment I saw Kohana, that she was also gone.

Her body may have remained, but the essence was missing. I gently removed the hardcover book she had on her tummy, with the title *La Tavola Ritonda*, which I placed at the foot of the bed.

I pulled her husk to me, and bawled for a long time. Yes, I felt overly sorry for myself. I'm not afraid to admit it. Life, or whatever existence this feigns to be, was unbearable without her here.

I don't know how long passed.

I lay there on my front, my hands holding hers. Sometimes, I nodded off. Other times, I shook her and begged her to return. I have no idea where all the tears came from, much like the electricity here and the running water. But I refused to move and refused to let her go, though she already had.

After a time, I did move.

I made cups of tea she didn't drink, told silly stories about anything and everything, forged empty plans for a future we would never have together, lay there for hours simply holding her.

I don't know when I became aware that the front door was open.

Brilliant, blinding sunshine was streaming in, and a figure, in armour, stood at the end of the bed, carrying white lilacs, rosemary, and a few branches of cherry blossoms.

I squinted, sheltering my eyes with my hand, and sat up between Kohana and this newcomer—trying, I gather, to block the view.

The longer I stared over at this person, behind burnished metal and leather, I could better see the face, beneath a samurai helmet tied with a red string under the chin.

Held fast, by a flexible bamboo pole on her back, was a large white banner. Two kanji symbols were splashed across the material, but I had misplaced my ability to read the language.

By the way, I did say 'her'.

I assumed this would be the boy from the alley behind

Kohana's okiya—I never did hear his name—but it wasn't.

Nor Pop, Shimada, O-tee-san, or Y.

I saw Kohana, returned to me, aged about nineteen, and my heart bucked. Then I understood my mistake.

'Tomeko.'

Of course.

Having placed her foliage on top of the book, she walked closer, touched my shoulder, and smiled.

There were no damned words necessary.

Straight after, this girl leaned over the bed to very gently embrace the unmoving body in the nightshirt that lay there.

I did not object when Tomeko then lifted her up and carried her out through the doorway.

I followed at a discreet distance, watching as they got onto a horse and rode away in the direction of a sun I hadn't seen for far too long, low on the horizon.

When I couldn't see them any more, I walked back into the hovel.

I was well and truly fed up with the beard hanging off my jowls.

I went into the bathroom and poked about for a reasonably sharp instrument. I would have used Shashin's sword, if need be, but luckily I discovered bounty in the hidden cabinet behind the mirror: a complete shaving kit, with my preferred Gillette razors and a tin of foam.

'You haven't used these to shave your legs, have you?'

Yes, I asked Kohana aloud. I removed my smoking jacket and slacks, wrapped a towel around myself, and started to work up lather.

I didn't expect any response.

'No,' I decided. 'I'm sure you'd prefer to use a butter knife, since it's more of a challenge.'

I laughed. Doing so was something of a coup, and I don't use the word lightly.

'Convenient,' I waffled on. 'I wish I knew about these razors before—I've been stumping about, looking like an unlaundered Moses character. Do you mind if I take a few minutes to freshen up?'

I could imagine her response: 'Help yourself. Let's not slip back into yawn-inspiring formality!'

'I'll give it my finest shot. Turns out, old habits do indeed die hard.'

I would have winked at the woman, if she were here.

She wasn't.

I ceased what I was doing, and stared at myself in the looking-glass for the longest time. White foam covered my lower face.

'You know, I think I've figured it out. When I was younger, my daughter said I looked like a fake Santa when I lathered up like this. Now, I resemble the real McCoy.'

'Profound stuff,' I could have sworn I heard Kohana deadpan from the other side of the door.

'No, no, not the Santa Claus thing,' I continued, sliding the razor across my left cheek. Nice to see I hadn't forgotten how to shave. 'Me. *Moi.* I'm not one for symbolism or religious claptrap, as you well know, but I think I've got it.'

This pronouncement was greeted with silence.

I finished shaving, and rinsed my face in water that came from some source unknown, and best to keep it that way.

The bathroom wardrobe was there, to my left. I went over, opened it, and discovered a black suit on a hanger, wrapped in plastic.

After I tore off the protective sheath, I was happier to see the label. It was a London job—Anthony Sinclair—not an offering from some twee Parisian haberdasher.

There was also a British-made white shirt, but the tie was my old favourite from the 1980s, the dark wine and black Christian Dior. So there was one last Frenchie jab. I laughed. The woman was marvellous.

When I returned to the living room, I found emptiness.

'My God, you do like your drama,' I sighed. 'Disappearing on me like this. Goodbye, Kohana.'

39 | 三十九

I walked a clay road, with yellow bricks marching alongside.

There were white stars of Bethlehem blooming all around, and they shimmered in the sudden depth of light.

Images from recent experience flooded through me, and ended with a grainy, slightly out-of-focus memory of Kohana seated at the Wagner concert, six years old, with her pageboy haircut, gazing intently at the mural on the ceiling.

I could almost make out the music too. Instead of any sorrow, or annoyance, I felt oddly uplifted.

Just then, skipping ahead of me, I spotted that familiar miniature person in the red cloak. Another six-year-old.

I hurried my step, and in a couple of minutes kept pace beside her.

The sun, a powerful thing, was now well above the horizon.

My daughter reached out and took my hand. I looked down at her face and I smiled. That face was the most beautiful, serene sight I've ever beheld.

Acknowledgments

Simply put, without the influence of two remarkable cities I've called home—Tokyo and Melbourne—this story would not exist.

Otherwise, artwork-wise, hefty nods go to designer Damian Stephens, and Julian Hebbrecht for his geisha image. Phil Jourdan also merits a big hand, having asked me to get involved with Perfect Edge Books, along with editors Trevor and Mollie.

Love to friends and family—of particular note, my wife Yoko and my daughter Cocoa, mum Fée and dad Des, and my four grandparents, including Les.

For culture tips and having organized Kyoto last September— when this novel was scribbled notes on bits of paper—bravo and hurrah to my mates Yoshiko, Toshie, Hashimoto-san, Tsukako, Hiroko, Yumiko, and Nonaka-san, from our movie class.

To those media people, and complete strangers, who supported my last novel *Tobacco-Stained Mountain Goat*, thereby inspiring me to get on with this one, I cannot (ever) thank you enough. Obviously. You are no longer strangers!

Japanese filmmakers, artists, actors, musicians and writers deserve grandstanding respect here. For starters, Satoshi Kon and Akira Kurosawa, whose respective movies, *Millennium Actress* and *Drunken Angel*, were a big influence on the story. Other vital directors include Seijun Suzuki, Kon Ichikawa, Yasujirō Ozu, Shunya Itō, Masayuki Suo, Mamoru Oshii and Masahiro Makino. Thanks also to manga artists Osamu Tezuka, Tōru Shinohara, Fujio Akatsuka, Shotaro Ishinomori, Hiroshi Fujimoto and Motoo Abiko; singers Shizuko Kasagi and Sayuri Ishikawa; writers Seishi Yokomizu, Yukio Mishima and Yasunari Kawabata; and actors Takashi Shimura, Toshiro Mifune, Meiko Kaji, Kazuo Hasegawa, Akiko Wakabayashi, Mie Hama, Mieko Harada, Hideki Takahashi, Setsuko Hara and Ken Takakura.

Yes, I'm Australian—so Western and 'other' cultural influences weigh in, referenced openly, or with a hopeful cheeky wink. Think writers like Raymond Chandler, Edgar Allan Poe, Dashiell Hammett, Lewis Carroll, Norman Lindsay, Arthemise Goertz, Roald Dahl, and Dante Alighieri; composer Richard Wagner; movies *You Only Live Twice*, *The Princess Bride*, *Swing Time*, *Apocalypse Now*, *The Maltese Falcon*, *Casablanca*, *20,000 Leagues Under the Sea*, *The Wizard of Oz*, and *Don't Look Now*.

As a side note, *One Hundred Years of Vicissitude* relates to my previous book, *Tobacco-Stained Mountain Goat*, a reading of which might add some clarity to the experience. It was published in 2011, via the cool cats at Another Sky Press (anothersky.org).

Also figuring in the blend are Greek myths, fairy tales, comics, *Star Trek*, actor Peter Lorre, Chinese philosopher Lao Tzu, MacArthur's pipe, Tristan and Iseult, Totoro, floriography, haiku (ta, David G. Lanoue), and—oh, yes—Sir Thomas Malory.

About the Author

Born in Melbourne, Andrez Bergen is an expatriate Australian author, journalist, DJ, photographer and musician, who has been based in Tokyo, Japan, over the past eleven years.

One Hundred Years of Vicissitude is his second novel.

Aside from specializing in Japanese culture, anime, movies, and electronic music's various tangents, Bergen has written fiction for Another Sky Press, Snubnose Press and Crime Factory. He did a book of prose in collaboration with Polish photographer Tomek Sikora, and published his debut novel, the noir/sci-fi-inclined *Tobacco-Stained Mountain Goat*, in 2011. He is currently putting together an anthology of short stories, by other writers and illustrators, that relates to the dystopia of *TSMG*.

Bergen makes music and videos under aliases Little Nobody, Slam-Dunk Ninja, and Funk Gadget, he ran indie/experimental record label IF? for fourteen years, he creates the occasional comic, and he's a self-professed amateur saké connoisseur.

Bergen is married to Japanese artist Yoko Umehara, and they have a daughter, Cocoa.

Find out more at www.facebook.com/andrezbergenauthor

**PERFECT
EDGE
BOOKS**

We live in uncertainty. New ways of committing crimes are discovered every day. Hackers and hit men are idolized. Writers have responded to this either by ignoring the harsher realities or by glorifying mindless violence for the sake of it. Atrocities (from the Holocaust to 9/11) are exploited in cheaply sentimental films and novels.

Perfect Edge Books proposes to find a balanced position. We publish fiction that doesn't revel in nihilism, doesn't go for gore at the cost of substance – yet we want to confront the world with its beauty as well as its ugliness. That means we want books about difficult topics, books with something to say.

We're open to dark comedies, "transgressive" novels, potboilers and tales of revenge. All we ask is that you don't try to shock for the sake of shocking – there is too much of that around. We are looking for intelligent young authors able to use the written word for changing how we read and write in dark times.